SPECIAL PLAY$

WIN THE GAME!

Bob McAndrew

Special Plays

By: Bob McAndrew

ISBN: 978-0-578-67239-7

All rights reserved

Copyright @ April 2020, Bob McAndrew

First Edition 2020

2011 W. Danforth Road

Ste 165

Edmond, OK 73003

To all the Commercial and Military Aircraft Salesmen

who travel the world working on the

"Deal of the Century"

Remember the 'Golden Rule'

The Customer may not always be right-

However, they will always be the Customer!

GAME BRIEF!

January 22 – Miami, Florida - **Super Bowl**

San Francisco 49ers vs the Cincinnati Bengals - - - 4th Quarter

49ers Quarterback, **Joe Montana** *passes* to *Wide Receiver* **Jerry Rice** who *scores the* **"Touchdown"** to *WIN* the **Super Bowl!**

January 22 - Cairo, Egypt – **Cargo Aircraft Company Super Sale**

Cargo Aircraft Company vs Egyptian Air Force - - - Final Contract Signing

Cargo Aircraft Company (CAC) Salesman *Quarterback,* **Larry Ray Hardy** *scores* the contract to sell six of their **CC-260 aircraft** to the Egyptian Air Force to *WIN* their Sales **"Game."** CAC's Egyptian **"Helper"** *passes* out **"reward$"** to his **Special Team** of local players. **CAC** *Corporate VP* **Ahmed Sharif** *runs* **"Special Plays"** to *pass* **"reward$"** from their Egyptian **"Helper"** to his home **"Team."**

Whereas, the *San Francisco 49ers* had to sign contracts with their key players and develop a **game plan** to ensure a **WIN** in **Super Bowl XXIII,** the *Cargo Aircraft Company* also had to sign-up a local **"Helper"** and develop **"Special Plays"** to *pass* **"reward$"** to the **"Helper's Team"** to **WIN** their Sales **"Game."**

1

The San Francisco 49ers *traveled* to New Orleans, New York, Los Angeles, Seattle, Detroit, Los Angeles, Chicago, and Phoenix, to **defeat** the competition. The ***CAC* Team** likewise *traveled* to Cairo, Paris, Zurich, Amman, and Washington to *run* their **"Special Plays"** to use US Foreign Military Sales funds to pay their **"Players."**

Here is your **ticket** to the **"Game"** of **International Military Aircraft Sales** where the **"Special Plays"** by the Team of Cargo Aircraft Company Executives and Egyptian Officials result in **"Extra Point$$$"** to them. The CAC *Quarterback* (salesman) and the *Coaches* (CAC Executives and Egyptian Officials) are crooks, and the game isn't over until the US Federal *Referees*/Prosecutors **"Rest their Case!"**

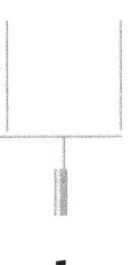

1
SCOUT THE TERRITORY!

Fall

The San Francisco 49ers had almost forty seasons with the National Football League. The 49ers had recently won the division for the second consecutive season, and ended the last season as the top seed in the NFC playoffs. Their season ended with an upset loss to the Minnesota Vikings **in the divisional round of the playoffs.**

This fall, the San Francisco 49ers know that they have the right team, coaches, and plays to win the Super Bowl.

During the previous sales campaign year, the Cargo Aircraft Company CC-260 cargo aircraft sales team lost more sales than they won. Like any team, the CC-260 sales team was under extreme pressure by their senior management to do better.

This fall, the Cargo Aircraft Company CC-260 sales team and Company management have an opportunity to score the most profitable sale in the Company's history.

Prior to the start of any sport season, team owners send out staff to scout the competition. In business, prior to the start of a sales campaign, the management conducts a market assessment and sends out salesmen to assess the opportunity. The management of the Cargo Aircraft Company had sent out their star salesman/player, Larry Ray Hardy, to look for and evaluate a sales opportunity in Egypt for their CC-260 military cargo aircraft. This wasn't Larry Ray's "first rodeo," a catchy idiom used by CAC that had become the new pet phrase throughout the political and international circles that CAC staff frequented.

Here is his scouting report !

Cairo - US Embassy Reception

The setting sun made the Cairo Marriott Hotel look like a modern pyramid on its own island in the middle of the Nile River. Flames from the gas torches lining the walkways cast an ancient light-shadow on the guests arriving for the US Embassy reception on the lawn by the main swimming pool. The waiters and servers were dressed in Anthony and Cleopatra era outfits. It was a time when western business culture ruled Egypt and the locals were anxious to do business the "Western" way. On the other hand, Western businessmen were going to be surprised to learn the hard way on how to do business the "Egyptian" way.

Larry Ray Hardy had just arrived on the scene. He was the new salesman covering Egypt for the Cargo Aircraft Company. Larry Ray wore his forty years well, a southern boy, easygoing, medium height, medium build, pleasant personality, slight southern accent, everybody's friend.

He knew these embassy receptions offered an opportunity to meet key officials of the Egyptian government. He also knew the rule of thumb for international salesmen of military equipment was to stay away from the US Embassy officials. They were either political appointee bureaucrats or undercover agents for US agencies looking for information for their weekly reports.

Larry Ray had been roaming the world for over ten years, selling military aircraft to third world governments. He knew more about third world military budgets, priorities, and the regional power brokers than any US Embassy bureaucrat. His target tonight was the Egyptian Minister of Defense, Helmy Mostafa, previously head of the Egyptian Air Force, and the key guy with the power and money to buy multimillion-dollar aircraft.

Larry Ray was well aware that the biggest challenge in selling military hardware to the third world was to find the right "facilitator" or "agent" or "consultant" or "helper" or, as they politically correctly said in the US, "lobbyist" to make a sale happen.

Larry Ray didn't have a degree in international business. He had learned by listening to his mentors and from on-site experience in the third world. Cargo Aircraft Company had one of the best international sales and profit records in the industry. Larry Ray had applied and improved the lessons of his bosses and sold a lot of aircraft throughout Africa. Egypt was an especially lucrative target as they actually had money. Well, not quite their own money. To keep a fair balance of arms in the region, the US Government gave both Israel and Egypt money, lots of it, to buy US military equipment.

He smiled as he sipped his first drink, thinking of his most recent sale. It always came down to being in the right place, a country that needed aircraft, at the right time, when they had the money. Of course, the right place and time was CAC's key to its success by being sure to have Larry Ray and the other international sales guys in a lot of countries, in a position to pounce on an opportunity.

Last year Larry Ray had a very profitable CC-260 aircraft sale to a small African country who was selling Russian military equipment captured (*OK, stolen*) from Libya to the US Government. He had endured many days in a country that barely had running water, but were awash in greenbacks. It was relatively easy to find the "Helper" in a small country. In fact, when he first met the buyers, in this case, the President and his Minister of Defense cousin, they strongly recommended CAC employ the services of a local businessman, another cousin who just happened to be in the same meeting. They also had expressed their concern that they didn't like to leave cash in the local bank, as the country had a history of coups on short notice. The math was very straight forward: sell XYZ country an aircraft at an exorbitant price and pay the local agent a "fee" to his Swiss bank account.

It was a win-win for both parties. With all the big money flowing around, Larry Ray was a little miffed that not a lot of money was coming his way. It was hard to stomach his aircraft bonus of three thousand dollars when the "Helper" would easily make over one million dollars per aircraft.

Now in Egypt, at this US Embassy reception, he used the salesman's basic butterfly approach at social functions. He fluttered around, making the usual courteous remarks, "Nice evening!", "Great reception!", "Good to see you!", whether he knew the person or not, all the while keeping one eye roving the crowd to pick out his target for the evening.

As he made his third tour of the reception area, he spotted the Egyptian Minister of Defense, Helmy Mostafa, and his entourage off to one side of the reception area near the banquet tables. It was Larry Ray's experience that the more financially third world a country was, the larger the number of hangers-on there were to the movers and shakers. Tonight's group really wasn't too large as compared to some he had to plow through in other countries in Africa.

Now was *kick off time*! He had done his homework and knew that the Minister had trained in the United States at Shepard Air Force base in Wichita Falls, Texas, and had attended Air Force Command school at Maxwell Air Force Base in Alabama. As always, the best move was a typical good old boy approach and a lot of BS. He placed his almost empty drink on a table, straightened his tie, adjusted his CC-260 airplane pin on his lapel, and inserted himself into the entourage,

"Minister Mostafa, so nice to see you again! I'm Larry Ray Hardy, Director of Business Development for Cargo Aircraft Company. Everyone knows our CC-260 aircraft." Larry Ray knew that you never used the words "sales" or "marketing," unless you were selling vacuum cleaners.

The Minister didn't recognize him at all. However, he was also very experienced at the reception game. "Nice to see you again, as well," he replied.

Larry Ray knew he had broken the ice, and had to quickly establish his credibility. "General Figgleman sends his best regards, and he regrets he couldn't be here himself."

Nice move, as Minister Mostafa and USAF Lt. General Figgleman were good friends and there was little chance that Mostafa would ever make the effort to check if General Figgleman actually knew Larry Ray Hardy

Larry Ray now had his proverbial *first down,* or foot in the door. On the reception field, you only had about two minutes to establish your credentials, pick the targets of interest, and obtain a commitment for the next meeting, before the next interruption,

So, he continued. "In fact, General Figgleman asked me to brief you on some special opportunities for the Egyptian Air Force in the upcoming Foreign Military Sales funding allocations to be made by the US Congress and Department of Defense. I'm here in Cairo for a few days to brief the EAF on our CC-260 aircraft, which are prime candidates for US Department of Defense FMS funding. Let me know when you would be like to hear about our aircraft and the amount of FMS funding Gen Figgleman endorses for Egypt.

Larry Ray handed him his card, where he had already written 'Friend of General Figgleman," and prepared to withdraw from the entourage. Just at that moment, a very attractive Egyptian woman approached, interrupting his farewell scene. She smiled at Minister Mostafa, and said, "Good evening, Brother. I have come to save you from all these business discussions and take you over to the banquet table so you don't faint from lack of food"

There was much laughter as the brother and sister left the group. One of the EAF Group Captains, a rank equivalent to a US Colonel, noticed that Larry Ray was staring at the very attractive lady. He broke the spell, saying, "As you Americans would say, for the Egyptian Air Force, she is the power behind the throne. She is his sister Tasha, who also happens to also be a Member of the Egyptian Government and head of the Military Procurement

Committee."

Larry Ray thanked the Group Captain and hoped that he had not heard the wheels turning in Larry Ray's head. What an interesting evening! A *first down* on making the contact, and possibly a set up for a score, in more ways than one.

Marriott Hotel Bar

As any salesman knows, the real opportunities for intelligence, and making plays for a deal, take place in hotel bars. Fortunately, Egypt was westernized enough to allow the serving of alcohol.

Later, as Larry Ray made his way up to the bar, he saw the US Embassy Air Attaché, Colonel Mike Barnes, off to one side with a couple of Egyptian Air Force senior officers. Colonel Barnes was in his USAF dress blues with enough ribbons to impress the cocktail waitresses, but not anyone who knew what good conduct and excellent marksman medals looked like.

However, Colonel Barnes did fill the Air Attaché image, tall and thin, slightly graying, nice tan from working out, or more likely, daily spending time by the Embassy pool. Plus, he had the ability to act like he knew the inside track when he didn't have a clue as to what was really going on.

Larry Ray had met Colonel Barnes when he made the compulsory visit to the Embassy last week to update them on Cargo Aircraft's interest in Egypt and obtain the latest intelligence on the country's military procurement plans. As usual, it was mainly a one-way conversation with Larry Ray telling the Colonel just a few of the things he knew about the Egyptian Air Force Procurement plans in order to give the Colonel some sensitive information to use in his weekly intelligence report. Well, it was time to run another play. At least buying the local Air Attaché a drink always looked good on the expense report.

"Colonel Barnes, great to see you again! It was another fantastic reception. I believe all the movers and shakers were there!" Might as well make him feel good in front of his EAF contacts.

"Larry Ray, thanks. Let me introduce you to a couple of friends. This is Air Marshal Saad and Air Commodore Riad." These guys were three-star and one-star ranks, respectively.

Larry Ray introduced himself and offered to buy the next round. Of course, he was immediately a welcome addition to the group. The key to this not-so-chance meeting was to find out if either of the Egyptian Air Force Officers had any clout, or were just marching in place, awaiting retirement.

By the time for yet another round, which Larry Ray again graciously offered to buy, he had discovered that Air Marshal Saad was active in establishing priorities and budgets for the Egyptian Air Force to qualify for US Foreign Military Sales funds. However, Air Marshal Saad was really awaiting retirement, and already promoting his new post-retirement business venture, a consulting company called "Pyramid Associates." *Really, someone needed to help him come up with a better name.*

However, Larry Ray was also planning to set up a consulting company when he retired. He'd already thought of a name, "International Redneck Services." Even though he liked it, he probably needed to come up with another, as the initials, IRS, would not play well with potential clients.

As usual, Colonel Barnes didn't have much news to offer and

was mainly taking mental notes for his weekly report.

To impress Larry Ray, Air Marshal Saad said, "I know that the CAC CC-260 aircraft is one of the many, many candidates for selection and grant funding in the upcoming Egyptian-US Foreign Military grants discussions. I can assure you it will receive fair consideration from me and my staff."

Larry Ray thought, *For sure.* He knew "grant" was really a buzz word for "free money." The key to moving a FMS military program forward in the EAF was finding a way to donate to the Air Marshal's future retirement fund.

Anyhow, no need to flip a coin to see who gets the ball.

Larry Ray responded, "Of course. I'm sure you'll do your usually thorough evaluation of the merits of each of the candidate aircraft. Here's my card. I'm in Cairo for a few days, so let me know if you need any information on our CC-260 aircraft"

Now for the aircraft salesman's hook. "We happen to be delivering a new CC-260 aircraft to the French Air Force next month. I will be in Paris at that time for a few days and it would be our pleasure to arrange for you to see the aircraft in Paris. At our expense, of course!"

Colonel Barnes almost choked on his drink.

Larry Ray could see the Air Marshal's eyes light up. An all-expense paid trip to Paris! Now the Air Marshal just needed to figure out a way to classify it as an official aircraft inspection trip.

Larry Ray decided to make it easy for him. Turning to Colonel Barnes, he added, "Colonel, you must plan to join us. It will give you the opportunity to fly the latest model of the CC-260 cargo aircraft."

How could the Colonel say no? All he had to do was figure out a way to call it an official trip. So as usual, the Egyptian's would call it a US sponsored trip and the USAF would call it an Egyptian Air Force sponsored trip. Win-win for both, with neither paying for any of it!

Larry Ray knew it was time to quit while he was ahead, and give the Colonel and Air Marshal an opportunity to conspire to make up a requirement for this upcoming aircraft inspection trip to Paris.

Larry Ray offered his good-byes and walked away thinking, *Not bad for the first scouting of the territory*!.

Larry Ray went up to his Executive Suite at the hotel. *Always good to stay where all the action was taking place.* His next move was to make up his roster for the "Teams."

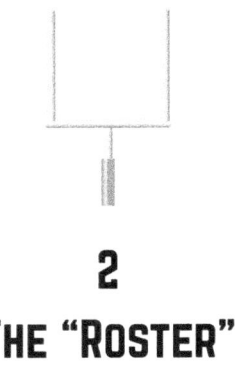

2
THE "ROSTER"

San Francisco 49ers

It was the forty-third season in the National Football League for the San Francisco 49ers. The highlight was their third Super Bowl victory. Throughout the season, the 49ers had concerns. They were six wins to five losses, and likely to miss the playoffs, but they defeated the Washington Redskins and finished the season at ten wins to six losses. In the playoffs, they defeated the Minnesota Vikings 34-9 in the first round. They defeated the Chicago Bears 28–3 in the NFC Championship.

Like any successful business, the 49ers had a Team of Owners, Coaches, and Key Players. They all had nicknames and other 'call signs.' A few of those …

Management Nicknames

Owner/President – Edward DeBartolo The Prince

Head Coach – Bill Walsh The Genius'

Key Players

Quarterback- Joe Montana Joe Cool, Bird Legs

Running Back – Roger Craig Catfish

Wide Receivers – Jerry Rice Flash 80, Gentlemen Jerry

Special Team Kicker – Mike Cofer Fleer

Cargo Aircraft Company and Corporation

The CAC CC-260 Cargo Aircraft Program was in financial difficulties with the Corporation due to poor international sales, which were the most lucrative for the Company, earning a profit of between twenty to twenty-five percent per aircraft. This was due to poor performances by their sales team in many key sales campaigns, or *games,* which had all failed to produce a single sale, or *score,* in the last eight months. The starting sales team were told they all would be made *free agents* if they didn't score some sales soon.

The Company had a secret play or code book for identifying key executives, customers, and contract terms since, when outside the US and especially in the third world, most business communications were monitored, along with the bugging of meeting rooms and even hotel rooms. These codes were so unusual that they sometimes raised more suspicion than clear language. These code books were restricted to only certain senior level executives.

The company and corporate marketing team also set up their own special code names for key company, corporate, and customer executives which only they knew. They believed these fake names would keep them from being terminated if somehow a sensitive internal marketing message was seen by others. According to the sales team, the key players on the CAC team were:

"Bigfoot" - Frank Moore - **President CAC**. Frank was over six feet tall and had the presence and personality of his code name. If his father had not pushed him into aerospace, he most likely would have had a good shot at a starring role in the "Jeremiah Johnson" movie. He was not really an airplane guy and his management style was similar to that of Attila the Hun. He only wanted results, and didn't want to be bothered with the details. Frank's career path had him passing through the airplane company on his way to a more coveted position at the corporate headquarters in Washington DC. To get there, he had to push the flyboys at this company to make more money and stop spending it on continuous upgrades to perfectly good airplanes. Frank had also previously held various administrative and finance positions at some of the other company offices, so he was sure that he knew all there was to know about any type of business. His code name should have been "Captain Ahab" as he was focused on chasing whale-size profits!

"Closer" - Mark Maddox - **VP Marketing.** Mark was a true good old boy from the deep South. He had a slow southern drawl and his beltline showed his weakness for family size platters of barbecued beef, pork, and chicken, with all the fixings. Mark had been around the aircraft international sales arena for a long time. He could smell the real deal from an exercise and get it closed quickly, as long as his team played by his rules. He had been at the Cargo Aircraft Company for over twenty years. Although his pay was not close to that of other Company VP's and Presidents, he had already bought his retirement retreat in the Cayman Islands with his "special play" bonuses from his many "helpers" around the world. Well, as his daddy used to say, "There's more than one way to skin a cat." *Or was that a possum?*

"Coach" - Robert McTelall - **Director of International Marketing**. He was one of the good guys, since he was the guy announcing these plays and games. Medium build, extremely handsome, good shape. Anyhow, he was the new arrival from the Washington DC corporate headquarters, being treated like any corporate visitor or addition. He was buried in BS and stuck in an out-of-the-way office. At least they hadn't given him the code name of the state bug – the cockroach. He had come to CAC to lend a hand in selling their whitetail aircraft, those unsold aircraft sitting on the flight line. He found out quickly that this team had made up some new rules for their sales game.

"Roadrunner" -- Larry Ray Hardy - **Marketing Manager - Mid-East.** Larry Ray was the penultimate salesman. He was tall and good looking, with just enough of a mustache to accent his good looks. Larry Ray had just gone through his second divorce. Apparently, his inordinate amount of time away from home only made his heart grow fonder for other woman. He had worked his way up through the ranks, knew the product well, understood the contract process, and could smoothly manipulate the "Helper," or consultant, approval process to get the people he needed at the price they required to get the sale. More importantly, he understood the US Government process of funding the purchase of military equipment through the US Government Foreign Military Sales program. Larry Ray of course knew the Foreign Corporate Practices Act and the obvious methods the US Government and the company watchdogs would be using to monitor international sales campaigns. He and his company and customer teams believed they had developed "special plays" to reward the key players without being penalized.

"Black Cloud" - Jim Smith - **VP Finance.** How fitting a name for the person that always played poor boy, never having enough money to fund essential sales activities like the Paris Air Show, or trips to Monte Carlo to meet customers, or paying international consultants what was needed to make thing happen. Jim certainly looked the part, short stature, cheap suits, eyeglasses, and no sense of humor. He made few friends, especially when his comment at every meeting was that he worked by the "Golden Rule"— that is, "He who has the gold, rules!" Of course, his plan was to keep the gold.

"Snake" – Vince Holliday – **General Counsel**. The name "Shark" would also have applied. When you were in the swamp, that is, foreign countries, up to your you-know-what in contract problems, his help usually killed the deal. Vince was a Yankee lawyer acting like a southern lawyer, always trying to be the smooth talking good old boy. He always had a legal opinion on every issue which was non-supportive of getting international business accomplished. Vince was small and beady-eyed, always nervous, like he expected the Federal Attorney General to just be waiting for him to make a mistake. Of course, he would never make a mistake, but many others would, and he would be the first to blow the whistle on his fellow executives.

"Sphinx" – Ahmed Sharif - **Corp VP Middle East- Zurich Office.** Ahmed fit the image of a true international mid-eastern business man. Olive complexion, medium build with an expanded waistline to reflect his good life style, Rolex watch, heavy gold chain around his neck, four-thousand-dollar suits, one-thousand-dollar shoes, and an expense account that would cause Black Cloud to have a heart attack. It was interesting that Ahmed had total support. In fact, he walked on water as far as **Bigfoot** and **Closer** were concerned. Ahmed really "knew his territory," as the Music Man had stated. However, it was clear he had never read the US Foreign Corrupt Practices Act. Or, if he had, he certainly had no intention of complying with it. Ahmed was a crook with a corporate badge and unlimited expense account.

"Eagle" – Ken Doyle - **Corp VP International Business-Washington DC office**. Ken was a true southern politician. He made all the rounds of the Washington DC social circuit. He always had a contact for whatever was required, and probably worked for the CIA. Ken was a smooth operator, medium height, was ex-USAF, and kept in good shape. He dressed the part for the territory. Probably one of the smartest players on the team. Smart enough to know what was going on, but never touched that southern tar baby, unless there was in something in it for him, as in $omething.

The Egyptian Roster

Additionally, the Marketing team also had special code names for the key players in Egypt.

"Tut" – Helmy Mostafa - **Minister of Defense**. He had held this position for many years, after a long career in the Egyptian Air Force. He had been key to supporting the past change, actually overthrow, of the government. It was amazing how flying scores of fighter aircraft over a city could influence voters! Although he was looking forward to his retirement, he was concerned on how he could afford the life he deserved and desired.

"Cleopatra" - Tasha Mostafa – **Egyptian Government Official**. She was smart and good looking. She used her charms to influence her government to procure military equipment which would be the best for Egypt, as well as the best for her brother and other players.

"Karnak" – Air Marshal Saad (Three Star General) - **Egyptian Air Force**. Although not as large as the Army, the EAF had over seven hundred military aircraft and was key to discouraging attacks by their neighbors. Saad was also soon to retire and looking for a well-paying senior position with a company that appreciated his experience and influence.

"Darius" – Air Commodore Riad (One Star General) - **Egyptian Air Force**. He was a close friend of Air Marshal Saad. He followed the direction of the Air Marshal on how to justify all of the Air Marshal's procurement decisions, whether they made sense for the EAF or not. Like Larry Ray, he felt that he was not given his due reward for his dedicated service.

"Ramses" – Ali Omar- President of **Military Aviation Parts & Service Company**, one of many Egyptian companies supporting the largest Army, Navy, and Air Forces in the region. MAPS did OK; however, Omar had many competitors and the profits were low, due to having so many small programs. He was looking for a bigger score for his team! He just also happened to be Cleopatra's friend.

Flip the Coin and Let the Game Begin!

First Game --- San Francisco 49ers at New Orleans Saints

49ers Win 34 to 33

The Saints just had their first winning season. They had a 17–10 halftime lead. Then Joe Montana, in the third quarter, had three touchdown passes. Coach Bill Walsh put Steve Young in for the fourth quarter; he was sacked in the end zone for a safety, and the

Saints went on to score seven more points after that. However, they still lost 34–33 to the 49ers.

Doing Business Internationally

Selling military equipment internationally required the hiring of local people to not only offer advice, but most importantly, to know how to make it happen. It was remarkable how many local and US laws limited who you could hire and how you could pay them. Companies usually spent a lot of time acquiring the in-country legal knowledge and advice, and having many internal reviews before hiring local support or "Helpers." The "In-Country Team" was the key for a successful sale. Internationally they were labeled as consultants; in Washington DC they were called lobbyists.

The main restrictions for selling internationally were defined in the Foreign Corrupt Practices Act: "This law makes it unlawful for persons and companies to make payments to foreign government officials to assist in obtaining business. Specifically, the anti-bribery provisions of the FCPA prohibit any offer, payment, promise to pay, or authorization of the payment of money or anything of value to any person, while knowing that all or a portion of such money or thing of value will be offered, given or promised, directly or indirectly, to a foreign official to influence the foreign official in his or her official capacity, induce the foreign official to secure any improper advantage in order to assist in obtaining or retaining business."

Essentially, that outlawed all the ways to easily do business internationally!

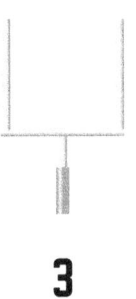

3

SECOND GAME · SAN FRANCISCO 49ERS AT NEW YORK GIANTS

49ers win 20 to 17

Walsh started Steve Young against the Giants. Young's inexperience with the 49ers' offensive plays limited him to 115 yards passing and the 49ers trailed 17–13 in the fourth quarter. Then Walsh sent Montana in and he made a 77 yard touchdown pass in the final minutes to Jerry Rice for the win.

Cairo – Marriott Hotel

Larry Ray had been busy over the days immediately following the US Embassy reception, sketching out his "Game" plan. His "Goal" was to sell six CC-260 aircraft to the Egyptian Air Force for around four hundred million dollars.

Teams with Key Players and Plays

Egypt

a. Egyptian Air Force requests the 6 CC-260 aircraft.

Air Marshal Saad runs the requirement for CC-260s thru the procurement line.

b. Ministry of Defense approves the purchase.

Helmy Mostafa tells the EAF they need to score the purchase of the CC-260s.

c. Government Committee approves release of US provided FMS funds.

Tasha Mostafa runs the CC-260 purchase thru the government committees.

d. Local "Helper" makes sure all players and coaches are "rewarded" for the efforts!

Alabama: Cargo Aircraft Company

Sales

a. Sales Manager - Larry Ray Hardy makes the sales plays in Egypt.

He passes the CC-260 Offer to the EAF. He works with Corp VP to recruit local "helper." He scores the contract

b. Sales Director - Robert McTelall manages Larry Ray.

c. Sales VP Mark - Maddox coaches Larry Ray and "Helper" through the CRM Plays.

Consultant Review Meeting (CRM)- Key Members

d. VP Finance - Jim Smith approves passing the ball to the "Helper."

e. General Counsel - Vince Holliday confirms "Helper" passes US and Egyptian laws.

Senior Management

f. CAC President - Frank Moore coaches both teams on how to win and score four hundred million dollars on the sale to Egypt. He runs "special plays" at his company and the corporation to score extra points for his team and the "Helper."

Cargo Aircraft Corporation

g. Corporate VP International - Ken Doyle of the DC office recruits US Government players.

h. Corporate VP Middle East - Ahmed Sharif runs the "special plays" in Egypt.

Now that Larry Ray had his teams, plays, and players' assignments, he was ready to start the game!

1st Play – Huddle with the US Embassy in Cairo.

Although the bureaucrats at the US Embassy really had little influence to make a military equipment sale happen, they certainly could delay the process if you couldn't get them on board. The key players at the Cairo US Embassy for a military aircraft sale were the Ambassador and the Air Attaché. Larry Ray made a call to Colonel Barnes to invite him to lunch to follow up on their discussion at the reception. Larry Ray knew from his many years in sales to third world countries that a salesman didn't want to highlight having any special contacts, better known as "friends," at the Embassy.

He needed to choose a place for lunch with a low probability of anyone recognizing him meeting with Colonel Barnes. Fortunately, the military executives at an embassy only wore their uniforms to formal functions, and not for day-to-day business. Larry Ray was not sure if Colonel Barnes would support his sale, so he needed to find out if the Colonel was supporting any of his competitors who were selling fighters, tankers, missiles, or tactical support.

The US Embassy was located on the east side of the Nile River.

Therefore, Larry Ray selected a restaurant on the west side of the Nile over by the pyramids, a good distance from the embassy. The Umami Sushi & Teppanyaki Restaurant at the Le Méridien Pyramids Hotel was today's choice. The location near the pyramids ensured it would be overwhelmed with tourists, but few locals. Moreover, not many Americans, Europeans, or Egyptians were generally going to eat at a Japanese restaurant in Egypt.

When in Cairo or any third world city, Larry Ray always had a local taxi on full time standby. Today he arranged for his special taxi to pick up Colonel Barnes to avoid using an embassy driver. Colonel Barnes preferred not to use his own car, which had a GPS tracker installed.

One other factor he'd learned the hard way was to use a brand name establishment, since the CAC finance bean counters, that is, the expense approvers, matched his expenses to known suitable business entities. He had made that mistake in N'Djamena, Chad, when he hosted a party for the Chief of the Air Force at the Au Bout Topless Lounge. For some reason they did not believe the name only meant it was a rooftop restaurant!

He was seated at a small table towards the back of the restaurant and waved at the Colonel when he entered. After a pleasant greeting, Colonel Barnes mentioned he had never been to this place, which further ensured no one would notice them here.

While they briefly discussed the weather and traffic, Larry Ray suggested they try the lamb teppanyaki, as no one wanted to risk having sushi in Egypt. Because the Colonel had to return to the embassy, he declined the complementary sake. Of course, Larry Ray had never declined a free drink in his life. During their barbecued lamb lunch, which was not baaad!!, they both expounded on how well they were enjoying their jobs and what fun it was to travel the world.

Once they finished and had ordered coffee, which Larry Ray really needed, as the complimentary sake was very good and plentiful, Larry Ray presented his case to the Colonel. Fortunately, the Colonel had not been a fighter pilot like many third world Air Force chiefs who only wanted more fast movers. Therefore, he was interested in discussing cargo aircraft.

Larry Ray started his pitch. "Colonel Barnes, as a senior US Air Force Officer, I know you appreciate the value to a third world country to have a fleet of multipurpose cargo aircraft like the CC-260 ZEUS. It not only fulfills all military cargo and troop transport missions, it is also a country builder. The ZEUS can conduct many humanitarian missions such as disaster relief, search and rescue, evacuations, and critical resupply in remote areas. It is clear that our own government would like to provide Foreign Military Sales funds for equipment which can be of service to a country other than fighting or killing their neighbors."

Larry Ray paused for a moment to let that sink in. Then he continued. "I have it on good authority from our Washington office that a request from Egypt for six CC- 260 aircraft would receive quick approval and FMS funding. Accordingly, we would appreciate your and the Ambassador's support of this purchase by the EAF. I certainly hope you can accompany Air Marshal Saad and Air Commodore Riad to Paris to see and fly the latest model of the CC-260 ZEUS."

More than likely, the Colonel had heard a similar pitch from several other US defense companies. He replied, "Larry Ray, first I want to thank you for a delicious lunch. And I do appreciate you keeping me apprised of your business initiatives here in Egypt. As you are aware, we at the Embassy are required to treat all US military equipment sales activities the same, and we cannot show any favoritism. But you'll be glad to know that the Ambassador has approved my joining the EAF for the CC-260 Inspection meeting in France."

Now that they had each made their positions clear, it was time to get down to the main business.

Larry Ray began his real pitch. "Colonel, you clearly are having a great career with the USAF. Your experience as a third world Air Attaché certainly prepares you for your next position, if you ever consider retiring. In fact, CAC and our corporate office in Washington DC are always on the lookout for people with your experience. So, if you ever plan to retire, please let us know, so we can discuss your interest in a senior position with our company. Our corporate VP of International Business, Ken Doyle, is a good friend of the Ambassador." Larry Ray didn't know if Ken even knew the Ambassador, but the Colonel would never ask, as it would reveal his retirement play.

The old friends in high places always helped, even though it probably wasn't the first time an opportunity had been dangled in front of the Colonel. Still, Larry Ray's timing may have been very good, because the Colonel replied, "Interesting you mention retirement, as I am planning to submit my retirement paperwork early next year and move back to the good ol' USA! With my extensive Air Force and international experience, I expect many US aviation companies will have an interest in what I can bring to the table."

Enough said! They leisurely finished their coffee, making more small talk, but the pipe had been laid. Larry Ray, of course, paid the bill, then walked the Colonel to his waiting taxi. "Colonel, you take this one. It's already paid for, and I want to go back to check on the corporate rate at this very impressive hotel."

In reality, Larry Ray did not want to take the chance of anyone seeing him return the Colonel to the embassy, as he expected the Colonel to become a strong supporter for the EAF to purchase the CC-260s.

After another night of working in his luxury suite, but mainly at the bar at the Marriott hotel, Larry Ray was ready for the next play.

2nd Play - Lay out the "Run" to Paris

The EAF headquarters was in eastern Cairo at the Almaza Air Base, located in the Heliopolis area adjacent to the Cairo International Airport. Larry Ray had been there many times, so he knew the drill. He had called the Air Marshal's assistant, Air Commodore Riad, to set up the meeting with his boss, but since Riad was unavailable, Larry Ray had ended up speaking directly with the Air Marshal himself. In passing, Larry Ray had mentioned that CAC was always looking to hire local companies to support their aircraft business activities. Dangling that possibility in front of the Air Marshal secured his meeting. He could sense the Air Marshal thinking, *First client for my new, yet to be established, consulting company.*

He arrived at the main gate to the headquarters in his private taxi. They were expecting him and had a car waiting to take him to the main offices. No outside private vehicles, especially taxis, were allowed on the base. *Guess in this country you really can't tell who your enemies are, so better to be cautious.*

Larry Ray was dressed for the meeting in a blue blazer, gray slacks, white shirt, well-shined shoes, Company tie, and, of course, the CC-260 lapel pin. He was ushered into the Air Marshal's private office, instead of going to a conference room. This meant it was probably going to be more than a sales call.

The Air Marshal's aide arranged for tea, during which the Air Marshal spent the first twenty minutes on the usual social conversation involving weather, accommodations, and local sites. Larry Ray had learned the patience required for a third world salesman.

Eventually the Air Marshal got down to business. "Mr. Hardy, please appreciate I am somewhat familiar with your CC-260 aircraft. The inspection of the aircraft in France will be very helpful in my understanding of all that it can do for my country. Thank you for the invitation. Please work out all the arrangements with my assistant, Air Commodore Riad. I expect he will also be included in this aircraft inspection visit!"

Larry Ray had already concluded that the Air Commodore would also be very helpful in assisting him to arrange for and influence the Air Marshal's support in the purchase of six aircraft, as well as providing inside information of the status of the CC-260 purchase program within the EAF. Too bad the Air Commodore wasn't also setting up a company that Larry Ray could help him out with. Larry Ray would just have to keep his ears open to any possible incentives to smooth his dealings with the Air Commodore.

The Air Marshal and Larry Ray ended their discussion by agreeing to have the inspection in two weeks, with all the arrangements, meaning expenses, to be paid by CAC!

3rd Play - Interception at the Marriott Hotel!!

Larry Ray was sitting at Harry's Pub, an English pub in a hotel in the middle of Cairo with imported English beer, ale and stout, to match the traditional pub menu. The Egyptian Government only allowed alcohol to be served in first class western-owned hotels. He liked this bar as there was very little chance that any of his contacts or potential customers would ever frequent it. He was currently going over an unofficial review of the last two plays.

However, when a light and airy voice from behind him said, "Mr. Hardy, what a pleasant surprise," he turned and almost fell off the bar stool. Directly behind him stood Tasha Mostafa dressed to kill, or at least take a prisoner.

She added, "Imagine running into you here at Harry's! I just finished a business meeting upstairs and thought an English beer was exactly what I needed to quench my thirst."

Larry Ray, the penultimate salesman, was never at a loss for words. He quickly responded, "Miss Mostafa, so nice to see you. Looks like we are both in the same thirsty condition. Please join me in a thirst quencher, or two."

She nodded, and they moved to a quiet table for two in the corner of the pub.

After the usual small talk on the weather and the quality of English beer, they discovered that they both preferred to be on a first name basis. After they ordered their beers, Tasha said, "I hope that your business meetings are going well. My brother tells me that you represent the Cargo Aircraft Company and are discussing the sale of your aircraft to the Egyptian Air Force."

Larry Ray was thinking, *What an amazing coincidence that a member of the Egyptian government, who is on the military procurement committee, happens to run into me at an out of the way bar in Cairo.* Of course, he knew that this wasn't a coincidence.

Larry Ray had seen this play before, so he knew which move to make. "Tasha, I expect you know the CC-260 cargo aircraft is the favorite military cargo aircraft for over sixty countries. Along with key support for any military operation, the ZEUS is the best aircraft for humanitarian relief, country building, and a host of other non-military activities. We at CAC are so proud of our aircraft and what it can do for everyone."

He took a sip of his beer and continued with his run. "It is clear to me that the Egyptian Air Force would like to have a fleet of CC-260 airplanes. Of course, money is always an issue. Plus, as you know, the heads of a lot of Air Forces are ex-fighter pilots, so they tend to want to spend their money on more fighter aircraft, which will hopefully never be used. I'm sure you are very aware that there is always a "funding and priority" issue with every military purchase."

Before she could comment, he made his end run, the free money play. "Tasha, I have it on good authority from our Washington DC office—in fact, I've just confirmed with Colonel Barnes here at the US Embassy—that there is US Government Foreign Military Sales grant funding available to encourage Egypt to purchase cargo aircraft instead of fighters and tanks."

Now was the time to "fumble," or play dumb, and let her pick up the ball. She replied, "Larry Ray, that is very interesting. I know from past experience that the allocation of US Government FMS funds is only for very good friends of the USA. I'm pleased to hear we are being considered for this funding. I agree that a fleet of CC-260 cargo aircraft would be good for my country, so I also would be pleased to help in any way to support this process and have my country buy your aircraft."

Looks like the ball had been passed back to Larry Ray. "Well, Tasha, it looks like we are both on the same page to provide the ZEUS to Egypt. Since I am new to Egypt, I certainly would appreciate your advice and council on all the steps in Egypt that will be needed to accomplish this sale. I and my associates in Washington can assist in assuring the FMS funding for these aircraft." What Larry was really saying was that Tasha and he were on the same team, and that he was counting on her strategy to help win the game!

Larry Ray knew from past experience that any one offering support expected to be rewarded for their efforts. So, it was time to establish the rules for Tasha's entry into the game. "Tasha, I would appreciate and could really use your advice, council, and support for the sale of our aircraft to the EAF. However, you know that Cargo Aircraft Company, as a foreign company, cannot act or even appear to unduly influence the decision process of your government."

Of course, he knew, like any politician anywhere in the world, that she knew exactly how this game was played. True to his expectations, she answered, "Of course. Therefore, may I recommend that I arrange to have you meet a very good friend of mine, Mr. Ali Omar. He is President of Military Aircraft Parts and Services Company, which is locally known as MAPS. Ali and I have worked together before to ensure the procurement of only the best military equipment for Egypt."

So now they had established the middle man. Amazing how the all the world used the same process! Larry Ray smiled. "Excellent, what a great idea. Please let him know that I'll be back in Cairo in a few weeks to present the EAF our proposal for the new aircraft. I can meet with him then to review the pricing and delivery details. Also, I expect he can arrange meetings between you and me so I can keep you up to speed." *And get to know you a LOT better.*

4

Third Game - San Francisco 49ers host Atlanta Falcons

49ers lose 17 to 34

The Atlanta Falcons' season was the franchise's twenty-third in the National Football League (NFL). The team was marred by tragedy when cornerback David Croudip died on October 10 after a cocaine overdose. It would be the first of three player deaths for the team in the space of two seasons.

The 49ers lost to the Falcons for only the fourth time since 1981. Joe Montana was intercepted three times *and* sacked three times in a 34–17 rout. Gerald Riggs of the Falcons rushed for 115 yard and a touchdown.

Zurich and Game Plan Review with Corp VP

The corporate "consultant/helper" playbook required the CAC "quarterback/salesman" to consult with the corporate regional Marketing VP prior to starting the play to find and select a "Helper!"

Therefore, Larry Ray needed to meet with and discuss his "Helper" requirement with Ahmed Sharif, the corporate VP for the Middle East. Interestingly, Ahmed had his office in Zurich.

Larry Ray thought, *Why would the Corporation have the Middle East marking office in Zurich, Switzerland?* Oh well, at least going up to Zurich was sure more enjoyable then going to some Middle East desert outpost!

Again, keeping in mind that all communications would be monitored, he needed to send a message that Ahmed would understand and not bring any undue attention to himself.

Even though he had met Ahmed many times at corporate and regional events, he carefully worded his message:

"Mr. Sharif, Greetings. Larry Ray Hardy here in Cairo. I have just completed my business and will be stopping in Zurich later this week to take a few days off before returning home. Hopefully we can meet for lunch. I know you plan to take a vacation to Cairo soon, so I would like to provide you with a list of some local sites you should see. I'll call you when I get settled in Zurich. Best Regards, Larry Ray."

The real succinct message, salesman to salesman was, *I'm planning to do CAC business in Egypt and need to brief you. I have already identified some of the players.*

Larry Ray didn't need to wait for a reply, as he already knew Ahmed was in his office this week. Next morning, he checked out of the Cairo Marriott and had his favorite taxi driver take him to the airport. He checked in at the EgyptAir first class counter. One of his rules was always to fly the local airline as a show of confidence in the country. EgyptAir had a fairly good safety record as compared to some of the crop duster airlines he had flown in various countries in central Africa. However, even in first class, EgyptAir didn't serve alcohol. On the plus side, the non-stop flight to Zurich was only a little over four hours. He would work up a thirst for some of the excellent Swiss wine!

Pleased that the flight was on time, Larry Ray sat back in his first class seat and considered his agenda for the meeting with Ahmed. He was aware that Ahmed had a good reputation for knowing his territory. So, the usual subject would be who was going to select and control the "Helper." Since Larry Ray already had a good idea of his team, he needed to have Ahmed pick the same team.

He landed just after midday in Zurich. The airport was close to the city center, so it was a short taxi ride to his hotel. Ahmed booked all his company visitors at the upscale and expensive Park Hyatt Hotel Zurich. Larry Ray liked his logic. If you are going to play in a big bucks game, you need to act like the big boy$ and fly first class, stay upscale, and eat and drink where they do.

The hotel was near the Zurich See, the Swiss name for Lake Zurich, just south of Ahmed's office. Again, Ahmed played the big money card in an exclusive high-rise office building. Not so coincidently, his office was near the Swiss branch of the Danish Saxo Bank, a large investment bank which was even more secure with account information than the usual Swiss banks. *Guess he liked to stay close to his money*!

After checking in and grabbing a short rest at the hotel, Larry Ray put on his big bucks game jersey—a dark blue suit, white shirt, and red power tie, just like in Alabama. *Ha!* Then he set out to meet Ahmed at the very high-end wine bar of the Mediterranean restaurant Terrasse, which overlooked the lake. Larry Ray knew they probably would not be serving his favorite food of fried catfish with hushpuppies!

Ahmed was also dressed to the nines in a most probably four-thousand-dollar suit. Larry Ray was not sure what category that was covered on the corporate expense report. *Maybe miscellaneous?*

Sharing a few remarks about the weather, the rigors of international business and travel, as well as the usual name dropping regarding their close personal relationships with the senior executives of the Corporation and its companies, they finished off a couple of glasses of wine, then got down to business.

Larry Ray explained that his goal, which was also the CAC goal, was to sell six CC-260 cargo aircraft and spares to Egypt for around four hundred million dollars. He mentioned that if the corporate Washington office could work their magic, the money could be available via FMS grant funds. This would be a great deal for Egypt. However, even if the corporate Washington lobbyist arranged that these funds could be applied to the CC-260 purchase, other corporate lobbyists in DC would also be trying to get these funds allocated to other military equipment like fighters, tanks, ships, or other arms. Therefore, it was essential that the Egyptian government direct that these available FMS funds be applied to the CC-260 purchase.

The players never knew who might be listening to their conversation, since they could not inspect the restaurant for surveillance microphones, such as taking apart the table or lights. Larry Ray recalled a company security briefing a few years ago about the discovery that an airline had all first class seats wired with hidden microphones to record conversations of businessmen enroute to the Paris Air Show, which is attended by all the world's aviation executives.

Not to be overly paranoid, but aware there might be an eavesdropper, Larry Ray passed Ahmed a sheet of paper which listed all the key players and their code names. He then outlined his Egyptian roster using vague language. But Ahmed could see from the paper that the key military players were TUT (MOD), key decision maker on airplanes verses other military equipment, and Karnak (EAF Air Marshal), key to selecting CC-260 cargo aircraft over fighters or helicopters. Darius (EAF Air Commodore) was a potential source to supply CAC with EAF insider information. The key government player, Cleopatra, would influence her government committee to favor using the US FMS funds to purchase CC-260 aircraft. He didn't mention his meetings with Colonel Barnes, or especially Cleopatra, as he wanted Ahmed to earn his big corporate salary. That meant not doing his job for him.

Lastly, he indicated to Ahmed that he understood that the company MAPS might be a good candidate as the local support contractor, the latest title for consultants, helpers, or fixers!

Ahmed apparently appreciated all the information Larry Ray had provided, as he offered to pick up the bill for dinner. Larry Ray wondered what name Ahmed would use for him on his expense report. *Probably "His Excellency Whoever."*

Ahmed stated that he was going to make a visit to Cairo the next week to meet with the US Ambassador and a couple of Egyptian government officials regarding setting up a corporate office in Cairo. This would give him the opportunity to review with some of his other sources to see what team it would take to score Larry Ray's deal.

They parted company in high spirits. It was amazing how good that bottle of wine made them feel when they both believed they each had an opportunity to make a score in more ways than one.

Next morning, Larry Ray returned to the airport for his first class Swiss Air flight back to the US. *Happy days!* Swiss Air did serve alcohol on its flights, and lots of it.

Meanwhile, Ahmed was in his office preparing his own game plan.

Corp VP Develops His "Own" Game Plan

This was not Ahmed Sharif's "first rodeo" or game! He was born in Amman, Jordan, into a very wealthy and politically well-connected family. He attended private schools in Jordan, received his second level or bachelor's degree at Cambridge in the UK and his third level or master's degree in political science at Georgetown in Washington DC, a course he himself could have taught. He was fluent in Arabic, English, and French. Switzerland had three official languages: French, German, and Italian. Although German was the official language in Zurich, French was extremely popular, so it worked well to have his office in Zurich, close to the money.

He was a true international businessman. Ahmed carried two passports, one American, the other Jordanian. Besides his Cargo Aircraft Corporate VP business card, he also carried a business card that indicated he was Executive VP of a Jordanian Export-Import Company named Jordanian Enterprise Team, or JET for short.

Now from time to time, usually after a few, *OK, quite a few*, drinks, Ahmed would hint that his Jordanian company was founded by a three letter agency that only handles offshore accounts. He never actually said CIA; however, he never denied the initials were CIA. So, Ahmed was not only a highly paid CAC corporate executive, he was moonlighting for another company! Calls to his office in Amman were answered in Arabic by an off-site receptionist and forwarded to his office in Zurich or mobile phone.

Actually, there was a JET office set up for him in Amman if he ever needed to have visitors or a meeting there. And it was smart and more politically beneficial to travel throughout the Middle East as a Jordanian, rather than an American, businessman. Moreover, being Jordanian, he could meet with government officials and military officers without raising any eyebrows or suspicions!

Ahmed made a few calls to set up his appointments in Cairo, then left the next morning for Egypt. For this trip he was the Jordanian JET executive, so he flew to Cairo through Amman on Royal Jordanian Airlines.

Ahmed checked into the Steigenberger Hotel El Tahrir, keeping his apparent loyalty to non-American chains. It was located near the government office buildings in central Cairo. He had a full schedule for the next two days, so he quickly unpacked and went down to the elegant restaurant located off the lobby. He settled into a small table, and ordered a glass of his favorite French red wine, while he perused the menu. At least he could have some authentic Middle-Eastern food. After the wine was served and he had ordered his favorite Arab dish, lamb kebab halabi, with falafel and hummus as a starter, he started going over some of the notes from the meeting with Larry Ray, as well as reviewing key contacts from his previous business dealings in Cairo.

Just as he was finishing his dinner, a beautiful Egyptian woman walked over to his table and sat down. She exclaimed, "Ahmed, how naughty of you to not let me know you were coming to town! Worse yet, you are here in my city having dinner by yourself."

Ahmed replied, "Tasha, this is a pleasant surprise," while he thought, *Either the international visitor tracking system at the Cairo airport is better than I expected, or the word was out that I was coming to town.*

Tasha said, "My brother mentioned you were coming to meet with him, and I know you always stay at this hotel, since it is close to his office. I just finished a meeting across the street, so thought I would stop over to see if you were here. What an amazing coincidence!"

Ahmed thought, *Sure, an amazing coincidence!*

He recalled they had first met over a year ago at her brother's house for a small private dinner party. Both she and her brother knew he had dual citizenships as well as dual business representations. They also respected that while in Cairo, he played only his Jordanian role. Well, as someone once said 'The plot thickens," *or certainly gets more interesting.*

He ordered a glass of wine for Tasha, and they went through the pleasantries about the weather, airline flights, hotels, and traffic.

Getting down to business, Tasha began, "Talk about a small world! Would you believe that a couple of days ago I happened to meet Mr. Hardy, the Cargo Aircraft Company salesman who was here to start a sales campaign to sell his, or should I say, your, CC-260 cargo aircraft to the Egyptian Air Force. Do you know him?"

What an opening! Ahmed knew this was going to be a fruitful evening. Fortunately, the wine was good, and there was lots of it. He noticed that Tasha had placed a small metal box in the center of the table. He knew it was an electronic signal jamming device. That meant that this conversation was going to be private and get serious.

Ahmed answered, "I know Larry Ray Hardy very well. In fact,

he visited me in Zurich right after his visit to Cairo to discuss this sale and request my help in making the in-country support arrangements." He knew this was exactly what Tasha wanted to hear.

Now she made her play. "You know, Ahmed, that Egyptian military purchases are much more complicated than just having a good product at a fair price! I expect this is not, as the Americans say, your first rodeo! Also, this is not my first rodeo, so let's get to the point. For starters, I assume you have not made any local support contacts or commitments for this sale?"

Ahmed responded, "Tasha, that is exactly why I am here. How fortunate that you are my first contact!"

Tasha smiled. "As you would expect, in my position on the Government Defense Procurement Committee, I know how the system works, or better yet, how to work the system. In Egyptian defense purchases there are three critical steps. In your case we need to ensure that the Egyptian Air Force selects your airplane and that the Minister of Defense supports and approves the purchase. Finally, my government committee would approve the funding, whether using Egyptian money or US-offered FMS funds."

Tasha paused to take a sip of wine, and then she continued. "So, before we discuss how to work the system, I need your commitment that we will work together on this project, unless you wish to spend your precious time and money looking for a better advisor. Additionally, let me assure you that my team does include my brother. Your word is good enough for me at this time. And I'm sure you know that if you commit to me and later change your mind to use someone else to facilitate your deal, I can also ensure that deal never happens."

Ahmed took a long drink of his wine while thinking, *She's the sister of the Minister of Defense and on the Government Military Procurement Committee, so she could certainly make or break the deal.* Since she had approached him this early in the process, it was a good indication that the purchase of the CC-260 airplanes already had good traction in their system. So again, as those Americans say, 'Don't look a gift horse in the mouth." He laughed and almost choked on his wine at the thought of Tasha as a horse.

He also knew this would be a very interesting and very sensitive arrangement, as she was a government official. In the United States, the Foreign Corrupt Practices Act prohibited the use and compensation of government officials to obtain business. He knew that Egypt also had restrictions on "baksheesh," also known as bribery. However, they were seldom enforced, especially at the senior government official level.

Ahmed replied, "Tasha, as you said, this is not my first rodeo. I am the Cargo Aircraft Corporate VP with the responsibility not only to recommend a "Helper," but also to have the final say on whomever any of our companies nominate to assist them to sell their products or services in the Middle East. That's why Mr. Hardy came to me to ask me to recommend the local support for his sale. More importantly, I am very aware of the restrictions of the Foreign Corrupt Practices Act." But he expected she already knew about the FCPA, implied in her comment that this wasn't her first rodeo either.

Tasha nodded her head. "Ahmed, it is clear that we both know how to play this game, so let's discuss our strategy and plan the expenses required to win."

They clinked their wine glasses and got down to business.

She opened. "First, tell me how much we have to work with, so I can judge if this is worth my team's time and effort."

Ahmed said, "One sure play we have is that our Washington DC corporate office can arrange for the availability of FMF-FMS funding for the aircraft purchase and a significant spares package. The price of each aircraft for the Egyptian Air Force will be around sixty million dollars. Six times that amount equals three hundred sixty million. Spares packages are usually around ten percent, so add another thirty-six million, for a total of three hundred ninety-six million dollars."

Ahmed paused for a moment to let that amount sink in, then went on. "The final price will be basically non-negotiable as the Cargo Aircraft Company will tell the Egyptian Air Force that in order to use US FMS funds CAC must sell the aircraft at the same price as they do to the US Air Force. However, this is also not CAC's first rodeo. Although they will confirm that the EAF aircraft configuration is the same as an existing US Air Force configuration, there has never been an airplane delivered in a basic configuration. Also, there are a multitude of USAF standard options included in this price. No USAF or Pentagon bean counter would ever be able to determine an USAF equivalent price. More importantly, the six aircraft have already been built and are ready for immediate delivery, so we have the opportunity for a quick score."

Ahmed could see from Tasha's enthusiastic expression, that she was probably already thinking about how she was going to spend her big reward. "Tasha, I have put together "Helper" agreements in over twenty Mid-East and African countries, so before you go out to buy that Rolls Royce, let me explain what levels of compensation are achievable from CAC and the Corporation. Please appreciate there is a lot of company and corporate oversight and approvals for any agreement for an in-country support of a sale. With the use of FMS funds. the Company is required to certify to the US Government that no portion of US FMS funds were used for a commission, fee, award, or bonus associated with a purchase. However, the Company and Corporation know how to work the system."

Tasha looked intrigued. Ahmed came to the heart of the matter. "Here are my thoughts for our "Helper" strategy. The Company is willing to certify that a fee per aircraft—they dislike using the word commission—of up to three percent will be identified as being paid out of Company overall profits, but not related to the profit on the actual sale. So that would provide you with almost eleven million dollars to work with! Again, before you spend it all, I expect that here in Egypt, like in every other country, it will require more than a single person to make this sale happen. Plus, I will need some incentives for my CAC executive team to get the FMS funds approved and to obtain company and corporate approval of your team."

Tasha appeared a little irritated at being lectured to, and snapped, "Ahmed, please don't treat me like the new kid on the block. I have just as much experience as you in establishing the right team and making deals happen. Since the amount available is significant, I suggest we also include incentives on the spares package. In my experience, they are more profitable and have less oversight associated with them."

Ahmed thought, *Score one for the "Helper" team.* She was already a step or two ahead of him. He apologized. "Please pardon me, I did not mean to insult your intelligence or business experience. You are entirely correct. With a spares package of thirty-six million there is considerably more latitude on the amount we can work with. Spares are the most profitable portion of any aircraft sale. No one can ever audit spares prices, as they can vary by configuration from day to day. In several other countries, based on my recommendation the Corporation has used a local support contractor to handle the spares business for the company and in some cases, again based on my recommendation, the support contractor is also the "Helper."

Ahmed was about to mention the support contractor candidate, MAPS, that Larry Ray had mentioned, when Tasha said," I know just the perfect company to be your support contractor. My close friend Ali Omar is the president of the company, Military Parts and Services, and has worked with me on some other projects."

Ahmed again almost choked on his wine at her mention of MAPS. He thought, *Isn't it an amazing coincidence that Larry Ray, and now Tasha, just happen to recommend the same company as the support contractor*. Since he knew there was no such thing in this business for this type of coincidence, it was clear that Larry Ray might be making an "end run" to score some extra points for himself.

Ahmed knew it was time to place a few more cards on the table so that he and Tasha could start with a clean slate, or game plan. "Tasha, by any chance, have you met with Larry Ray Hardy?"

"Why, yes. Last week at the US Embassy reception. I did happen to run into him again a couple of days later. I expected that he had briefed you on our discussion. However, it appears from your question that he did not share all we discussed."

Ahmed frowned. "Tasha, let me clarify how this works. Larry Ray is the airplane salesman. His responsibility is to convince the Egyptian Air Force to buy the CAC CC-260 airplanes. The identification and selection of a local "Helper" or support contractor is my responsibility. Larry Ray knows this and last week, per company and corporate procedure, asked me to come to Cairo to do just that. Between you and me, my concern is he may be thinking of some sort of "Special Play" where he obtains a share of your fee. However, for the time being, let's be extra careful what you commit to him, while still encouraging him, as he is a key element to making the sale happen. So, let's allow him to run his "Special Play" with you for the time being. Again, keep in mind that Larry Ray is not included in my incentive team."

"So, let me summarize how I see the game scores for both of our teams. It will take some time to prepare and obtain approval of all the support contractor contracts. However, here are my best estimates of the bottom lines for each." Ahmed took out a pen and wrote on a cocktail napkin:

6 x CC-260 Purchase "Support" funds at around 3% = $10 + m

Spares "Support" funds at around 15% = $5 + m

Total = $ 15 + m Estimate
- may vary slightly by final contract

Egyptian Team – X players = 75% so approx. $ 10m

Ahmed's Team - CAC* Exec's + Corp Exec's = 25% so approx. $ 5m

*does not include Larry Ray

46

Ahmed could see he certainly had her interest, so he said, "Tasha, it's getting late and since I'll be here a couple more days, I suggest you review our arrangement with your players, and that we meet before I leave to confirm we are using the same playbook."

Her look of approval indicated that this meeting had gone better than she had expected. "Ahmed, I believe we are off to a good start. Let's plan to meet again the day after tomorrow. I'll let you know the time and place." With that, Tasha stood up and quickly left the restaurant.

Ahmed smiled as he paid the bill, thinking, *Now that was a true business meeting*! Since he could never use her name on his expense report. he asked the name of the waiter. Ahmed would give him an appropriate title which no bean counter would be able to trace.

Cairo – Working the Territory-The US Embassy

The next morning, Ahmed, as the Cargo Aircraft Corporate VP, visited the US Embassy to meet with the Ambassador to advise him of the possibility for the sale of CC-260 aircraft to the Egyptian Air Force. Of course, he would ask the Ambassador for his support, even though he knew the Ambassador was a political appointee who had no idea how to make things happen in the third world.

Upon reaching the Ambassador's corner office on the top floor of the Embassy, he was immediately ushered in. The office was overly-decorated with Egyptian artifacts, which probably were there to make the Ambassador feel like he was imbedded in the country. As Ahmed entered, he was not surprised to see that the Air Attaché', a USAF officer, would also be included in the meeting, since the meeting subject was military aircraft.

Ahmed started with, "Ambassador Knox, it is a pleasure to see you again. Thanks for seeing me on short notice."

The Ambassador replied, "Mr. Sharif, welcome to Egypt. Please appreciate that we are here to provide advice and support to all American companies, especially those like Cargo Aircraft, that offer American products which can strengthen the position of Egypt in the region. Accordingly, I have invited my Air Attaché, Colonel Barnes, to join us for this meeting."

Ahmed shook hands with the Ambassador and Colonel Barnes. They all took seats around a large conference table, with the Ambassador taking command by sitting at the head of the table. A secretary served coffee and they went through the standard discussion of weather and the rigors of international travel.

The Ambassador eventually asked, "Mr. Sharif, what can the US Embassy here in Egypt do for the Cargo Aircraft Corporation?"

Ahmed launched into his "We need your help" pitch. "As you know, the Cargo Aircraft CC-260 military cargo aircraft are able, not only to fulfill all military cargo and troop transport missions, but they are also country builders. The ZEUS can conduct many humanitarian missions, such as disaster relief, search and rescue, evacuations, and critical resupply in remote areas. There is no question that Egypt, like many developing countries, can certainly make good use of a fleet of CC-260 aircraft. I'm sure Colonel Barnes can confirm the exceptional role of our aircraft."

Colonel Barnes nodded his head. "I do confirm that the CC-260 provides exceptional capabilities to the US Air Force and it would be of great service to any country. I am very familiar with the CC-260 and will encourage my contacts in the Egyptian Air Force to give your aircraft due consideration."

Ahmed had heard this support speech from many ambassadors and staff. After all, it was what they were paid to do. He might as well tell them how CAC was going to make their job easier.

He replied, "We at CAC appreciate and thank you for your support. As you both know, the US Government provides Foreign Military Sales funds to many countries to support the addition of equipment that both makes the country militarily stronger, as well as supports the US objectives in their region. I have it on very good authority that there will be FMS grant funds made available to Egypt for only the purchase of CC-260 aircraft."

Both the Ambassador and the Colonel were a little taken aback. It was usually the embassy that advised US companies of the availability of FMS funds. Additionally, the embassy usually recommended the product or service to receive such funds. Although most businessmen would be upset at being blindsided, these two were true politicians who had learned to "Go with the flow." So, in the spirit of being on the team, the Ambassador stated, "Well, that certainly will make out job easier. However, I need to await official notification from Washington on FMS funds specifically for CC-260 aircraft before I can pull strings over here."

Ahmed thought, *Ha! Pull strings!* The only strings these two could pull would be to run the American flag up the pole on top of the embassy! However, being the diplomatic corporate visitor, he answered, "Mr. Ambassador and Colonel Barnes, please be assured the Cargo Aircraft Corporation will keep you informed on both the status of our EAF sales campaign, as well as any information our Washington office has on the status of FMS funding for Egypt's purchase of CC260 aircraft."

Ahmed knew it was time to leave, having reassured them they would be kept in the loop. He arose, and parted with, "I know you are very busy. Thank you for your time."

As Ahmed left the embassy, he was comfortable that he had made the Ambassador aware that a CC-260 sale was in the works. Ahmed expected that the Ambassador, being a political appointee, would not do anything to rock the boat. Ahmed also found it interesting that Colonel Barnes did not mention that he had already met with Larry Ray. Ahmed again felt concern that Larry Ray was making some of his own plays.

Cairo – Working the Territory-The Helper.

Upon returning to his hotel, Ahmed had an unsigned message waiting for him which said, "If convenient, can you meet with your new friend at the Military Aircraft Parts and Services Company office adjacent to the Almaza Air Base on El-Nasr Rd at 6:00 PM this evening. Security will have your Jordanian info on their file, so please call them to confirm you will be arriving." This was followed by a local telephone number. Ahmed quickly understood that, in dealing with his Egyptian team, he would be using his Jordanian identity. He immediately called to confirm the appointment.

Since he had a free afternoon, he decided he should take care of some administrative business, as in open up a local bank account. Coincidently, an HSBC bank was located a block up the street from his hotel, another amazing coincidence, since his Jordanian Company already had an account at HSBC. It was surely convenient with his travels that this Chinese Bank had branches in over 50 countries.

He walked over to the bank and asked to meet with the manager. With his Jordanian HSBC well-endowed account, the manager was pleased to open another local account. He immediately transferred fifty thousand dollars into this Egyptian account. Then he withdrew ten thousand to buy ten American Express thousand-dollar gift cards.

He spent the rest of the afternoon working out his game strategy. Although he didn't necessarily have an offensive and defensive team, he did have an Egyptian and American team.

That evening, Ahmed arrived at the MAPS office building right on time, passed easily through security, and was escorted up to the top floor executive office area and ushered into a very pleasant conference room. Two people were there—Tasha, and a very tall, well-dressed Egyptian.

Tasha greeted him. "Ahmed, thank you for coming. Allow me to introduce you to Mr. Ali Omar, the President of Military Aviation Parts and Service Company."

Mr. Omar extended his hand, saying, "Mr. Sharif, a pleasure to meet you. Tasha tells me there is a very good business opportunity available for us. Please have a seat and allow me to provide you a short briefing on my company."

Ahmed thought, *I like him already because he is not playing the usual "Howdy to You" conversation game.*

Once they were all seated, Ali Omar continued. "Firstly, it's "Ali" among friends. I founded this company five years ago after many years working as a civilian executive in the Equipment Purchasing Division of the Egyptian Ministry of Defense. I have worked with many countries to acquire military equipment, spares, support, training, publications, and other related elements of logistics and program support. I have not had the opportunity to work with the Cargo Aircraft Company. However, we are very familiar with support for aviation products such as fighters, helicopters, and missiles. So, I already have a very good working relationship with the Egyptian Air Force and the Ministry of Defense. Of course, Tasha and I have a very close working relationship. You know the golden rule: "She who controls the gold, rules!"

Ahmed could see by the eye contact and expressions that there definitely was a close working relationship. He had also done some checking on MAPS since Larry Ray had already mentioned them. It was clear MAPS had a good track record and was the prime candidate as the CAC Egyptian Support Contractor on this deal. Also, with Tasha and apparently her brother on this team, he need not spend any more time looking for a "Helper."

Ahmed responded, "Ali, thank you. Based on MAPS considerable experience and strong local recommendation, I will propose to CAC and the Corporation that we use MAPS as our official support contractor for our CAC CC-260 Program in Egypt. I would appreciate receiving a summary of your capabilities, experience, staff, and facilities that you have to support our product, spares, training, and publications, as well as office space and local transportation."

Since he had already outlined the available "incentive$" with Tasha, he didn't wish to have another discussion or negotiation of payment for support in a possibly unsecure office. Also, there was usually a Statement of Work prior to discussing payments. However, he was sure that with their apparent relationship, Tasha had already laid the pipe. Maybe even laid more than the pipe!

Ahmed continued, "Once I receive your support proposal, I will meet with the Cargo Aircraft senior management to obtain their agreement to use MAPS. After I have the company agreement, I will then obtain approval of the Corporation. Following those approvals, I will come here to submit our support contractor agreement and discuss the compensation we can offer for the services you provide."

Ali replied, "Ahmed, I look forward to working with you and the Cargo Aircraft Corporation. I will have our CC-260 support proposal to you within a couple of days. Please do not hesitate to call me if you or your Corporation have any questions."

They shook hands again and Ahmed played his "Thank you" card. "Ali and Tasha, I truly appreciate the time you are spending to help me do my job here. Since I don't live here and therefore cannot show my appreciation with a few dinners or other get-togethers, please accept this little "Thank you" from me to you." He then gave them each a sealed envelope containing five American Express gift cards which he knew they wouldn't open in front of him.

Again, this was not Ahmed's first rodeo. These five thousand dollars in gift cards to each of them was really an insurance, or fall back, which he hoped he wouldn't have to use. However, if either of them attempted to turn on him later in this game, they had both just accepted money from Jordanian Enterprise Team, JET, which he would tell them was actually associated with the CIA. No foreign government official or business person ever would want it known publicly they had received money from the CIA. Again, Ahmed hoped he would never have to use that play.

Tasha left the conference room with Ahmed. Once they had exited the building and were clear of any listening devices, Ahmed said to Tasha, while they waited for their private taxis, "Tasha, it's clear to me that you have the right team. Please tell Ali to add an extra five percent to the price on his support contractor proposal and to spread it over ten years and request thirty percent on the spares package. This will allow us to let the CAC Finance VP show how good he is by negotiating MAPS down five percent on support and ten percent on spares handling. Then, when we spread the support over ten years, the yearly amounts of around one million dollars will not raise any eyebrows."

"Prior to the CC-260 contract being signed, we will arrange for an initial payment for the initial two years. Once the US Government funds and pays for the aircraft and the spares package, and you have transferred the reward for my team, we will then pay the remaining amount for the other eight years. Again, keep in mind that Larry Ray is not on my team, so you will need to take care of him." Ahmed thought, *Maybe in more ways than one*!

Tasha commented, "I knew I would like working with you. Don't worry. I will take care of Larry Ray to keep him happy." They laughed at their inside joke, then left in their respective taxis. Ahmed knew it was time to work his side of the field.

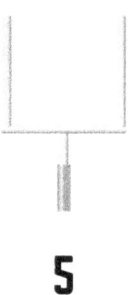

5

FOURTH GAME- SAN FRANCISCO 49ERS AT SEATTLE SEAHAWKS

49ers win 36 - 7

The 49ers attained 580 yards of offense to defeat the Seahawks. Montana threw four touchdown passes and Young added a fifth. Craig and Rathman made 186 rushing yards. The Seahawks quarterback Kemp was intercepted three times.

Mobile Alabama – Cargo Aircraft Company

After a first class Swiss Air flight across the Atlantic to Washington DC, Larry Ray had survived the American Airlines economy section one-stop flight to Mobile. Someday he hoped that someone would provide non-stop service with at least business class. He picked up his truck at the long-term lot and drove to his apartment in downtown Mobile on Georgia Avenue. He liked that the address reflected his redneck roots! He had a small apartment, as he was not left with a lot of spending money following the unpleasant divorces of his past two wives.

He thought, *I really need to find a way to supplement my CAC pay so I can get back to living the life style I deserve, or at least get a new pickup truck.* He hoped that his new Egyptian friend would be willing to score a few "extra point$" for him.

The next morning Larry Ray returned to his office at the CAC

CC-260 manufacturing plant at the Mobile Aeroplex-Airport. Once he got settled in and had a few cups of coffee, he called to schedule a meeting with the VP of Marketing, Mark Maddox. He would need to request that Mark's secretary ask his new next-level boss, Director of International Marketing, Robert McTelall, to join them. He was another one of those corporate guys down from Washington DC, who thought they knew it all. How many airplanes had he ever sold? Anyhow, Mark and Larry Ray already had a good working relationship. He expected that Mark could keep McTelall from interfering and messing up his sale.

They all met in Mark's office on the executive level. There was not much "Howdy Do" talk, as Larry Ray got right down to business. He summarized his meeting in Cairo with the US Ambassador. Although Larry Ray had only seen the ambassador at the embassy reception, and had not spoken directly to him, he informed the group that the ambassador fully supported the sale of the CC-260 to the EAF. He then exaggerated the extent of his meeting with the Minister of Defense. Listening to Larry Ray, you would think they were now drinking buddies. He highlighted his meeting with Colonel Barnes and the two senior EAF officers, saying that the Colonel suggested the trip to Paris with EAF senior staff to inspect the new CC-260 aircraft.

He reiterated what he knew from Ken Doyle, Corporate VP in the Washington office, relating that FMS funds were available for Egypt to purchase up to six CC-260 aircraft. Finally, he mentioned that the ambassador had suggested they contact a local company named Military Aviation Parts and Service to provide local support for their business. He added that Ahmed Sharif was currently in Cairo to follow up with his own contacts on the potential for the sale, as well as check out MAPS. Larry Ray knew that no one would check with Ambassador Knox or Colonel Barnes to verify his report. He deliberately did not mention Tasha Mostafa, since she was supposedly outside his area of responsibility. Plus, she was on his special team.

Mark thanked Larry Ray for his very detailed report and said it sure sounded like he had very good potential for a big sale.

Finally, it was time to hear from "the elephant in the room." Mark addressed the new guy from Corporate, hiding a smirk. "Robert, please give us your opinion based on your extensive experience in international sales."

Robert began, "Larry Ray, it appears to me that you certainly are off to a good start. In my experience, the customer, the EAF, will usually accept whatever the power players tell them to buy. I see the need for us to solidify support from four areas. The first would be to ensure that US Government FMS funds are available and directed specifically for the Egyptian purchase of six CC-260 aircraft in addition to the appropriate spares package. Second, we need the Egyptian Ministry of Defense to support the purchase of six CC-260 aircraft, but that shouldn't be too difficult if they are essentially free."

Robert looked around to see if everybody was on board so far. Satisfied they were in agreement on these two initial points, he continued. "Third, the Government Military Procurement Committee must support using FMS funds for this purchase, which shouldn't be too difficult, because the money is not theirs. Fourth, you are going to need a very well-connected local consultant, or agent, or support contractor, or whatever term this company uses. In Washington DC, we call them lobbyists. They are usually expensive and, as you both know, we cannot include commissions, fees, bonuses, or any kind of monetary award in a sale using FMS funds."

Both Mark and Larry Ray sat there looking sort of stunned. Robert could tell that they apparently hadn't taken the time to read his corporate résumé highlighting his four billion dollars' worth of corporate international sales to over twenty countries at high profits.

He was thinking, *And here they are sitting there with twelve completed, but unsold, CC-260 aircraft on their airport ramp. You would think they would appreciate some help in moving these whitetails.*

Mark recovered first and said, "Robert, this is not our first rodeo! All of the areas you mention are in work either thru Larry Ray, or our International VP, Ken Doyle and Mid-East VP, Ahmed Sharif. We know how to sell airplanes and would appreciate your advice on whatever local support agreement Ahmed recommends."

Since it was probably not the best time to remind them they had twelve unsold aircraft on the ramp, especially from the new guy, Robert responded, "Mark and Larry Ray, I'm just offering my understanding of the issues for a successful sale. If you already have this all in the works, then good for you. Mark, I am here to provide my assistance as you request and offer guidance to Larry Ray." It was looking to Robert like they really didn't want to have any further discussion on this subject.

Mark ended the meeting with, "Great! Both Larry Ray and I will be pleased to have your advice."

It appeared to Robert that they both knew he had a good working relationship with the corporate chairman, and didn't want to appear uncooperative. As he and Larry Ray were leaving the office, Mark called out to Larry Ray, "Hey, Larry Ray. Could you stay for a minute? I need your advice on where to go fishing this week-end."

With the new guy out of the office, Mark and Larry Ray got down to the real business discussion. Mark said, "OK, with that corporate spy gone, tell me how it's really going."

Larry Ray then reiterated a short version of his previous report. concluding that the EAF was on-board and the sale really hinged on Ahmed finding the right "Helper," and then getting both company and corporate approval of the incentives the "Helper" would need to get the sale approved.

Mark assured Larry Ray that he had the skids greased for approval of a "Helper" and was confident that Ahmed would select the best local team to score this sale. Of course, the sale was also dependent on getting FMS funds allocated to Egypt for this purchase of six CC-260 aircraft. Mark then mentioned that the allocation of FMS funds was being handled by his longtime friend, the Washington DC Corporate VP, Ken Doyle.

Mark concluded, "Larry Ray, I want you to continue to prepare the sales proposal and ignore the airplane configuration the EAF may want and write the proposal to exactly match the configuration of the CC-260 aircraft sitting on the ramp. Since they will be free gifts to the EAF via FMS funds, they will take what we give them. I'll check with Ahmed on his progress in selecting the "Helper." In the meantime, let's not share too many details with McTelall. I'll send him to Washington to work with Doyle to keep him out of our hair."

Larry Ray had already provided Mark the code names he and

Ahmed had established. However, since neither had mentioned their meetings with Tasha, "Cleopatra" was not in the game yet. Mark also had developed another code name list for the Cargo Aircraft Company, including corporate, players. He had certainly played this game before.

After Larry Ray left his office, Mark composed a message to Ahmed at his Jordanian office address which he would send himself.

(To the Ticket-Holders: The real names are inserted in parentheses to save you from flipping back to the roster.)

Mark wrote: "Sphinx (*Ahmed*). I just had a good report from Roadrunner (*Larry Ray*). Expect you are working on a local resource program with a plan to take care of Tut (*MOD Mostafa*), Karnak (*AM Saad*) and Montu (AC *Riad*), as well as select the Resource Program Manager (*Helper*). Once you make your recommendation, I can assure that both Undertaker *(President Frank Moore,)*, and Eagle (*Corporate VP Ken Doyle*) are on board as part of our team, and will approve your recommendation. Also, we will be able to direct the players not on our team, Roadrunner, Black Cloud (*VP Finance Jim Smith*), Snake (*General Counsel Vince Holliday*), and the new guy, Coach (*Robert McTelall*) to also approve what you propose. As in the past, let's be careful to keep our game plan closely held. Appears to me there can be a lot of "extra points" for our team in this game.

Later on, while Larry Ray went about his business of working with the technical and contract staff to prepare the proposal for the EAF, Mark arranged an off-site meeting with the CAC President. The company had a policy initiated by the legal department that the office secretary was to document all senior level meetings with the subject and attendees! Mark thought, *Those company lawyers are sure nosey*!

CAC - Off-Site – Strategy Meeting

As usual these special secretive off-site meetings were held at the president's home, an estate on the Dog River, an actual Alabama river not far from the CAC facility. Frank had a very large house on a couple of acres, which included a large boat house over the river. His current boat only required a small portion of the covered dock. Frank expected the "extra points" from this Egyptian game would allow him to upgrade to a more suitable boat, maybe even a yacht.

On this sunny afternoon, the two co-conspirators, as they thought of themselves humorously, settled into lounge chairs with their bourbons, neat. Mark led off with, "It's been a long dry spell, and I'm not talking about when we both had our last drink." This caused them both to chuckle.

Mark continued, "My sales boys have not been doing very well, or actually doing much at all. But we've just been given a great opportunity to unload six of those whitetails to the Egyptian Air Force at a good price in the next couple of months. Larry Ray is working the basics, and our first-string team member Ahmed is laying the pipe in Egypt. Frank, as you know, it's going to take a team effort here and at Corporate to approve the local support package that Ahmed needs to get the sale accomplished. It appears that with FMS funding and the customer encouraged to accept six of the whitetails as they sit, we can have a very profitable sale, which will make our corporate fathers happy and improve our chance for those small corporate bonuses."

Now Frank smiled, because he knew what was coming next. Sure enough, Mark didn't miss a beat. "Now you know that we also have our own bonus program that I call "extra points," which rewards the home team's key players. As in the past, I will work with Ahmed to set up the "extra points" for the two of us, plus Ken Doyle, who is our special team member in the Washington DC corporate office. No one else is participating in our special bonus program, so mum is the word with Larry Ray, Smith, Holliday, and especially, McTelall."

Frank drained his drink, and sat forward. "Mark, any idea yet of the value of this sale?"

Mark settled more comfortably in his chair, looking very pleased with himself. He replied, "Looks like we can get full price for all six aircraft. So, six times sixty million equals three hundred sixty million dollars. Plus I expect we can get the EAF to request a ten percent spares package for another thirty-six million. That puts us close to four hundred million!"

Frank knew that CC-260 international sales were the highest profit maker for the company at around twenty-two percent, and usually around forty percent on a spare's sale. He quickly calculated a potential profit of over ninety-five million. He knew that Ahmed would probably need ten to fifteen percent of that for his teams, which would include the "extra points" for the home team. Even with that, the Corporation would be happy just getting rid of half of the whitetails at a still very high profit.

Mark laid out the immediate plans. "Once Ahmed has the local "Helper" selected, I'll have him come over here to help us sell the "Helper" package to finance and legal. I expect we should have his selection package by next week. In the meantime, please see what you can do to have the Washington corporate office confirm the availability of the FMS funds for these aircraft and spares, and expedite their allocation."

Mark then wrapped it up. "I know you and our Washington office team member Ken Doyle have done all this before, so it should be a slam dunk, or should I say, touchdown. I am going to send McTelall up to DC to monitor this process. Not much he can do up there, but it gets him out of our way for a while. I'm still not sure whether he was sent here to help us, or to spy on us. We'll just have to see if he is a player or a referee."

The next day Mark sent a message to Ken Doyle, a member of his team, advising him that he was sending Robert McTelall up to work with him to secure the FMS funding for the six CC-260 aircraft and spares. He had already briefed Doyle on the game strategy, so he was aware that McTelall was not a member of the team, and only needed to be briefed on the standard process of obtaining FMS funding.

He then called McTelall on the phone and simply say, "Robert, I have advised Ken Doyle that you will be coming up to assist them in ensuring that FMS funds will be made available, and specifically allocated to the Egyptian CC-260 aircraft and spares purchase very soon. I suggest you go up to DC tomorrow. I can handle any of the international sales campaigns while you are away. Don't worry, I'll keep you informed on any important activity."

McTelall thought, *I'm sure you will, except anything to do with Egypt.* However, he replied cordially, "Mark, I'll do my best to work with Ken to get the FMS funds allocated ASAP."

The next morning McTelall went to the adjacent Mobile airport main terminal. As he waited in the security line, he wondered who was using the CAC Company Biz Jet today. It was authorized by the Corporation to provide speedy transportation to Washington DC and other major US and international cities, since there were not many non-stop flights out of MOB. He expected it was on standby for Frank Moore and Mark Maddox in case they had to flee the country prior to being indicted for some of the under-the-table deals it was rumored they had made.

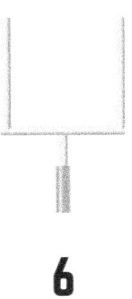

6

FIFTH GAME · SAN FRANCISCO 49ERS HOST DETROIT LIONS

49ers win 20 to 13

San Francisco led the entire game. There was no score in the first quarter. In the second quarter Rice ran for a touchdown and Cofer kicked a field goal. Then the Lions kicked a field goal. The score at the half was 10 to 3.

Early in the second half, 49er Taylor returned a punt seventy-seven yards for a touchdown. Also, Murry kicked a second field goal to make it 17 to 6 at the end of the third quarter. In the fourth quarter, Cofer kicked another field goal and Lion Mandley scored a touchdown.

Washington DC- CAC Corp Headquarters

The CAC Corporate office was located on the top floor of a high-rise office building in Pentagon City. Whereas most executives would like an office with a spectacular view of the city, the CAC Corporate executives were pleased that they had a great view of the headquarters of their main customer, the Pentagon. Additionally, the office was adjacent to Reagan National Airport, which kept visitors from spending hours experiencing the beltway traffic jams.

Ken Doyle, Corporate VP International Business, had initially worked for several years for Frank Moore at CAC. He, with some covert support from Frank, had been promoted to the corporate office with a clear understanding between himself and Frank that CAC interest always came first. Moreover, Frank had made him a player on his "extra points" team. When McTelall was at the corporate office, he had a slightly lower level position as Director International Marketing, so he did not know Ken very well. McTelall was usually absent, being directly involved in the international sales campaigns for the various companies. Ken really didn't like to travel. He preferred that those people needing help come to see him at his office.

After landing at Reagan, McTelall took the free shuttle to the Crystal Gateway Marriott hotel, which could actually be seen from the airport. Since the hotel was adjacent to the corporate office, McTelall proceeded to walk over to the office after checking in. As he entered, he received a warm reception from various staff and secretaries. When he reached Doyle's office for his scheduled meeting, the secretary advised him that Ken was still at another meeting, and she would call McTelall when Ken was available. This was not unusual, so McTelall put the time to good use to visit with several good friends. After an hour or so, Doyle's secretary called to tell him Ken was now available.

As McTelall walked into Doyle's office, he was again amazed at the number of pictures of Doyle with senior government senators, congressmen, congresswomen, and military generals, as well as various certificates and awards. It sure looked like he liked what he was doing!

Ken stood to shake his hand. "Robert, great to see you. Thanks for coming up. It will be good to compare thoughts on how we can secure the FMF-FMS funding for Mark's Egyptian CC-260 sale. As you know there are no sure things when you are relying on politicians and government bureaucrats to keep their word. Fortunately, since President Carter's peace accord between Egypt and Israel, Egypt is now a favored nation as far as the provision of US FMF-FMS funds for their military."

McTelall was impressed in that Doyle appeared to be one of the few people who could discriminate between FMS and FMF funds!

To the Ticket-Holders: Here is a brief tutorial on the FMF-FMS process.

The Foreign Military Financing (FMF) program provides grants to help countries purchase weapons and defense equipment produced in the United States as well as acquiring defense services and military training. FMF funds purchases are made through the Foreign Military Sales (FMS) program, which manages government-to-government sales.

On a much less frequent basis, FMF also funds purchases made through the Direct Commercial Sales (DCS) program, which oversees sales directly between foreign governments and private U.S. companies.

The State Department's Bureau of Political-Military Affairs and the latter›s Office of Security Assistance set policy for the FMF program, while the Defense Security Cooperation Agency (DSCA), within the Defense Department, manages it on a day-to-day basis.

Military personnel and attachés in US embassies overseas, play a key role in managing FMF within recipient countries. Congress appropriates grant funds for FMF.

OK, probably more than you ever wanted to know about FMF-

FMS funding!

Ken offered, "Let me bring you up to date on what we have so far. As I said, Egypt is a favored nation as far as FMF-FMS grants go. They have already received several hundreds of millions of dollars of FMS funds in military hardware for their Army and Navy. Accordingly, the EAF is well-positioned to receive the next big FMF-FMS grant. Of course, the EAF will have to request that they receive the CC-260 aircraft through the FMF process, which will fund the purchase directly from CAC. The advantage of going FMF verses FMS is it keeps the US Air Force from being involved and dictating the configuration and options for the aircraft. This will allow CAC to sell the EAF the CC-260 whitetails that are sitting on the ramp, which is one of the highest priorities of the Corporation. I understand that Larry Ray has laid the pipe at the EAF to request six CC-260 aircraft and for the US Embassy to support this purchase by the EAF."

It was clear to Robert that Ken was being kept up to date on the sales campaign in Egypt. Based on Robert's past experience with international sales, he knew that Ahmed was most likely in daily contact with Ken, as this sale was totally dependent on using US FMF funds. Everyone needed Ken to work his magic in DC, or there would not be any "extra points" this year.

Since they both knew how this all worked, McTelall said "I agree that the Egyptian ducks, or should I say sphinxes, are all in order. They just need a little incentive to make them move."

Ken smiled, then added something they both already knew. "I'm sure Ahmed has selected the local team to get the ducks moving. Of course, he, Mark, and Larry Ray will need support from both of us when he submits his "Helper" recommendation to the Company and Corporation."

McTelall nodded in agreement, and thought it was time to make sure he was coming along on his own assignment. "Ken, I agree that Ahmed will select the right local team in Egypt. Mark would like to have confirmation that the FMF funding will be available when Ahmed's team passes the ball to us. Can you give me a brief update so I can assure Mark and Larry Ray that all is in good order up here?"

Ken replied, "I'm glad you asked. There's something I want to show you."

The Cargo Aircraft Corporate Office "War" Room

Ken then walked Robert down the hall to the secure, windowless, restricted access Political Support Room. Once inside, Robert saw that one wall was covered with a map of the United States and another wall with a world map. The world map had colored flags on various countries to highlight company sales activities. They were like stoplights—red, yellow, and green. Most were green, indicating normal marketing contact. Several of the yellow indicated there was interest and that a sales campaign was being considered. There were only a couple of red ones, one of which was centered on Egypt.

On the US map there were many blue and gold circles around various towns across the country. Twenty-seven of the gold circles were around the home towns of each member of the Senate Armed Services Committee. Over fifty blue circles were around the home towns of the House Armed Services Committee members. In the center of all the gold circles and in about a third of the blue circles there were orange flags. McTelall already knew the Corporate lobbying strategy to place CAC subcontract work, meaning jobs, in the home towns of key Senate and Congressional Armed Service Committee members. This would certainly encourage them to fund CAC programs in order to keep or increase the local jobs.

While McTelall studied the US map, Ken said, "As you can see, we have all of the key members of both Committees on our team. They are already briefed to approve whatever FMF funding is requested for the Egyptian CC-260 aircraft and spares purchase."

Robert commented, "Ken, great work! You folks really know how to make things happen in this town."

While looking at the US map, Robert had noticed an orange flag on a very small town in a midwestern state. He asked about it.

Ken replied, "That is the hometown of the US Senator, who is the head of the Senate Armed Service Committee. We have established an airplane parts manufacturing facility there. The name of the town, Resume Speed, is a little hard to read. Years ago, the town was just a highway intersection. It didn't have a name and was so small it could not afford a name sign on the highway. So they switched the highway signs at the intersection to name the town!"

McTelall was pretty sure Ken was pulling his leg with that tale! The point was, it was clear that Ken Doyle had all of the Senate and Congressional ducks, chickens, turkeys, or whatever those southern boys called politicians, in a row. Since the Defense Security Cooperation Agency within the Defense Department managed the FMF programs on a day-to-day basis, McTelall asked if Ken had any indication of their position on using FMF funding for the EAF to buy the CC-260s.

Ken smiled. " You know, Robert, it is an amazing coincidence

70

that the recently retired Director of the DSCA has joined the Cargo Aircraft Corporation as our new VP of Defense Business and now has an office down the hall from me. I can assure you he maintains good contact with all the staff at DSCA that used to work for him. They still call him General, and still know how to follow orders!"

Robert chuckled, then thanked Ken for the briefing. It was time to get back to Mark with an update.

McTelall headed back to the hotel, where he reported back to Mark that Ken Doyle had all of the Senate and Congressional political support in order. He also mentioned that the Corporation had just added another VP to assure a good working relationship with the DSCA. They agreed the next step was for Ahmed to submit his recommendation for the "Helper." Mark said he would contact Ahmed and take care of that action. It appeared to McTelAll that Mark and Ahmed certainly had a close working relationship.

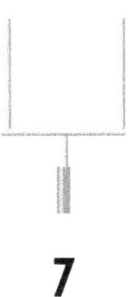

7

SIXTH GAME – SAN FRANCISCO 49ERS HOST DENVER BRONCOS

49ers lose 13 to 16 in Overtime

Montana passed for 191 yards, then had an interception. Walsh replaced him with Young as the Bronco's Elway tied the game 13–13 on a touchdown pass. In overtime a Young pass was intercepted and set up Karlis' winning field goal.

Cairo - CAC Egyptian "Helper" Strategy and Plays

The Minister of Defense, Helmy Mostafa, had a large villa on the golf course in Mirage City on the Ring Road, just a short distance from central Cairo. More importantly, it was adjacent to both the Almaza Air Base and the Cairo International Airport. As he had said many times, you never knew when you would need to make a quick departure on a business trip, or when the government might be overthrown again.

It was early evening. Helmy's sister Tasha and her close friend, Ali Omar, had joined him for light refreshments. Helmy was sort of an old school Egyptian and usually didn't include his wife in business meetings, even if it included other family members.

After one of his servants had served the expensive French merlot, along with a tray of hummus and pita bread, Helmy asked Tasha and Ali, "Before we get down to this Cargo Aircraft Company business, when are you two going to announce your engagement so we can all start planning the wedding?"

Tasha rolled her eyes. "Brother! Of course, Ali and I have deep feelings for each other, and do intend to marry as soon as we get certain affairs in order. But, as you know, we are involved with more than just being two people in love. Our mutual business activities, that is, my support for the approval and funding of military projects, which just happens to be linked to Ali's MAPS Company, requires a little discretion. We believe the incentives from this CC-260 aircraft program will make a very nice wedding gift. In fact, let's start discussing this wedding gift, so we can think about a wedding date."

Helmy smiled, thinking it was the first time she had mentioned a wedding date. He launched right in with, "OK, Tasha. You have met with their Corporate VP Ahmed Sharif. Please outline what we have to work with."

She removed a cocktail napkin from her purse and placed it on the small table in front of them. "This little paper may not look like much. However, I can assure you it is as good as any legal document, as it was written and signed by Ahmed at the end of our meeting. He knows we are all part of this team and is relying on me to handle the incentive disbursement, and relying on Ali to provide the Statement of Work-Support Contractor Proposal for the in-country support for their CC-260 Program."

"To begin with, Ahmed has already met with Ali and is confident he can get a MAPS Support Contractor Agreement approved by CAC Company and Corporate committees. He assured me he has, to use an American idiom, "the skids greased" at the Embassy here. He also has US Senate and Congressional Armed Service

Committees support and approval of the Foreign Military Grant Funding for six aircraft and a ten percent spares package. I'm sure your Ministry of Defense and my Aviation Committee will have no problem accepting free airplanes and spares."

Tasha took a moment to let them both process that information, then continued, "Let me outline the aircraft contract as Ahmed has explained it to me, and the incentive arrangement Ahmed and I have agreed upon. Understand that these numbers must not be discussed outside of this room. The contract will be for six CC-260 Aircraft as currently configured, which are immediately available at three hundred sixty million dollars."

Now she looked directly at Helmy. "Brother, your Air Force must take them "as is." Ahmed said they are already built, so CAC cannot make any changes. Again, I expect you can convince your Air Force to take free airplanes, as well as a free spares package. Ahmed said they can pay around three percent on the aircraft, which amounts to ten million dollars."

This caused both Helmy's and Ali's jaw to drop. Tasha laughed, then warned them, "OK, before you both go off to spend it all, keep in mind we will need to "grease the skids"—you know, I kind of like that term—with the EAF. Brother, that should not take a lot of incentive, since they work for you."

Both Helmy and Ali chuckled at that, then Tasha resumed her report. "Additionally, in the MAPS Support Agreement this ten million will be spread over ten years at one million per year so as not to raise too many eyebrows with their internal consultant committees and finance types. Ahmed and I have agreed they will pay the first two years up front and pay the remaining eight million shortly after we reward their team. I'll outline that plan now."

Tasha scooted forward in her seat and referred again to the cocktail napkin. "On the spares package of thirty-six million dollars, which is also FMF funds and so free to the EAF, Cargo Aircraft Company will arrange for MAPS to handle the EAF spares business with a fifteen percent support fee for MAPS, which amounts to around five million dollars. In order not to highlight CAC paying more to the local support contractor, we will arrange for the spares FMF payment be made directly to MAPS. MAPS can then transfer the payment to CAC for the EAF spares after deducting their fifteen percent. No one monitors the customer payments to CAC for spare parts."

She looked directly at both of them. "Again, before you spend it, this five million is the reward for Ahmed's team. He suggested that MAPS contract with his Jordanian Company, JET, as a consultant for five years with a one-time payment on contract signing of five million."

Although Helmy and Ali probably thought that a five-million-dollar kickback was a little steep, they couldn't be too greedy with a quick ten million between the three of them.

Tasha added, "Ahmed pointed out that the salesman, Larry Ray Hardy, was not part of his team, so he expected me to reward him. However, after meeting Larry Ray, I know what he would like." She raised her eyebrows. "Money and love. But I only plan to give him one of those!" As Ali started to object, she finished, "That is, only a little money!"

Helmy laughed. "Good work, Tasha. Since I control the EAF purchase, I feel that fifty percent for me and the other fifty percent for you two is fair!"

Tasha had played this game before with her brother, so she also laughed as she said, "Brother, in case you hadn't noticed there are three members on this team, and we all have a pivotal role in winning this game. Since Ali and I know you are wondering what to get us for a wedding gift, I suggest, in order to be fairer and to give us your blessing on our wedding, that we agree to a three-way split and get on with the game."

Helmy was proud of his sister's aggressive position, thinking that a little over three million dollars was not bad for his job of convincing the EAF to accept some free airplanes, so he willingly accepted her proposal. "Tasha, you and Ali sure drive a hard bargain. I agree. Happy Wedding! Please set a date before you spend my gift."

Tasha smiled at him. "Brother, thank you for this generous wedding gift."

Helmy nodded, then said, "OK, let's layout the next steps."

Tasha quickly replied, "Here's the schedule that Ahmed and I discussed. There are three initial steps. First, Larry Ray will have the proposal prepared at CAC for the six aircraft and spares package, then deliver it to the EAF immediately prior to the EAF visit to Paris to inspect the CC-260 this month. Next, Ali will prepare the MAPS CAC Support Contractor Proposal along the lines that Ahmed suggested and review it with Ahmed in Zurich."

"Third, Ali will then accompany Ahmed to the CAC Company headquarters in Mobile, Alabama, to personally present it to their management. Now, based on Ahmed's advice, as he has been through this process many times, Ali will have submitted a proposal which will allow him to be negotiated down to the numbers we have agreed upon."

"This will begin the next set of steps, or what I call the Washington phase. Once CAC management approves the MAPS Support Contractor Agreement, Ahmed, Ali, and Larry Ray will travel to Washington DC to present and obtain Corporate approval of the MAPS support agreement. I also believe Ahmed has one or two team members at the Corporate headquarters. While there, Ahmed will obtain confirmation from his DC team that the FMF funding for Egypt to purchase the aircraft and spares has also been approved and is available."

"Once the MAPS Support Contractor Agreement is signed and it is confirmed that FMF funds are available, CAC will pay the initial two million on the MAPS agreement. With MAPS being paid before the CC-260 contract is signed, there will be no connection with paying a commission on the upcoming CC-260 sale. That completes the Washington phase."

Tasha looked directly at Helmy. "Brother, please appreciate that Ahmed and Mark Maddox are going out on a limb supporting the advance payment, and they will expect that we keep our end of the bargain. Now, if you have any concern that you cannot guarantee the EAF will take these free airplanes, then we should stop now, because I do not want to pull the tigers tail, as the Americans say."

Helmy responded, "So my job is to get the EAF Generals who work for me to take free airplanes? Well, I have one-hundred-percent confidence of success!"

Tasha nodded and continued, "Good! Let's talk about the end goal. Once MAPS is approved, Larry Ray and Ali will return to Cairo and Larry Ray will submit the proposal to the EAF for the aircraft. At that time, it will be OK for Ali to provide support to CAC. Brother, you will need to encourage the EAF buyers to take just a little time to finalize the contract, as we do not want it to look too easy. Then, once the contract is signed, the US Embassy here in Cairo will coordinate with the Defense Security Cooperation Agency in Washington to coordinate the transfer of the funds for the aircraft and the spares."

Tasha glanced confidently at both Helmy and Ali. "Now for the final step. Once Ahmed confirms that CAC has received the aircraft payment, and we confirm that MAPS has received the spares payment, we'll start the "pass the incentives" play. Since the airplanes are already built and there is FMF money available, this entire process should only take a couple of months."

She beamed at her fiancé. "Ali, my love, you will be the banker for us all. But I don't want you taking off to Rio with our money. Well, not without me!" This made them all laugh.

Tasha took a sip of wine, then finished her lengthy presentation. " If this meets with your approval, I will send a message to Ahmed that the home team is briefed and ready to start the game!"

8

SEVENTH GAME – SAN FRANCISCO 49ERS AT LOS ANGELES RAMS

49ers win 24 to 21

49er had a great game with 199 yards of runs as he scored three touchdowns. Despite the Rams' three Everett touchdowns, the Rams still lost to San Francisco.

Mobile, Alabama- Cargo Aircraft Company

The Company and Corporation had a formal process to approve the hiring of consultants to support their international business activities. It was called the Consultant Review Meetings, or CRM. It was well-known that in Washington DC these consultants or "Helpers" were called lobbyists. Regardless of the term used, they were paid a lot of money to make things happen. In this case, the sale of CAC aircraft to Egypt, being paid for by FMF-FMS funds, would require the influence of both consultants and lobbyists.

The CAC Corporate Washington, DC office already had their politicians, or ducks, in a row. Obtaining CAC approval for International Consultants was sometimes difficult, since many CAC executives still remembered that a few years ago their Corporate Chairman and President had both been indicted by the Feds for their role in influencing, that is, passing money, to the king of an Asian country to encourage them to buy CAC aircraft.

Although they both were fired by the Board of Directors, at their trial they were only given probation for this victimless crime. The judge, previously a Senator, had a $oft $pot for the Corporation. It was hard enough to convince the CAC Finance VP to invest in a "Helper," but the Company lawyer, or legal beagle, didn't want anyone to go to jail, most especially himself.

Mark and Larry Ray knew that getting both Company and Corporate CRM approval was going to be a tough sell. So, it was time to start the CRM play. Mark started it off by sending a private message to Ahmed.

(To the Ticket-Holders: Again the real names are inserted to avoid having to flip back to the Roster. Remember, it had to be written so that only Ahmed would understand the message.)

"Sphinx *(Ahmed)*, the team in Washington says that all of the Tidal Basin ducks have been fed and are presently in a row. Now is a good time for you to visit us. Please bring along your new friend, Ramses *(Ali Omar)*. I expect in our activities at this location we will need to be on the lookout for problems with Black Cloud *(Jim Smith -VP Finance)* and Snake *(Vince Holliday-General Counsel)*. I will show my copy of the visit Agenda *(MAPS Proposal)* to our friends here. Look forward to seeing you soon."

Mark then asked his secretary to have Larry Ray come to his office. Once Larry Ray had arrived, and was seated at Mark's office table, Mark started his CRM play.

"Larry Ray, you need to prepare the request to the CRM to have MAPS as our 'Helper' in Egypt, but let's not use that term around here. Those bureaucrats in our CRM don't even like using consultant, since that was the title our previous Corporate senior management used for their Asian "Helper." So, let's go with the now politically correct term Support Contractor. I'm having Ahmed bring Ali Omar over with him when he comes for the CRM meeting. Ahmed can provide his usual Corporate assurance that all is above board, not that Holliday or Smith will believe him." Mark rolled his eyes as he said this.

Then he picked up where he left off. "Ali can brief the CRM on his company's history and experience of supporting military projects in Egypt. That will give us credible name recognition, which should assure the CRM that you have not created a "Ghost Helper." Also, keep the payments as MAPS proposed, as we can set up Jim for a negotiation where he can claim a big win, that is, savings based on his negotiating expertise. Since we have the potential for an imminent sale, I'll get with Frank to be sure this CRM approval is expedited so we can get it up to Washington ASAP for their approval."

Larry Ray answered, "OK. I'll have the formal request ready by the end of today. Mark, there is one issue. Normally a CRM request goes thru my direct boss, McTelall, before you can approve it for submittal to the CRM. As you know, we are not sure whether he will sign it, or want to do his own research before signing it."

"Good point," Mark said. "Back-date the request to last week when McTelall was in Washington and I'll sign it and send him a copy next week for his file, but not his comment. It will probably be on the CRM meeting schedule before he reads it."

Larry Ray returned to his office and finalized the Marketing request to the CRM to hire a support contractor for Egypt. He had made this play before and knew, no matter how they arrange the fee for support contractor services, the CRM, especially VP

Finance Jim, would immediately compare the service fee to the expected income on the upcoming sale of six airplanes and calculate a commission amount.

Larry Ray knew that Ali had inflated the requested amount. Therefore, in his head Larry Ray figured the initial request to be a million and a quarter dollars times ten years, which equaled twelve and a half million dollars, not counting the spares package. With the expected contract to be around three hundred sixty million dollars, the estimated commission would actually come to around three and a half percent. This was not an unrealistic commission. However, Larry Ray knew that was around the amount of the Asian deal, so no one would agree to that level of payment these days.

He thought that Ahmed's plan for Ali to let Jim negotiate him down by twenty-five percent was an excellent strategy, and would play to Jim's ego. Ali would emphasize that the payments were for services over ten years. Therefore, the so-called equivalent commission of less than three-tenths percent a year would certainly not raise any eyebrows, and would also get approval for what Ali needed to get the job done in Egypt.

Although Larry Ray knew there would be a spares package, it was prepared by the Product Support Department and not his responsibility. He expected that Mark and Ahmed would arrange for MAPS to be the local distributor for CC-260 spares. No one seemed to pay too much attention to spares other than it was an accepted industry standard for customers to pay exorbitant mark-ups for spares.

There had been a very public case some years ago when a US Government whistleblower revealed that the USAF had paid five thousand dollars for an aircraft lavatory sink. Of course, no one had pointed out that the manufacturer was located in the hometown of the Senate Armed Services Committee Chairman. Some thought it was actually his very own company.

What Larry Ray didn't know was that, with Mark and Ahmed's recommendation, Frank had agreed to direct that a boatload of CC-260 spares would be delivered directly to MAPS on consignment, prior to delivery of the first aircraft. This would allow the spares payment to be made directly to MAPs with the FMF-FMS money. Although the US usually only paid FMF Funds directly to the US manufacturer like CAC, as many politicians say, "Where there is a will, there is a way." Or more to the point, "Where there is an incentive, there is a way." Of course, Maps would transfer to CAC the agreed price for the spares after deducting their twenty percent handling fee. Spares were so lucrative, that even with this pass-through, CAC would make their twenty-plus percent!

In case anyone missed it, Ali had slipped in another five percent, or a little over one and three-quarters million dollars for spares handling in the MAPS Agreement, which would probably cover the cost of the wedding and honeymoon, plus a couple of Rolls-Royces! It was interesting that no one hardly ever read the fine print.

The Cargo Aircraft Company CRM Huddle

The CAC Consultant Review Meeting was composed of four attendees: President Frank Moore, VP of Finance Jim Smith, General Counsel Vince Holliday, and VP of Marketing Mark Maddox. They would all have reviewed the request written by Larry Ray, and previously approved by Mark. So, already one vote for MAPS! In addition, Mark knew Frank was on board, so they were half-way there.

As time was of the essence, it was smart for Frank to have Ahmed attend the meeting, as well as having Ali standing by to provide a briefing on the capabilities and experience of MAPS. Mark wanted to wrap up all the issues addressed and have all the questions answered in one single CRM meeting. Both Larry Ray and McTelall were invited be in attendance. However, they were to only speak when spoken to!

The group met in the CAC executive conference room with Ali having coffee in a small side room while waiting to be called into the meeting.

Frank's Pre-Game Opener

Frank called the meeting to order, then stated, "First of all, I would I expect you are all aware that the Company and Corporation are in financial difficulty due to the lack of sales of our highly profitable CC-260 aircraft."

Frank decided he might as well put pressure on Jim and Vince that the financial welfare of both the Company and Corporation would rest on the results of this meeting. If they were not supportive of this sale to Egypt, then they would be to blame for further poor financial results.

Frank continued his opening remarks. "Second, you all can look out the window and see the twelve, I repeat twelve, whitetail aircraft sitting on the ramp. The cost to carry that inventory is what is dragging the Company and Corporation down. I have emphasized to Mark and his salesman that they had better move those aircraft or else! Don't ask what the else means." Frank frowned at Mark as he said this.

"Third, Larry Ray has spent most of his recent time overseas and has brought us a deal that will remove six of the whitetails at full price. I emphasize, full price, and, just as importantly, right away. Larry Ray, thanks for a good job."

Frank was really laying it on thick for Jim and Vince. McTelall thought maybe he would just call for a vote without any further discussion.

However, Frank wanted them to really buy into this deal. "Fourth, we have never sold an aircraft to a third world country without obtaining some local . . ." Frank had started to say "help," but because the word was so close to "Helper," he instead quickly ended his sentence with, ". . . advice on working with their organizations."

Seeing that no one had caught this slight hiccup, Frank turned his attention to his VP of Marketing. "Mark, please start with a brief overview of this potential sale to Egypt"

Mark's Kick-Off

"Well, like Frank said, all the credit goes to Larry Ray, who has brought us the "deal of the century," well OK, "deal of the year." As you all know, selling cargo aircraft to third world countries isn't easy, since most generals want guns, missiles, or fighter aircraft. Larry Ray has worked his magic at the senior levels of the Egyptian Ministry of Defense, the Egyptian Air Force, and the US Embassy, to obtain high level support for the purchase of six of our whitetail aircraft."

He paused while the others nodded their approval toward Larry Ray, who was soaking up the recognition. "To make it even better for the Egyptians and ourselves, our Washington office has positioned Egypt to receive FMF-FMS grant funding for these airplanes, as well as a significant spares package to Egypt. Please appreciate that to preclude the Egyptians from changing their minds, the DC team has arranged that the FMF-FMS finds can only be used for the CC-260 purchase."

Mark stopped and cleared his throat for effect, in order to deliver the details they had all been waiting for. "The contract amount is three hundred sixty million dollars for the six aircraft and another thirty-six million for the spares package. Not to steal Jim's thunder, but with the aircraft at full price and a big spares package, I think we can look forward to a very good profit! Now, before you head for the bank, remember that in the third world, there is no such expectation as a sure thing. Once the word gets out that free money is available for a military purchase, there will be other politicians, generals and aerospace companies trying to upset our apple cart. As usual in third world countries, we need to enlist a local entity to support our case, just like we do in Washington DC with lobbyists."

"Both Larry Ray and Ahmed have done their due diligence and are recommending a well-established and respected local company, Military Aviation Parts and Services, which has the experience and reputation to represent CAC interest in Egypt. As time is of the essence to both us and the Egyptian Air Force, Ahmed has invited the President of MAPS to be here to brief us on their experience and capability, as well as to answer any questions you may have on their Support Contractor Proposal."

At this point Mark directed their attention to Ahmed, who nodded in agreement and held up his copy of the proposal for the rest to see. After a low murmur of discussion between the others, Mark continued on.

"I expect you have all read it. You may wonder why they have proposed such a long term agreement covering ten years. Ahmed and I agree with MAPS that it is important to show the Egyptian government and the EAF that we plan to be there for the long haul. And as you all know, no doubt some finance or legal type will try to equate a support contractor payment to some sort of commission. By the way, I intend no offense to present company. To avoid this situation, this ten-year agreement keeps the dollar amounts in the acceptable range for an in-country contractor for a major aerospace company."

The VP Finance Jim could not sit any longer without inserting his foot in the aisle, and interrupted, "Just a minute! The finance department will provide the financial overview and determine the profit level for this sale, and the legal department, under Vince Holliday, will rule on the legality of the amounts of payments to an overseas contractor."

Before a fight could break out, Frank held up his hand and interjected, "Gentlemen, calm down! I'm the one who asked Mark to summarize this matter. That is all he has done, so let's let him finish the summary I requested."

Jim, with Vince in his corner, looked daggers at Mark, who ignored them and continued, with a nod from Frank. "Well, I certainly am not trying to tell Finance or Legal how to run their business! The purpose of this meeting is to provide everyone with a complete overview of all aspects of this sale. Larry Ray, Ahmed, and I have done the best we can to present you with a potential sale which we believe will be of great benefit to the Company and Corporation. However, Finance and Legal are certainly at liberty to object to what we are proposing."

Mark was really thinking, *Might as well as put them both on the spot as the ones who may kill the best deal in a long time.*

It was time for Mark to wrap it up. "Finally, the six aircraft spares package is intended to be consigned to MAPS if we hire them as our Egyptian Support Contractor. I expect the consignment terms and conditions will be generally the same as our other international support contractors."

Mark sat down and Frank then opened the meeting for questions and comment, while reminding all that Ahmed and Larry Ray were there to answer questions on specific items, and not there to offer opinions on any finance or legal matters.

Jim's Return

When Jim finally had the floor, it was obvious that he intended to make it clear that he was the key vote on hiring this Support Contractor. He had reviewed the MAPS proposal and, considering the asking price, he already knew he would be able to show his negotiating expertise. However, the boss, Frank, was strongly supporting the Sales guys and the Company desperately need this sale, so maybe he shouldn't come on too strong.

Jim began with, "Gentlemen. If, and I do emphasize "if," Larry Ray can get a contract for six of our whitetails at the asking price, then I will personally give him a pat on the back." Jim looked over at Larry Ray with a cold smile.

Larry Ray smiled back, thinking, *How about a decent bonus for once!*

Jim continued, "Even at full price we do not have a large amount to pay for local support. The Company is in serious financial trouble due to the lack of CC-260 sales."

He thought, *Might as well place the blame on the sales guys*. He also knew that remark would take the wind out of Mark's sails.

"Give me a little time to negotiate with the MAPS President to see how low he will go. I agree time is of the essence, so I'm glad he's here in order to move this agreement forward ASAP. I would encourage the sales and contracts team to hold the line on full price, especially since it will be US taxpayer money coming back to us! That's all for now."

Larry Ray's Play Review

Now it was time for Legal Beagle Vince to throw his usual bucket of cold water on the deal and make it clear that Legal really held the key to the sale. "Before we all head for the bank, or, as Larry Ray would say, count our chickens before they hatch," said Vince, "we need to be sure we have played by all the rules, as well as thoroughly vetted any local assistance. Larry Ray, please go through all the contacts you have made in Egypt."

This was not unexpected by Larry Ray, and he was well-prepared.

"Vince, you and Jim were copied on all of my trip reports, so I will just summarize what they say. First, I made documented sales calls on the senior staff at the Egyptian Air Force, who confirmed their interest in acquiring several CC-260 aircraft. Since the Air Marshal and Air Commodore, the two most senior positions in the EAF, indicated that they were not very familiar with the CC-260, they requested we arrange an inspection-demo of a CC-260 aircraft. Currently, the best way to accomplish that is to use the new CC-260 that is being delivered to the French Air Force next week. I will be hosting that visit next week in France, after I deliver the formal proposal for six CC-260 aircraft to the EAF in

Cairo. As you all know, we host many inspection visits mainly at international air shows, so this is not anything different from our usual sales activities."

Larry had intentionally omitted mentioning Paris as he knew they would all like a free trip to Paris. However, although Larry Ray knew he really shouldn't add this next bit, he just had to make a point. "Of course, you are welcome to join us if you think a few drinks and a dinner are going to have an influence on a general as to what military equipment he buys."

Well, that certainly earned me a few glares, he thought.

"Secondly, I followed company protocol and met with the Air Attaché', a Colonel Barnes, at the US Embassy in Cairo to brief him of our business activities. It's not surprising that when he heard about the inspection trip to France, he invited himself to go along. Of course, he will be paying his own expenses."

Larry Ray almost choked when he said that, since all sales people knew these attaches expected a free ride. *That would probably be a good pass to throw to MAPS.*

"Back to my conversation with the Air Marshal. He mentioned that the other aerospace and military suppliers they buy from usually have a local company to handle a lot of the day-to-day support requests and other business, especially considering the eight-hour time difference between Egypt and Alabama. He also mentioned that they already had a very good working relationship with MAPS. So, I passed this info on to Ahmed, as he has the responsibility to sort out any local help."

"I would recommend,' Larry concluded, "that we proceed as quickly as possible since it appears to me that we have the ducks, or should I say sphinxes, all in a row."

Vince Throws a Flag

Vince wasn't about to be rushed, because everyone knows that when someone is being paid by the minute or page, they talk a lot and write slow. Now he gave the "I warned you all" speech.

"You are all aware that the Corporation suffered a great loss both financially and to its reputation by previously violating the Foreign Corrupt Practices Act. I can assure you that nothing like that will ever happen on my watch. I insist that both Larry Ray and Ahmed verify that all of their contacts and discussions in Egypt have been in strict compliance to the FCPA. Also, it must be certain that this agreement with MAPS has no hidden payoffs to any Egyptian Government official or military person."

Frank cut him off. "Vince, get off your high horse! The CRM request for MAPS, which they both have already signed, includes written statements to that effect. Let's have Ahmed provide us with an overview of his due diligence in selecting MAPS."

It was clear that Vince didn't like being spoken to in that tone. However, since Frank was his boss, he swallowed his irritation, and simply answered, "OK."

Ahmed's Sweep

To say this was not Ahmed's first rodeo was an understatement. He not only had played this "Helper" game before, he had also accumulated, through rewards from "Helpers," several very large Swiss bank accounts—and no one had ever thrown the flag on him! However, he needed to get this CAC CRM approval right away before the FMF money was intercepted by another team.

Ahmed made his basic play. "Gentlemen, we make a good team and we have won many games, that is, sales, all by playing by the rules. As you all know, the Middle-East is my home ground. I have been to Egypt many, many times and have a lot of high-level business contacts and friends there. We are fortunate that the EAF mentioned MAPS. As their President, Ali Omar, will show you, his company has a long history of providing exactly the services to the EAF that your aircraft require."

To drive his point home, Ahmed added, "He is well known and respected in Cairo for his honesty and hard work. As I said, he is already working with the EAF, so what we propose is simply an expansion of his current business. That means we do not have to introduce a new player in this game. Of all the possible candidates of which I am aware, MAPS is the best local player we can have to assure we win this game."

Ahmed realized that Jim and Vince didn't know all of the special plays MAPS brought to the game, but that was beside the point. Therefore, he made his final play. "I suggest we allow Ali to brief us on his company and I'm sure you'll see the benefit of working with him."

McTelall's Replay Review

Before Jim, or especially Vince, could give Ahmed the third degree, Frank interposed, "I agree. But wait, we haven't let our newest team member provide us with his perspective. McTelall, what is your position on this?"

McTelall knew that in any third world sale, money had to flow to the local decision makers for that sale to happen. But the key to staying out of jail was to never ask the "Helper" what they did with any of the money paid to them. This was the time to just play along.

So McTelall responded, "I certainly agree with Ahmed that it is really fortunate to find a local contractor who is already in business with our potential customer. I'm sure that with his in-country expertise, Ahmed has brought us the right man for the job. I'll leave the amount of payment up to the financial experts, as I'm sure Jim will get us the best deal possible."

Frank thought, *That's what I like—a "yes" man.* Aloud he announced, "We'll take a short break and then hear from MAPS!"

MAPS Makes a Play

Like all the others, this was not Ali's first rodeo. Ahmed had coached Ali on this play as to what to say, what to emphasize, and more importantly, what NOT to say!

Once he was introduced, the group all got seated with their second round of coffee. Ali's first move was the old "death by power point." So, he started through his 25 PP slides presentation.

Basically, Ali covered the history of MAPS. IIis numerous slides showed all the critical components of MAPS support. This included various military programs support, spares, supply of support services, support equipment, identifying manufacturing sources, sustaining engineering services, sustaining engineering and technical services, hosting and supporting field service representatives, logistics service representatives, contract field team, field service representative deployment and travel, technical order updates, technical order print and distribution, country standard time compliance technical orders, depot maintenance, aircraft modifications, and, finally, data and configuration management programs.

Once he had delivered his data and was surprised they were all still awake, he made his final pitch. "As you can see, MAPS is a full-service aviation support company, and we would be honored to represent the Cargo Aircraft Company CC-260 Aircraft program in Egypt."

He had certainly shown them that MAPS was well-experienced to support the CAC program. Plus, in his presentation, he emphasized he already represented an American military helicopter manufacturer, a European business jet company, as well as providing logistics services at Almaza Air Base. He also knew when to "quit while you're ahead."

He couldn't resist commenting that he had another couple of hours of power point slides, if the committee wished more details of his business. That worked!

Frank smiled at him, saying, "Ali, thank you. I believed that is sufficient background for us. We are impressed with MAPS."

Then Frank turned to the rest of the group. "Any questions?"

When they remained silent, Frank turned back to Ali and said, "The next step is to have you and Mr. Smith discuss and agree on the compensation for your services. Assuming you and Jim reach an agreement, then the Committee can vote on retaining MAPS as the CAC Support Contractor for Egypt. I need to mention that the Corporation must also approve this agreement. However, they usually rubber stamp our recommendation."

Ali nodded his assent.

Frank continued, "Now, I would like to invite you to join me for lunch, and then you and Jim can meet after lunch to discuss the price for your services."

With that, the group, knowing that was their cue to exit, filed out. The Helper play had been made!

Frank's Post Play Review

Frank had a corner alcove in his office which served as a very private dining area. Once he and Ali sat down, they did the usual small talk until lunch was served. Frank waited until they had finished eating and were on their after-lunch coffee to be sure Ali understood the game! He also knew that there were no listening devices in his office.

"Ali, thanks for coming and also for the very good overview of your company. Ahmed and I have worked together as a team for many years. We have made some very good and beneficial business deals for the Corporation."

He was thinking, *And ourselves.*

Frank went on. "I assure you that both of us know how the world works and what it takes to do business in other countries. I expect you also are aware that we do not wish to discuss the details of how you play the game in Egypt, or how we make scores in Washington. So, when you meet with Mr. Finance, I hope you have some flexibility on your Support Contractor pricing, because Jim needs to have you give him something to feed his ego. Moreover, it is none of his business who your friends are in the EAF or the Egyptian Government, or if you incentivize anyone. My team suggests you stay close to your fee on the spares business so you can meet all of your commitments, as there is more flexibility in spare price mark-up."

Ali smiled. "Frank, to use a term you all seem very familiar with, this isn't my first rodeo, even though I have never been on a horse."

That made Frank laugh. "It's clear you've played this game before so I'll leave you to agree to a price with Jim. Then we can vote to approve your contract and get it up to the Corporate CRM committee, which, again, will be just a rubber stamp of what we recommend."

The luncheon and conversation having come to an end, Frank's secretary then escorted Ali down to Jim's office.

The Final MAPS Play

Ali and Jim took a seat at Jim's very small conference table. Just as Jim was about to make his "we do not have any money" speech, Mark walked in and sat down.

Jim snapped, "Mark, this is a Finance meeting, not a Sales meeting!"

Mark had a ready come-back. "Sorry to intrude, Jim. However, Frank instructed me to attend in order to be sure that, in these discussions, we do not reduce the work scope for what MAPS needs to do to support our aircraft just to save a few bucks."

Of course, Jim was upset. But he knew better than to challenge the President. He also knew Mark was sent to spy on him so he could not use his usual heavy-handed treatment of Ali. Well, he would show Mark his art of negotiating!

Mark knew what Jim was up to, and also knew that a very long drawn out negotiation with Jim would certainly drive you to drink, or at least make you need a drink!

So, Jim started out by giving his usual "poor man" speech, the one that said the Company was in dire financial straits mainly due to lack of aircraft sales. Mark grimaced, but held his tongue. Jim also highlighted that the MAPS proposal as the most expensive he had ever seen. Of course, he was lying.

Before Jim asked for donations from MAPS, Ali decided to cut to the chase. "Jim, MAPS, like CAC, is in business to make money. I have obligations, also like CAC, to my shareholders to only enter into fair business deals. Please appreciate that my support proposal is very similar to the rates MAPS is charging current customers. However. . ."

Now came the big "however," as Ali paused for a moment for effect.

Then Ali made his final run. "I would like to have CAC as a customer! Therefore, I am willing to make a significant new client "friendship" discount of twenty-five percent."

He had subtly emphasized that this was truly the best he could do without saying "take it or leave it."

Mark gave Jim his best "don't be stupid" stare, and Jim got the message. In order to play up to Mark, who would report all this back to Frank, he responded, "Ali, it is clear that our team desires that your company provide our in-country support. Therefore, I am pleased to accept your offer. Please revise your pricing as you proposed, and I will approve it."

Touchdown!

Mark smiled a little too smugly, as he said, "Good deal! Ali, thanks for working with us. I'll get with Frank to get everything signed off here, and forwarded up to the Corporate office for final approval. We should have that within a week, so let's all focus on getting those aircraft sold!"

The CAC CRM approval to hire MAPS was signed off the next day! Amazing how fast things could get done when the President walked the document around for sign off.

The next plays would be in Washington DC!

9

EIGHTH GAME – SAN FRANCISCO 49ERS AT CHICAGO BEARS

49ers lose 9 to 10

On Monday Night TV, the 49ers lost to the Bears . San Francisco had ten penalties for 57 yards and Montana was sacked four times.

Washington, D.C.- Cargo Aircraft Corporate Office

Mark and Ahmed had convinced Frank that "time was of the essence," in order to obtain his OK to use the Cargo Aircraft Company biz jet, a very nice Gulfstream G-IV with international range, to take Ahmed, Larry Ray, and Ali from Alabama to Washington. Frank had called his Corporate colleagues to set up a Corporate CRM committee meeting the next day. This meeting would be chaired by his friend, and co-conspirator, International VP Ken Doyle. Consequently, CRM approval should be a rubber stamp.

Following the Corporate CRM approval, Larry Ray and Ali would take the Corporate jet to Cairo to submit the formal Sales Proposal to the Egyptian Air Force for the six aircraft, after which they would offer free executive transportation to the EAF Air Marshal, Air Commodore, and Colonel Barnes for their trip to Paris for the CC-260 inspection and demo flight. This was the actual reason they were using the Company jet. Larry Ray would also be able to include Ali in the Paris trip. Nothing like a male bonding trip to develop close working relationships! The Paris trip was just getting better and better. Ahmed would stay in DC to work with Doyle to be sure all the money ducks were in a row!

After landing at Reagan, a company limo delivered them to the adjacent Crystal Gateway Marriott hotel. Ahmed needed to have a Special Play discussion with Ali and Ken Doyle. The problem was that Larry Ray was not on the "extra points" team, so Ahmed had Ken arrange a diversion. Ken had advised the Corporate HR Director that he was considering adding to his office staff and asked her, as a favor, to interview Larry Ray, while not publicizing the possibility of this expansion around the office.

Ken had called Larry Ray and indicated that the Corporation was considering expanding the Washington office and might be adding a senior Director of International Marketing. He told Larry Ray that he had arranged dinner that evening as an informal interview with the very attractive Corporate HR VP, Kathy Nix, to discuss his interest in the position. Ken also told Larry Ray that he, Ahmed, and Ali would just be having a couple of drinks to provide Ken a brief overview of MAPS. No need for Larry Ray to sit through that again.

Larry Ray thought that having dinner with Kathy Nix could be a lot more interesting in a couple of ways! She had suggested they meet right after work at the restaurant, The 15th & Eads, in the Marriott. He was already at the bar working on his second whiskey on the rocks when Kathy walked up to him. They had met once or twice before in Company meetings. However, he had never been given the opportunity for a one-on-one.

Kathy was dressed in her formal DC office attire, consisting of a black low-cut dress, a string of pearls, and high heels. She wasn't sure what game Ken was playing, since she, as head of HR, was not aware of any indication to add to the DC office. So, her play was to make this a "quickie," meaning a short meeting!

"Larry Ray, how nice to see you again," said Kathy, as she held out her hand. "I see you are already getting into the DC swing of things. It's true that this town can drive you to drink!"

They both laughed.

Larry Ray then responded, "Kathy, nice to see you too. You not only look great; you look like you are ready for a drink! I have reserved a table over there in the corner."

Larry Ray got up, grabbed his drink, and showed her over to a small corner booth where they could sit at a ninety-degree angle to each other. Larry Ray though it was a rather intimate arrangement, which he hoped would get more intimate. The waiter came immediately and Kathy ordered her normal glass of chardonnay. Larry Ray ordered another whiskey, making it clear he was drinking American bourbon, and not Scotch whiskey!

They did the usual "how's work?" talk until her wine was served. Then Kathy started with, "Ken Doyle has mentioned he may, and I have to emphasize "may," be expanding his DC office staff and asked that I meet with you to discuss your interest in joining the Corporate office. Please appreciate that we do not have an open requisition yet, so this is sort of an informal interview. So please give me a one-drink overview of your international experience."

Larry Ray nodded, and clinked her wine glass. After taking a deep swig, he began, "Kathy, I have been in international sales at CAC for over ten years. As you may be aware, prior to joining sales, I was in CC-260 Customer Service for five years. That gave me both a detailed knowledge of the aircraft, as well as experience in working with international customers. Of course, when I moved into sales, I was assigned the prime territory reserved for new sales guys—West Africa! I can assure you that nothing happens quickly in that part of the world. I did spend a lot of time in some challenging countries like Ghana, Nigeria, Chad, and Guinea. I was successful in making sales to a couple of those countries. My very profitable sale to Chad was my ticket out of West Africa and into the Middle East."

With that, he finished his drink and waved the waiter down for another round. Kathy indicated that two was her limit.

He continued, "Kathy, it was an education to see how much these in-country "Helpers" make on the sale of our aircraft. I really don't know why we pay them so much! You may be aware that CAC salesman do receive a bonus on each sale. However, in most cases, its only peanuts compared to what we pay those "Helpers." Anyway, I am currently working Egypt and it looks good to sell them six of our whitetail aircraft for over three hundred fifty million. Again, I expect the "Helper" will make a fortune and I'll be lucky to get enough to buy a used truck! As you can understand, it's a lot of work, especially traveling seventy-five percent of the time with little monetary appreciation. So, yes, I am interested in making a change."

Kathy was a little taken back by his attitude towards his company. She wasn't sure he would be any happier at, or even a good addition to the Corporate office. She really wanted to get this over with before he had too much more to drink.

"Larry Ray, that's very interesting! I certainly can't comment on CAC salary matters. You already know the job description and responsibilities by working with Ken. If we do open a requisition to recruit for this Director level position at our office, the pay is a salary grade fifteen, one up from your current level. That would be around a twenty percent pay increase. Since the cost of living in the DC metro area is significantly higher than Mobile, Alabama, the Corporation will give you another twenty percent as a cost-of-living allowance. However, this is only in effect as long as you live within twenty-five miles of the office. We do have a Corporate Management Incentive Program, which is actually a bonus to all Corporate senior staff based on the profitably of the Corporation. Unfortunately, due to the last few years of our dire financial performance, there has been no MIP distributed."

After hearing this, Larry Ray thought he was a lot better off to stay with CAC and work his magic on getting an real bonus from his "Helpers."

He kind of slurred, "Kathy, thanks for this overview and information. Let me know if Ken does open a req for this position as I would like to discuss it further."

He was really thinking, *Yes, the further away from DC that I can get.*

Then he added, "Would you like to join me for dinner?"

Kathy thought it looked like he was going to have a liquid dinner. She answered, "Larry Ray, I would love to. However, I need to get home to my family"

She got up, and thanked him for the drinks and his time. Larry Ray wasn't quite able to get up, so he waved from his seat. As she walked away, she wondered what Ken was up to, as there was no way this guy would be lucky enough to keep his current job, let alone be promoted to a Corporate position. Well, Ken would owe her for wasting her time tonight.

Somehow, Larry Ray made it through a couple more drinks and staggered up to his room. He wasn't sure how much of the interview he would remember in the morning.

Meanwhile Ahmed, Ali, and Ken were having their own private dinner party to work on their political game plan. Of course, the game in Washington is "see, and be seen." Ken had reserved his usual table downtown at the very exclusive Capital Grille just down the street from the Capitol and a hangout for the movers and shakers, or a lot of those who thought they were. Once they were seated at Ken's very strategic table, where he could "see, and be seen" by other diners, he launched into his discussion. He wanted to get business out of the way before the place got too crowded and some of his many, many friends started showing up.

After their drinks were served, He said, "Ali, thank you for coming up to DC. Ahmed and Frank have briefed me on the experience and capabilities of your company. Plus, now that you have agreed on the compensation with Jim, and the CAC CRM approval has been signed, there should be no issue with obtaining Corporate approval. I expect I can have your agreement signed within the next couple of days."

Then he leaned over to Ali and said in a lower voice. "Ali, please appreciate that Ahmed, Frank, and I are on the same team. so whatever you and Ahmed have agreed for the home team is OK with me."

Ali replied loud enough for Ahmed to hear, "Gentlemen, I am

106

pleased to be on your team!" He did wonder what team Mark Maddox and Larry Ray were on. But since he was working with the first string, it was not his concern.

The rest of the evening was a lot of "stop and go" with many of Ken's political friends, congressmen, and senators, who kept stopping by to introduce themselves and always hinting that another campaign was approaching which would need funding!

Corporate Office –CRM Approval

The next morning, Larry Ray had the assignment to keep Ali busy by showing him the sights of Washington DC. In the past, the Corporate officers always wanted to meet the "Helpers." However, ever since a couple of Corporate executives went to jail by being directly linked to "Helpers," the senior execs liked to play plausible deniability! They had delegated Corporate CRM approval responsibility to Ken Doyle, leaving all legal and financial responsibility at the Company level. Ken had approved the CAC CRM request and faxed copies back to all the CAC committee members. Ken had also arranged to meet with Ahmed, Larry Ray and Ali after lunch in the Corporations' main conference room.

Once they all arrived and were seated, Ken announced, "Ali, I am pleased to advise you that the Corporation has approved your Support Contractor Agreement with CAC. Here is your signed copy. Again, you are working for CAC, so all contacts will be directly with the Marketing, Product Support, and Finance Departments at CAC. The agreed two-million-dollar initial payment should be paid to MAPS by CAC within the next couple of days."

"Also, please appreciate that, although we have high level assurances that the FMF-FMS funds are currently allocated to the EAF for the six CC-260 aircraft and spares, there is always a risk of a "claim jumper" or "pirate" going after these funds. Once more, time is of the essence, so I suggest you and Larry Ray go do your stuff."

Ali smiled. "Ken, Ahmed, and Larry Ray, thank you for your confidence in MAPS. Larry Ray and I will be leaving this evening for Cairo to submit the formal CC-260 proposal to the EAF. And, by the way, thanks for the use of your Company jet."

"Once we have returned to Cairo, we will start our first play, which is to take two key senior EAF officers, along with the US Embassy Air Attaché, to Paris to inspect your aircraft and, as you say, seal the deal with them. At the same time, my team in Cairo will be working to expedite the Egyptian Parliamentary Committee and Ministry of Defense request to allocate FMF funding for Egypt for the six CC-260 aircraft and spares."

It was time for Larry Ray and Ali to exit the meeting and leave the office to check out of their hotel, then go to the airport and board the Company jet. It would be a long, but very comfortable, flight to Cairo via Paris, since they were the only passengers. Still, with the stop in Paris and time change, they would not arrive in Cairo until the next evening.

Corporate Office – The FMF Play

To the Ticket-Holders: Here's a short refresher on obtaining FMF-FMS from Chapter 6.

Congress appropriates funds for FMF through the yearly Foreign Operations Appropriations Act. The Senate State and Foreign Operations Appropriations Subcommittee recommends to the Defense Security Cooperation Agency, which is under the Department of Defense, the funding for countries they select.

It was an amazing coincidence that the Head of the Foreign Operations Appropriations Subcommittee just happened to have a factory that made the cargo loading system for CAC aircraft and employed over 200 locals in his hometown. The Corporate Office had already lobbied to have the Committee allocate four hundred million dollars to Egypt and had linked it to a CC-260 purchase. This linking was unusual. Still, it was very interesting what effect a promise of more CC-260 aircraft work, and therefore jobs, could have on a politician.

The next hurdle was the Defense Security Cooperation Agency, known as the DSCA. It was currently led by a two-star Air Force General. This Security Cooperation workforce had both military and civilian personnel located all around the world. They managed a diverse portfolio of Security Cooperation programs including Foreign Military Sales, Foreign Military Financing, International Military Education and Training, Defense Institution Building, and Humanitarian Assistance and Disaster Relief.

It was another amazing coincidence that the current CAC Corporate VP of Defense Business had recently retired from being the head of the DSCA. As was normal around the Washington Beltway, friends and business associates tended to remain in contact and continued to do each other favors in return for expected future favors. Therefore, the direction from the Foreign Operations Appropriations Subcommittee on Egypt was already in the works. This was because the DSCA Director had already told the manager of the office of Security Assistance, which was responsible for the global execution of security assistance activities that included foreign military Sales, to expedite the funding for the EAF CC-260 purchase

The DC ducks were in a row and ready to make their play!

While Larry Ray and Ali were winging their way to Paris, Ahmed stayed in DC another day to meet with Ken to assure him that Ken was signed up as a member of the "extra points" team. Ahmed then prepared to return to Zurich to develop his play that involved bank transfer plays.

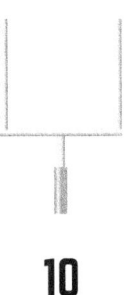

10

Ninth Game – San Francisco 49ers hosts Minnesota Vikings

49ers win 24 to 21

The Vikings had won in the playoff against San Francisco the previous season. Walsh started Young, who was berated repeatedly by the crowd. At about the two-minute warning in the fourth quarter, Minnesota was ahead 21–17. Then Young avoided a sack and ran the game-winning touchdown, earning a big applause from the crowd.

Washington to Cairo, via Paris

Larry Ray and Ali arrived at the Signature Executive Jet terminal at Regan National where the CAC Corporate Gulfstream G-IV was fully fueled, and the two pilots were waiting for them. Since they had the 11-passenger jet to themselves, they would be able to stretch out and get some rest during the overnight flight. Larry Ray was a little miffed that there was not the usual flight attendant on board to serve the Corporate executives. Oh well, he certainly could pour his own drinks and open the box meals without a lot of help. They would be stopping in Paris to refuel. There they would meet with the Paris Office Corporate VP and maybe add a few amenities prior to departing for Cairo.

Soon after takeoff Larry Ray opened his carry-on and pulled out a bottle of his favorite bourbon. Well, one of his favorites, as he hadn't yet found any bourbon he didn't like. He found a couple of glasses and some ice in the small galley in the forward area just aft of the flight station. After pouring two large portions, he went to sit across from Ali.

"Ali," he said, " I hope bourbon is OK with you. You'll find that us southern boys from CAC do like our bourbon."

Ali was a true international businessman and could handle most of the world's local drinks. He could certainly drink bourbon and was thankful that Larry Ray was not from eastern Europe where they drank the very hard to swallow plum schnapps brandy called Slivovitz.

Larry Ray wasn't aware of what sort of team Ali and Ahmed had discussed or organized, and wanted to be assured of a winning team. On the other hand, Ali had been warned by Ahmed and Frank that Larry Ray was not a player on the "extra points" team, so he needed to limit his drinks to avoid carelessly saying too much to Larry Ray about the actual game plan. This discussion was going to be a real poker game, played with a poker face, and each having hidden cards!

Larry Ray started. "Ali, we should review our game plan for Cairo and Paris, since we are both on the same team. As I mentioned, I have already met with both Air Marshal Saad and Air Commodore Riad to encourage them to support the CC-260 purchase. I believe the trip to Paris will go far to ensure that support. However, I am in no position to reward them for their assistance other than a free trip to Paris, plus a few drinks and meals in Cairo."

Larry Ray was really thinking, *Talk about throwing Ali a pass!*

Of course, Ali had been around the "pyramid" a few times too. He replied, "Larry Ray, as you Americans say, this is not my first rodeo. I know both the Air Marshal and the Commodore very well. I have done business with both of them many times,". . . *both over and under the table,* Ali added to himself

Aloud, Ali continued, "Now that I am on the CAC Team, I can assure you I can influence them to play ball with us. However, you know it's going to take more than two EAF Officers to get this deal done. Have you signed up any other players for us?" Again, Ali was thinking, *Over and under the table?*

Larry Ray answered, "I have met with the US Air Attaché at the Embassy, Colonel Barnes. As you know, he will be going on the trip to Paris with us and, as expected, will actively support the EAF decision to buy the American aircraft. All we can do to reward him is the all-expense paid trip to Paris, although I have also hinted there could be a job for him at CAC when he retires, *if* he actively backs our Company! At the minimum, he will not object to the sale, and he will OK the allocation of the FMF funds for the aircraft."

Larry Ray didn't want to mention the end run he was making with Tasha. However, he needed Ali to reward Tasha, and hopefully brother Helmy, for their aid. So, he carefully passed this assignment over to Ali. "I know that, along with the EAF, this sale will require the co-operation of the Minister of Defense, as well as approval by the Egyptian Government Military Procurement Committee. I expect and trust that you, as our Support Contractor, can obtain both of these."

Ali wasn't about to disclose any more information to Larry Ray, and was ready to end the conversation. "Larry Ray, I assure you that I have a good working relationship at all levels of the Egyptian military and political decision makers. I am sure I have the right team in Cairo to make this sale. Now, let's get some rest so we are ready to run some plays when we get to Cairo."

With that, Ali reclined his seat and closed his eyes. Larry Ray decided to have another drink while he considered how to be sure that Tasha was drafted as a player on Ali's team, since Ali had been rather vague regarding that probe. After another drink or two . . . *OK, who's counting*, Larry Ray fell asleep.

It was light when Larry Ray woke up, feeling a little hungover. Across from him Ali's was having coffee and a light breakfast.

Ali greeted him. "Larry Ray, Good Morning! I made some coffee and found a box of croissants in the galley. Allow me to play flight attendant and serve you some." He stood up and went to the galley, returning shortly with hot coffee and a croissant for Larry Ray.

"Thank you, Ali," murmured Larry Ray. "You're a great teammate!"

A little later they landed at the Paris Le Bourget Airport, which is the busiest airport dedicated to general aviation in Europe, and located a few miles from the center of Paris. The pilot taxied to the exclusive Jetex terminal. Once they were parked, the door opened and the stairs were extended. Larry Ray and Ali debarked and walked into the Jetex business lounge to wait while the jet was refueled. One of the nice advantages of using Jetex was that they had their own dedicated immigration and customs staff. It only required about a minute to have their passports stamped, with a "Welcome to France," without anyone checking their briefcases.

As they walked over to the coffee bar, Ali was surprised to be met by a man in a business suit and two very attractive young women who looked like models. They were dressed in outfits that looked similar to flight attendant uniforms.

Larry Ray said, "Ali, allow me to introduce you to Ted Tanner, our Corporate VP for Europe, who has his office here in Paris."

They all shook hands, and Ted followed with, "Gentlemen, please meet Belle and Denise. They will be accompanying you for the rest of your journey to Cairo, your return to Paris, and will also act as your guides while you and your guests are here in Paris."

Ted thought he probably didn't need to mention that their names, Belle and Denise, meant, respectively, *beautiful,* and *goddess of wine* in English. Their Egyptian guests would certainly find out on their own!

Before Ali could ask why they needed to have escorts with them at all times, Ted interjected, "Please, don't be fooled by their appearance. They are first class security guards, a service which we provide for all of our high-level executive visitors to Paris. Their main function is to provide security for your two EAF officer guests."

Ali was not sure that Ted hadn't really meant something else starting with "se-" as their true service for the Generals. Anyhow, he liked what he saw and, since this was a CAC play, he certainly would go with it.

Once the "security guards" left to board the jet, Ted said, "Larry Ray, the new CC-260 we are delivering to the French Air Force will arrive the day after tomorrow at the French Air Force Base in Villacoublay, which is about eight miles southwest of Paris. We plan to use our CAC delivery flight crew to provide the aircraft briefing and make the demonstration flight to your Egyptian Air

Force guests. Accordingly, we will delay the aircraft hand-over to the French until after the EAF visit. I understand the schedule specifies that you all will arrive three days from now around ten in the morning?"

Larry Ray nodded his head to confirm Ted's information.

Ted continued. "Good. At that time, we will provide executive transportation to the George V Hotel and give you time to get settled. I reserved a very nice conference room, where a light luncheon will be served while the chief CAC CC-260 pilot provides a briefing on the aircraft's capabilities and an overview of the demo flight. We'll leave you on your own for the evening, as I know this is not Larry Ray's first rodeo in Paris!"

Ali thought, *Again with the rodeo talk. I didn't know that Mobile, Alabama, qualified as the wild west, with its share of cowboys!*

Ted added, "Of course, the "security guards" will be with you at all times, except for the trip to the Air Base and the demo flight. For that event, a coach limo will pick you up at 11:00 AM the next morning to go to Villacoublay, where our crew will have already pre-flighted the aircraft. We are planning about a two-hour flight. The EAF guests may take a session in the right-hand seat in the copilot's position, if they wish to fly the aircraft. After lunch and refreshments, the limo will return you all to the hotel in the afternoon. As for the evening, I know Larry Ray will be able to find plenty to see and do in Paris."

They all chuckled at this while Ted finished his rundown. "The CAC jet will depart Le Bourget the next morning to return you and your guests to Cairo. Unfortunately, the "security guards" are off that day, so you both will have to play flight attendants. I understand the Corporate jet will drop you all off in Cairo and then depart for the return flight to the US. So that about wraps it up. I wish you a successful business visit to Paris. I trust you will find a little time to enjoy the Paris sights."

Paris To Cairo

Larry Ray and Ali thanked Ted for his briefing and making the Paris arrangements for them and their guests. They then left the executive terminal to board their jet. Once they were settled in their seats, the plane taxied out and headed for Cairo. As they leveled off, both Belle and Denise came up from their seats in the aft section.

Belle addressed them in a charming French accent. "Gentlemen, please be assured, no matter what Mr. Tanner says, we can do more than just provide security. *Pour commencer,* let us show you how we can mix some drinks and prepare lunch for you. Since we will be working together, please, just call us "Bea" and "Dee.""

Belle and Denise then returned to the galley. Larry Ray and Ali smiled at each other, both thinking that they might have the opportunity to try out all of Bea's and Dee's services. However, their flight to Cairo was scheduled for only about four and one-half hours. It was the first time Larry Ray had ever hoped for a longer flight!

They wined and dined all the way until landing at Cairo International Airport. Both Bea and Dee had catered to their every desire…*well, almost everyone.* Upon arrival, they taxied up to and parked at the FBO, Executive Sky Flight Support.

For this stopover, since he would be meeting with the EAF the next day, Larry Ray booked himself, along with Bea and Dee, into the five-star Heliopolis Towers Hotel, which was conveniently located between Cairo International and the EAF Almaza Air Base, about a mile away. Larry Ray then sent Bea and Dee over to the hotel via the FBO limo.

As for Ali, once inside the FBO executive terminal, he made a quick call and arranged an all-day guided tour for the "security guards," which would take them to the Cairo Museum, the Pyramids of Giza, and the Khan el-Khalili bazaar, better known as the souq, one of the world's great shopping experiences. Since Larry Ray and Ali were going to be in meetings all the next day, they then adjourned to a small executive conference room to discuss their game plan for tomorrow, as they had been too distracted during the flight to have a serious conversation.

Larry Ray started first. "Ali, thanks for making the tour arrangements for Bea and Dee. Just between us boys, I suggest we do not make any further plays with them, since they work for Ted Tanner and he doesn't like other employees playing with his toys, or should I say, his employees."

Ali thought, *Probably Larry Ray is really only trying to keep them for himself.* But aloud he said, "Of course. Let's not get distracted. In fact, let's get down to business. I agree with your plan to have me join you for the meetings at the EAF tomorrow and accompany you and the Air Marshal and Air Commodore to Paris. That way they will know for sure that I am well-connected to CAC and will expect I have the means to reward them for their support for your deal. So please, leave any reward discussions to me. I plan to wait until after the Paris briefing, demo flight, and special security work by Bea and Dee to get them in the mood for discussing other incentives to encourage them to support your deal. Of course, I expect by then that Bea and Dee will already have, as you say, laid the pipes… no pun intended!"

"Also, please be assured I will also be working the Egyptian system that is well above their pay grade to ensure and expedite the purchase. I'll only share those plays with my own team, so that you Americans can maintain your plausible deniability—whatever that is—that you tend to prefer!"

Larry Ray smiled and responded, "Ali, we make a good team! After we meet with the EAF and I formally submit the offer for the six CC-260s in the morning, I'm scheduled to meet in the afternoon with Colonel Barnes at the Embassy. As you know, he will be accompanying us on the trip to Paris, officially to oversee the demo, but really because, as you also know, Air Attachés generally never pass up a free all-expense paid trip."

Ali nodded his agreement, and Larry added, "I will inform Colonel Barnes that you, representing MAPS, are also going along as our new local Support Contractor to learn about the aircraft and to act as translator on any technical discussions where the EAF may have questions. It doesn't take a lot of special treatment to have him support our project, as he'll be receiving direction from his boss in Washington to lobby the EAF on our behalf."

Ali and Larry Ray then agreed to call it a day and to meet for coffee in the morning prior to going over to the EAF headquarters next door. Larry Ray took the FBO limo over to the hotel. As he was checking in, there was a note waiting for him. It simply said "Harry's Pub has a beer reserved for you at 7:00 PM tomorrow evening" Since he had only met one person, Tasha, at Harry's, Larry Ray smiled as he thought how good she looked holding a beer. Actually, the beer never entered the picture. He ordered room service and decided he had better get a lot of rest, because tomorrow would be very busy, and could just turn out to be a rewarding day, or better yet, evening!

Home At Last

Ali took a taxi to his home and was pleased to see Tasha sitting in his living room next to two glasses of wine. After a hug and a few kisses, she smiled and said, "Let's have a glass of wine, maybe even a couple, while you tell me all about your business trip to the US and Paris."

Sitting beside Tasha on the comfortable sofa, Ali took a long sip of wine. "It all went extremely well, just like Ahmed said it would. The contract negotiations were not difficult and we will receive what we and Ahmed agreed upon. MAPS was approved by both of their Company and Corporate international Committees, so MAPS is now the CAC Egyptian Support Contractor and we should receive the initial payment shortly. This will give us a little working capital to take care of business here."

They clinked their wine glasses together, then Tasha asked, "Was there any discussion on how to take care of Larry Ray?"

Ali replied, "Their senior executives confirmed directly to me, in no uncertain words, that he was not a player on their team. So, my dear, it appears you yourself will have to figure out how to reward him. I trust you can figure out a way without exposing yourself, and I mean that physically, not just literally." He finished with a laugh.

She grinned. "I already have started that play. I will meet with him tomorrow evening and convince him he will be rewarded, all the while keeping my clothes on!"

That remark made them laugh again. They were getting giddy either from too much wine or, more likely, because they were on track to win the local game with a big score.

Tasha then said, in a more serious tone, "Getting down to the real business, I suggest we hold on to any rewards to your new EAF friends until we are assured that they are playing on our team. The same goes for Larry Ray, as he won't be expecting the big reward until after the contract is signed. The only risk I foresee is our home team getting that final big reward."

When Ali looked concerned, Tasha quickly added, "However, I trust Ahmed and the way he has it set up. We also get the bonus on the spares package right away. When we make the reward for his team, then they will make the long-term contract payment to MAPS. If they don't, then we can call foul and make a lot of trouble for them. I'll talk to my brother and let him know that the game is underway and to expedite his plays."

Tasha set her wine glass down and snuggled close to Ali. "OK, that's enough business for tonight. Let's get down to some serious loving!"

Starting a New Day

Ali and Larry Ray were having coffee in the Heliopolis Towers Hotel when Bea and Dee sauntered into the coffee shop like two models on the fashion runway. The conversation level in the area dropped considerably as the girls stopped by their table.

Dee greeted them. "Ali and Larry Ray, how nice to see you again! We were hoping it would have been sooner." She obviously meant the previous night.

Bea murmured, "*Oui.* Ali, how can we thank you for arranging the tour today?"

No one was going to try to answer that question!

Dee purred, "Hopefully, we will see you both this evening. Also, we will be ready to provide our special security services to your clients starting tomorrow."

Bea and Dee then strolled provocatively to another table. Ali was grateful he would be at home that night with Tasha, but he didn't think Larry Ray would be able to resist their "services," especially after Tasha warmed him up!

Larry Ray raised an eyebrow and smiled. "I think I need to switch hotels, or else I'm going to owe Ted Tanner big time!"

This drew a laugh from Ali.

Placing his napkin on the table, Larry Ray scooted back his chair. "Meanwhile, let's get on with our day job."

EAF Headquarters

A MAPS car was waiting for them in front of the hotel. MAPS already had all the base entry passes for them and their vehicle.

Larry Ray thought, *I'm going to like working with these guys as they sure know how to cut through the red tape.*

Larry and Ali easily cleared security at the main gate of Almaza Air Base. They then pulled up to the entrance of the headquarters building. Once through the front door, they were immediately escorted up to Air Marshal Saad's office on the top floor. As they entered, Saad came and greeted them like old friends. Air Commodore Riad was also there and offered his greetings.

They moved to a sitting area where, once they were comfortable, an assistant served them all tea. Larry Ray was experienced with Arab hospitality and knew it would take several cups of tea and lots of small talk before they would be able to get down to business.

After about an hour of visiting, Ali took the initiative to get things moving. "Air Marshal and Air Commodore, both Larry Ray and I would truly enjoy visiting with you for the rest for the day. However, you both know how our American friends are anxious to keep the ball rolling. Plus, you will be leaving for Paris in the morning for the CC-260 inspection and demo flight. Allow us bring you up to date on our Project."

"First of all, I am pleased to announce that my Company, MAPS, has been appointed the Egyptian Support Contractor for the Cargo Aircraft Company. This means that as we go forward, you have a local business and, more importantly, a friend, to assist the EAF in all its dealings with CAC. I recently returned from a visit to the CAC factory in Mobile, Alabama, as well as their Corporate headquarters in Washington DC, where I met with all of their senior management."

"Secondly, and also of great importance, I am assured that the CAC Washington team have influenced the US Department of Defense and the key US politicians to provide a Foreign Military Financing grant for a Direct Commercial Sale of six CC-260 aircraft, plus a significant spares package to the EAF. I am sure I do not need to point out that a FMF Grant means the US pays directly to CAC for the aircraft and spares. All you need to do is sign the contract which Larry Ray just happens to have with him."

The Air Marshal and Air Commodore tried not to look too pleased, since they still wanted to play hard to get, or perhaps really wanted to hear what was in this deal for them. They had all played this game before.

The Air Marshal responded, "Ali and Mr. Hardy. That all sounds very good. However, the Air Commodore and I must review our requirements to be sure the CC-260 aircraft fit into our long-term strategic plan. We cannot introduce new equipment onto our aircraft fleet just because they are free."

This position was not unexpected by either Ali or Larry Ray, as they hadn't yet decided how much incentive these two would need to join the local team.

Larry Ray decided it was time to make a strategic play. "Air Marshal and Air Commodore, please appreciate we are only bringing you what we believe is an excellent opportunity to add the world's best military and humanitarian cargo aircraft to your Air Force. You certainly can take the time you need to evaluate our offer."

But before they became too comfortable thinking they had all the time in the world, Larry Ray added, "However, I must mention that there are twenty other CAC salesmen traveling around the word offering these same six aircraft to other Air Forces. Granted, they are not able to offer free aircraft in the same way as we are offering them to the EAF, yet, as you know, many countries have the money to buy the aircraft outright. Furthermore, as with any money provided by politicians, their commitment can change on short notice. We strongly recommend that if you wish to have the CC-260 aircraft for free, it would be wise to expedite this purchase, and we can work with you on that. We believe the CC-260 inspection and demonstration flight in France will convince you of the value of adding our aircraft to your fleet."

Larry nodded to both Saad and Riad. "Thank you for your time today. We will be departing for Paris from the Executive Sky Flight Support FBO over at Cairo International at ten tomorrow morning on our Company jet. Colonel Barnes will also be joining us for this aircraft inspection and demo flight."

The Air Marshal and Air Commodore stood up, giving nothing away, and indicating the meeting was over.

"We look forward to our trip tomorrow," was all that the Air Marshal said.

Ali's driver dropped Larry Ray back at his hotel. On leaving the car, Larry Ray remarked, "Ali, it appears our EAF friends have played the hard to get game before. I'm sure they will be more enthusiastic once you give them your incentive briefing. As I mentioned, I'm going over to the US Embassy to see Colonel Barnes to make sure he has received his game brief from his boss in Washington. I'll see you at the FBO around nine in the morning so that we can provide Bea and Dee with a little background on their assignment."

As Ali rode away, hc hoped that Larry Ray didn't make too many end runs that night, especially on his fiancée, although he knew Tasha could handle him. He just wasn't sure that Larry Ray wasn't also going to try to score on Bea and Dee.

Back at his hotel, Larry Ray had a quick lunch while trying to decide his play for the evening. He was very pleased that Tasha had made the effort to meet with him. He couldn't decide if it was business or pleasure, or maybe both. If it turned out to be pleasure, there was a logistics problem, since he just couldn't walk into any major hotel taking a member of the government to his room.

Likewise, he wouldn't expect her to take him home with her, as servants can have loose lips. He and Ahmed hadn't yet set up the usual Corporate secret apartment, which was standard in most major cities where they were doing business. Of course, if Tasha didn't want to play tonight, then there were always the backup players, Bea and Dee.

Larry finished his meal thinking that in this international aircraft sales business, it was really difficult to plan all the plays. Not only that, you also need to sell aircraft. Well, as they said in sales school, stay flexible and be prepared to improvise!

US Embassy

Larry Ray had his usual taxi take him over to the US Embassy. Since he had been there several times before, he was pre-cleared to enter, and was escorted to a small conference room off the main lobby. It seemed the US Government didn't trust a US citizen in their work spaces. Or more likely, didn't want a US taxpayer to see how good the government had it. He took a seat and served himself a cup of coffee from a hotel style coffee bar set up in a corner. He thought, *I bet they don't make or get their own coffee up on the top floor!*

Soon Colonel Barnes entered the room and shook hands with Larry Ray. After pouring himself a cup of coffee, he started with, "Larry Ray, nice to see you. And thanks for including me on the EAF CC-260 inspection and demo flight visit to France. I've already received comments from DC that there is strong support in Washington to have the EAF acquire your CC-260 aircraft. Also, my contacts at the EAF appear open, if not supportive, to have your aircraft. Appears you and your DC office have been working all the key players very well."

Larry Ray replied, "Colonel, that's good to hear. We all know the CC-260 will be a good addition to the EAF. The best part for Egypt, as you may know, is that the six aircraft and spares purchase is being funded by an FMF grant with a contract through the Direct Commercial Sales program. That cuts out a lot of red tape and provides for a quick sale, which is great, as we already have the aircraft sitting on the ramp in Mobile."

Colonel Barnes thought, *Wow! These guys have more clout in Washington than I thought.*

Larry Ray continued, "Additionally, we have already contracted with the local military aviation service company, MAPS, to be our CC-260 Support Contractor. Their President, Ali Omar, will also be joining us on the trip to France in order to become familiar with the CC-260 aircraft, as well as to assist in any required translation of the technical discussions. I believe you may know that MAPS already supports several EAF programs. I'm convinced it will be beneficial for you to get to know Ali, since I expect you and he will be interfacing on some of the aspects of this program in the future."

Colonel Barnes thought, *Wow again! These guys already have clout here in Cairo.* It was nice to see an American company that knew how to work the system. Some of them didn't even know what the Sphinx was!

Colonel Barnes took a sip of his coffee, then replied, "Looks like you have done a good job of getting all of the players running in the same direction. I look forward to the visit and will do my part to support your Program." What he didn't say, but insinuated was, *I expect there will be some reward, as you previously mentioned, when I retire.*

Larry Ray thought, *So far so good! Looks like he's on board.*

He then said, "Colonel, there is one sensitive area regarding our visit to France. I'm not sure if you have much experience working with the French. We find that during the bi-annual Paris Air Show they monitor all non-French industry competitors by bugging our chalet and even the hotel rooms of our senior executives. Sometimes they have even intercepted our key clients by having their female agents seduce them when we aren't with them. We suspect they then use these plays to encourage, or rather, bribe them to favor French industry. They sure have upped their game with these unique French plays!"

When Colonel Barnes didn't look particularly surprised, Larry Ray knew the door was open for his next pitch. "We have had a Corporate office in Paris for several years. You know we Americans sometimes say "the best defense is a better offense." Our Paris office has assigned two "Security Service" personnel to accompany us on this trip. They will be with our two EAF officers at all times during the visit, except during the CC-260 briefing and demo flight. And Colonel, I do mean at *all* times."

Again, Colonel Barnes didn't look surprised, but he definitely looked interested

Satisfied that he had the Colonel's undivided attention, Larry Ray finished off his briefing in top form. "Please appreciate that this is for the protection of our guests. Moreover, these Security Specialists, by their contract with us, are not allowed to disclose to anyone any conversations they overhear or other activities that may take place. I assure you we have a good track record in working with them. So, my friend, I'm sure you will appreciate the talents of the Misses Belle and Denise when you meet them tomorrow.

We will be advising the two EAG officers that the two women are security specialist escorts assigned to protect them at all times from any French spying, even when we are not working. Once you meet Bea and Dee, you'll understand why the Air Marshal and Air Commodore will not refuse their protection."

Now Colonel Barnes was looking almost a little stunned. Larry Ray thought, *He probably thinks I'm really the CIA, and that he had better watch his step and any other moves.*

Larry Ray got up and shook the Colonel's hand, while saying, "I expect that's enough details for now. I'll see you at the Executive Sky Flight Support FBO over at Cairo International in the morning. We plan to leave for Paris around ten on our Company jet."

As Larry Ray left, Colonel Barnes really was sort of overwhelmed with all that info. He surmised that this was certainly going to be a very interesting trip, especially for his friends at the EAF.

Harry's Pub

Larry Ray arrived at Harry's Pub a little before seven and was not surprised to see Tasha sitting at a corner table with two beers in front of her. As he reached her side, she got up and gave him a "Nice to see you" light kiss on his cheek. He gave her a warm look in return and said, "Tasha, what a pleasant surprise. I was wondering who my secret admirer was that wished to win me over with a few beers!"

As they sat down, Larry Ray again seated himself to her side and not across from her. He was as close as he could get without sitting right next to her.

Tasha gave him a flirtatious smile. "Larry Ray, I know it will take more than a few beers to win you over. Thanks for meeting with me."

Then putting on her "Let's get down to business" voice, Tasha said, "As you would expect, I am anxious to have an update on your Program. I have already heard that you were successful in having MAPS appointed as your local Agent, or as you call them, a Support Contractor. Actually, I do know Ali Omar." She added to herself, *That's quite an understatement, but let's keep Larry Ray's hopes up.* "I can assure you his local Team includes the key high-level players who can win this game for you."

Since Tasha knew all of this already, Larry Ray had to assume she was on Ali's Team, but didn't want to ask her directly, just in case someone later asked him that question when he was under oath to tell the truth and nothing but the truth.

Tasha could see that he wanted to know more, so before he could ask the question she didn't want to answer, she stated, " Also, let me assure you that our team has ways and the means to reward a key player who isn't a member on our local team, but assists in winning the game."

With that assurance, Larry Ray decided he might as well make his play with her to see if she herself also personally rewarded any of the players. "Tasha, I appreciate that Ali will thank me for his being selected as the well-paid coach for the local team. You know, you and I make great partners in putting together players and teams to win these sales games. I would recommend we have a few more private strategy sessions to discuss what else we can put together."

Tasha was pretty sure she knew what he wanted to "put together."

Since she and Ali had agreed with Ahmed that they would handle the incentive to keep Larry Ray in the game, which included money only, and no "putting together," it looked the time had come to make the "lead him on" play.

Tasha replied smoothly, "Larry Ray, what a good idea! I know you and I could develop some very interesting positions. . . oops, I mean interesting business plans."

From the look on Larry Ray's face, it was clear what business positions he was interested in. She quickly followed with, "Let's drink to our new partnership and plan to have a serious strategy session very soon. I know a quiet place where we can develop our business positions without being disturbed."

With that, she knew she had led him to believe that, sometime in the future, he would get what he desired, even lusted for. What he didn't know was that she was an expert at delaying the game.

She ended her little play of sensual sparring with, "Larry Ray, sorry. I must run, as I have a meeting tonight with my brother and I need to encourage, or as you say, "lobby" him to accept the free CC-260 aircraft from the USA. But that should not be a hard sell!"

They both got up, and Tasha gave him a more than affectionate kiss near his lips. Larry Ray sat back down, definitely aroused, and ordered another beer. He was sure he was going to score with Tasha, only just a little later than he had hoped. After a couple more beers, followed by a little food, he returned to his hotel to get ready to play the Paris game.

As he walked through the lobby, he did check the bar just in case Bea and Dee were in there and possibly ready for a strategy session. Fortunately for them, but unfortunately for him, they had apparently turned in early and wouldn't have to run any defensive plays tonight.

The next morning, when he had a clearer head, Larry Ray sent a short message to Ahmed, using only the code names for the players, as usual:

"Sphinx (*Ahmed*), the visit here went very well. I saw the local icons, Karnak (*AM Saad*) and Darius *(AC Riad)*, along with my guide Ramses (*Ali*), and they were very pleased to see us and encouraged us to visit more often. Also, our local US host (*They had forgotten to make up a code name for Colonel Barnes*), who will be on the visit to France, was also pleased to see us. All is well here!"

Larry Ray wasn't about to mention his meeting with Cleopatra, the lovely Tasha, as he believed only he was running that "Special Play."

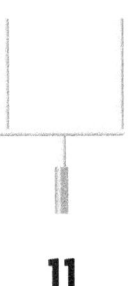

11

TENTH GAME – SAN FRANCISCO 49ERS AT PHOENIX CARDINALS

49ers lose 23 to 24

The 49ers advanced to a 23–0 lead in the third quarter. The Cardinals then began a comeback as quarterback Lomax passed for a pair of touchdowns. Additionally, San Francisco had fourteen penalties for 106 yards. On a kick return, Walsh was hit by a runner and suffered two cracked ribs. The Cardinals moved down the field in the final minute and scored on a nine-yard Lomax pass to Roy Green.

Cairo to Paris

As Larry Ray grabbed a quick breakfast in the hotel, he kept an eye out for Bea and Dee. He was getting concerned that they were avoiding him. What he didn't know was that Ted had instructed them to not get involved with Larry Ray, and that they had actually left some time ago to make sure the executive jet was stocked and ready for the trip to Paris.

By the time Larry Ray checked out of the hotel and made it over to Executive Sky Flight, both Ali and Colonel Barnes were already there waiting for him. He picked up a cup of coffee and joined them in the lounge.

Larry Ray greeted them pleasantly. "Colonel Barnes and Ali,

looks like you aviation types always like to get to the airport early. I see our EAF guests haven't arrived yet, but I expect, at their political level, no flights ever leave without them. Fortunately, it's our airplane, so we also will not leave without them."

Barnes and Ali smiled in return, just as Air Marshal Saad and AC Riad entered the executive terminal with two aids carrying their bags. Actually, they were right on time. They all said their hello's, while several of the FBO ground crew took their bags out to the plane. The CAC executive jet looked impressive sitting on the tarmac. Larry Ray thought, *Just wait until you get inside and see the interior layout, especially Belle and Denise!*

To the Ticket-Holders: For those that do not have your own Biz jet, and, although this is not a picture book, the following layout will help you keep up with the on-board activities.

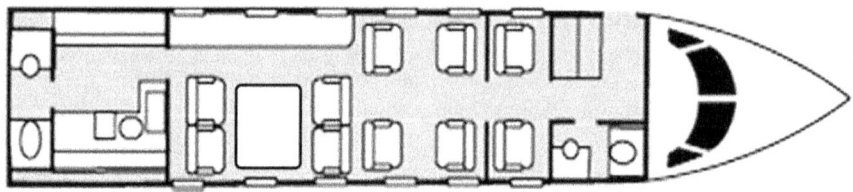

As the group walked up the airstairs and entered the cabin, Larry Ray could see that all three of the military guests were impressed with the looks of the flight attendants. Dee escorted Ali and Colonel Barnes to two facing seats in the mid cabin, and Bea escorted the two EAF officers and Larry Ray to the four-person conference and dining area in the aft section. This would allow Larry Ray the opportunity to explain the need for security guards when visiting the French on business, and also assure them both that Bea and Dee were working in that capacity. More importantly, Larry Ray would explain that the girls worked for CAC and had very strict non-disclosure agreements, meaning they would not and could not disclose any of their security work activities. Larry Ray knew this could be a difficult pass, so he would wait until Bea and Dee had smoothed the field with a few drinks.

Meanwhile, this would give Ali a little one-on-one time with Colonel Barnes to determine if he was on-board to truly support this game plan. Larry Ray had already informed Ali that, even though he had mentioned a potential job at CAC, the Colonel appeared to still be a little unsure of his plans after his upcoming retirement.

The two flight attendants, aka security guards, sat in the two forward seats for take-off. Once airborne they would have plenty of time to show their stuff.

Once the jet leveled out, Bea and Dee offered their guests mimosas, a combination of champagne and orange juice, as Larry Ray had told them the group had a business briefing just after they arrived in Paris, and he wanted everyone alert or at least looking alert. After a few glasses, Larry Ray made his pitch about how the French spy on business visitors. He was pleased that they seemed to believe him, or maybe the mimosas had smoothed the field.

Later, after a light snack had been served, Larry Ray asked Bea to sit with their guests to discuss the girls' roles and capabilities. *Well, most of their capabilities.*

In very good English, with a charming French accent, Bea began, "Gentlemen, I expect that Mr. Hardy has briefed you on some of the spying that the French conduct against foreign business visitors. I can assure you their spying is as bad, or even worse, than Mr. Hardy mentioned. Please do not be fooled by our appearance.

Dee and I are both ex-DGSE agents. That stands for the General Directorate for External Security, which is France's external intelligence agency. This is the French equivalent to the United Kingdom's MI6 and the United States' CIA. We are both fully trained in protective actions, including physical attacks and the use of all types of weapons. More importantly, we are both very familiar with the DSGE surveillance and eavesdropping bugging capabilities. It is important that Dee and I be at your side at all times, except when you are receiving military briefings or on the demo flight."

Then she smiled pertly, and with a wink, continued, "Of course, we expect you can attend to business in the toilet on your own! Again, I want to reassure you, as I'm sure Larry Ray has mentioned, both Dee and I are bound by a very strict non-disclosure agreement that assures you that we protect your privacy. This agreement is so binding, it carries the threat of jailtime, if it is violated. This means you can do whatever you want in Paris and there will not be any tattletales."

Both the Air Marshal and Air Commodore smiled, and Air Marshal Saad responded, "Thank you, Mademoiselle Bea, for your briefing. I assure you that the Air Commodore and I now understand the reason you are both with us. We appreciate your experience and capabilities. We look forward to having you, as our American friends say, babysit us."

This made them all laugh, and Bea got up and went for another round of mimosas.

Meanwhile, Ali and Colonel Barnes were enjoying their drinks and playing "Who knows the most influential people at the EAF" game. The conversation eventually led to Ali asking the Colonel,

"What are your plans after you retire?"

Colonel Barnes replied, "Well, I'm considering a lot of opportunities which make use of my very valuable experience in the US Air Force. I would like to continue being involved in a business that keeps me connected to military aviation."

Ali was a little surprised that the Colonel seemed to be looking intently in his direction. *OK, might as well incentivize him to support their plays.*

"Colonel, that's very interesting. As you know, MAPS, along with our recent sign-up with CAC, currently represents several other US military aviation companies. Actually, I have been discussing with my Board, that if the EAF obtains the CC-260, we will have a significant long-term relationship with CAC. Accordingly, we should consider setting up an office in the US to interface with CAC and our other US clients. If we decide to set up that office, we would like to talk to you regarding any interest you may have in running that operation."

The Colonel looked pleased at Ali's suggestion. "Ali, I would be very interested, as it would be the best of two worlds, using my international military aviation expertise, while working for a company involved in military aviation support. Since we are almost neighbors in Cairo, let's plan to get together when we get back, so I can become more familiar with your operation."

Ali was thinking, *Slow down a little, as this play is just beginning.* He closed the discussion with a final pass.

"Great! As you know, those two EAF officers will soon be our biggest customer in Egypt. I expect you know and get along well with them."

Ali was aware that if the Colonel wished to work for CAC, the job would depend on the EAF getting the CC-260. If he wished to work for MAPS, that job would also depend on the EAF getting the CC-260. Ali easily concluded that, either way, it looked like the Colonel needed to support the EAF getting the CC-260.

The rest of the flight went smoothly and quickly. The jet landed in Paris at Le Bourget and taxied to the Jetex ramp. They all deplaned and walked into the executive terminal. Again, immigration and customs clearance were a rubber stamp. In fact, their luggage was moved directly from the airplane to the waiting executive coach. They all, including Bea and Dee, boarded the coach and headed for the center of Paris.

The coach pulled up at the main entrance to the very exclusive Hotel George V, just off the Avenue Champs-Elysees on the Avenue George V, which made the hotel easy to find. Again, the Paris VP, Ted Tanner, had made all the arrangements. The hotel manager was waiting for them in the lobby and personally handed each one their room key, along with his business card with his direct number.

Larry Ray thought, *Sure, makes traveling easier when you know, or incentivize somebody to handle the small stuff.*

Was it another amazing coincidence that Bea's room was adjacent to the Air Marshal's, and Dee's room was adjacent to the Air Commodore's, with connecting doors? It sure looked like Ted Tanner was really concerned about their guests' security.

As they had discussed on the flight, the schedule was to get settled in their rooms and then meet for a luncheon and CC-260 briefing in a top floor conference room. Additionally, both Bea and Dee had advised their EAF assignees that they would need to accompany them to their rooms and sweep the rooms for listening devices.

The Air Marshal countered with, "OK. Then in return we will accompany you ladies to your rooms and inspect them." No one was sure whether he meant the rooms or the ladies.

They all laughed at his comeback. It looked like the Air Marshal was getting into the Paris spirit of mixing business with fun.

A short time later, everyone, except Bea and Dee, met in the top floor executive conference room. Apparently, Ted trusted the girls with only so much information. The group was met by the CAC CC-260 delivery flight crew, and they were all served drinks of coffee, tea, and sodas, because it was too early for anything stronger. Well, because it was France, they also did serve wine. Of course, this gave Bea and Dee time to set up their personal secret cameras in the EAF Officers rooms. You never know when the French might develop a military cargo aircraft and need a little leverage to sell them to Egypt. The French, after all, were the French!

The CAC flight crew provided a long Power Point briefing on the aircraft's technical and operational capabilities, too long to be included in a novel with a page limitation. However, the wine sure made the drawn-out presentation more enjoyable.

After the aircraft briefing, it was suggested that everyone take a break so as to be well-rested for a special dinner party later that evening. Bea and Dee arrived to escort their assigned guests, and left immediately with the two EAF generals. Air Marshal Saad was overheard saying he suspected his bed was bugged and perhaps needed Bea to inspect it again. No one was going to touch that line.

Of course, there were many, many great restaurants in Paris. However, the only one with the best view in Paris, the most excellent wine, and the best food and service was the very expensive Le Jules Verne Restaurant on the second level of the Eiffel Tower. The general tab per person was around four hundred dollars, not including the wine. The restaurant only took reservations if one was a close friend of the French President, a member of the French Government, or had a special monetary relationship with the manager of the George V.

The group all met around eight that evening in the hotel lobby. The hotel executive coach limo was waiting to take them on the short ride over to the Eiffel Tower. No one asked if Bea had found any bed bugs in the Air Marshal's bed. He looked very relaxed, so he must not have been bothered by any Bea-bugs while he rested.

The restaurant had its own dedicated elevator. Busts of Jules Verne and Gustave Eiffel greeted them as they entered the private lobby. A professional attendant guided them to the elevator, which had windows on both sides to let its passengers see the inner workings of the Eiffel Tower, with views of Paris beyond. A display told them how far above the ground they were at each stage of the ride. Approximately four hundred feet above the ground, the elevator stopped, and the doors opened into the magical kingdom of Restaurant Le Jules Verne.

The exemplary service began as soon as they left the elevator. The young and dynamic staff greeted them warmly, as if they were regulars, and escorted them to their reserved private dining area, which was light and airy. Its palette of steel, accompanied by white and gold accents, presented a sharp contrast to the heavy upholstery and dark color scheme of the hotel.

The group was cordially seated at a round table, with Bea and Dee to the right of each of their charges, not necessarily to help them eat, but just to be sure their champagne and wine glasses were never empty. Although Colonel Barnes looked a little jealous, he knew he would not be able to get away with playing that game.

All the champagne, wine, appetizers, main courses, and desserts, as well as the special attention of the very attractive waitresses, would defy the page limit to any novel. Throughout the dinner, Larry Ray made many comments of the special treatment CC-260 customers and operators receive, not only at the Paris Air Show but also at Farnborugh, Dubai, Singapore, or any others they might attend! He indicated that their Corporate jets would be used to take key customers to these air shows. He failed to mention that Corporate policy was to advise any hopeful customers that it was already committed whenever they requested a ride.

After dinner they enjoyed a couple rounds of Remy Martin Louis XIII cognac, one of the most expensive cognacs in the world. All in all, it was a very pleasant evening for everyone except for Larry Ray's expense account. He thought that he had better wait until after the sale to submit it, so that there would be enough money to pay this bill.

They called it an early night for Paris, as they were going on the demo flight the next day. Because Larry Ray had conducted this Paris dinner tour before, he had scheduled the demo flight after lunch so that everyone could have a long night's rest, assuming Bea and Dee let the two officers have any rest.

The hotel coach was waiting for them below, and, since there was very little traffic, made a quick trip of it back to the hotel, not that any of this group would notice or, at this point, even be able to tell the time. They all said their goodnights in the lobby and went to their suites.

It was hard to imagine, but Larry Ray was still thirsty, so he left the hotel and walked the short distance down to the Avenue Champs-Elysees. He secured a small table at Fouquet's, his favorite people-watching place on the corner. He had really had his fill of wine. Nevertheless, because the waiter didn't understand his pronunciation of bourbon, he ended up with a large glass of wine after all.

Just as he was taking his first sip, a voice next to him exclaimed, 'Larry Ray! What an amazing coincidence to run into you tonight!"

Larry Ray turned and saw Ted Tanner smiling at him as he took a seat across from him. Larry Ray thought, *Ted certainly keeps a close watch on all of the visitors to his turf.* Aloud, Larry Ray made the salesman's reply, "Ted! Nice to see you! I was hoping I wouldn't have to drink alone."

There followed the usual small talk as Ted ordered and the waiter delivered his glass of wine. Then Ted said, "Larry Ray, I trust all is going well with your sale and that my security staff are doing a good job for you."

Larry Ray was sure that Ted was receiving a daily, probably hourly, report from his staff, so he replied, "Ted, all the arrangements you have made, including the limo service, hotel reservations, getting us into the Jules Verne, and certainly Belle and Denise, have been extremely helpful to my sales campaign."

Immediately after he said that, he knew he would probably regret it, as the world runs on "quid pro quo."

Not to miss an opportunity, Ted quickly responded, "I hear that this may be one of the most profitable sales in years for CAC. My friends in Washington say you also have arranged a big reward for your "Helper.""

Larry Ray knew what was coming next, so he took a big swig of wine and sat back.

Ted continued on. "I'm sure you are as frustrated as I am at the small rewards that your Company and the Corporation give to their own people, such as you and myself, who are the ones that make the sales happen. I would like to think that, even though our bosses don't reward us, people like your "Helper" must appreciate all we do to make this happen."

Larry Ray wasn't sure whether Ted was trying to shake him down, or this was a test from Corporate HR to test his ethics. However, he had known Ted for several years and, like all the people that ran the Corporate International offices, he knew how to work the territory. So, after another large drink of wine, Larry Ray decided to deflect this pass.

"Ted, please appreciate that MAPS was interviewed and selected by your fellow Corporate VP, Ahmed, and your buddy in DC, Ken Doyle, who worked closely with Ahmed to have MAPS approved. Also, I know that Ahmed and Ali discussed and agreed the "Helper" reward long before it was approved by the CRMs. It appears to me that Ali, Ahmed, and Ken may already have already arranged for some "Extra Points" in this game. I will make a run by Ali to be sure that he is fully aware of your and my efforts. I suggest you do the same with Ahmed and Ken."

Of course, Larry Ray was not going to say a word to Ali, as he was already expecting to be rewarded by Tasha, and hopefully in more ways than one. But he would let Ted make his play with Ahmed and Ken. And Ted could do OK. On the other hand, if either one blew the whistle on him. it could shorten his career.

Ted nodded, got up abruptly, and left without another word. Larry Ray leisurely finished his wine and asked the waiter his name and rank for his expense report. Then he got up and strolled, almost in a straight line, back to the hotel

Paris – CC-260 Demo Day

They all met for a late breakfast in the heart of the hotel at the exclusive Le Cinq restaurant, which they had all to themselves. There was even one waitress for each of them. Both of the EAF Officers looked extremely rested. Apparently, Bea and Dee were earning their pay. After breakfast everyone, except Bea and Dee, walked thru the lobby to board the executive coach for the trip to the French Air Force base in Villacoublay, just a short distance southeast of Paris near Versailles.

Upon arrival, Ted had again worked his magic. They were pre-cleared for access to the Air Base and were escorted to the flight line, where a new CC-260 was waiting. The CAC flight crew, who had briefed them the day before, were standing by the aircraft. The CAC chief pilot immediately took charge and asked them all to follow him as he conducted the pre-flight walk-around inspection. Once that was completed, they all climbed up the ramp into the cargo area.

"There are only three observer seats in the flight station," the pilot informed them. "I suggest the Air Marshal, Air Commodore, and Colonel Barnes join the co-pilot and myself up there. Mr.

Hardy and Mr. Omar, sorry, but you will have to make yourself as comfortable as possible on the canvas seats along the cargo compartment wall. Mr. Turner, our loadmaster, will get you settled and arrange a visit for each of you to the flight station once we get airborne. Please appreciate, he has not had any flight attendant training, so you may have to get your own coffee."

Everyone chuckled as the "Flyboys" headed toward the steps up to the flight station at the front of the aircraft.

Larry Ray and Ali strapped themselves into the very uncomfortable canvas seats. They had both considered just staying in the Officers Club. However, they knew they had to act like this demo flight was going to sell the aircraft. With both of their "Special Plays," they knew the sale was a done deal as long as these guys didn't crash the aircraft today.

Up in the flight station the pilots were briefing the guests on all of the advanced features of the CC-260. They emphasized that it only required two pilots. The flight engineer, navigator, and radio operator had been replaced by automated electronic systems. Of course, they just had to mention that the next generation CC-260 would have only one pilot and a dog. It would be so automatic that the pilot was only there to feed the dog, and the dog was there to bite the pilot if he touched anything.

That broke the ice and drew laughter from their guests.

The plane took off and headed southeast towards Nantes, passing on by it to the Bay of Biscay. It was best to be over the water when showing what the aircraft could do, especially when conducting low-level maneuvers. The CAC pilots clearly demonstrated the exceptional capabilities of the CC-260. Because it was a medium size two-engine aircraft, it had more than sufficient power for these low-level operations. Off and on during the flight, the co-pilot let the EAF Officers, as well as Colonel Barnes, sit in the right-hand seat and fly the aircraft.

Meanwhile, back in the cargo compartment, both Larry Ray and Ali were wondering if there were any barf bags on the aircraft. The continuous maneuvers, including the power-on stalls, caused an effect similar to seasickness.

To reward them for their patience and suffering, on the return to Villacoublay, Larry Ray and Ali were permitted to go up to the flight station to have a look around. They could tell that their three guests were extremely pleased with the flight by the many compliments they were handing out.

After landing at the Air Base, they taxied over to where the hotel coach was waiting. As they departed the aircraft, the EAF Officers and Colonel Barnes thanked the CAC flight crew profusely for the demo flight. It appeared the demo flight play had worked well.

The group arrived back to the George V at mid-afternoon. As they walked into the lobby, Bea and Dee were waiting to escort their EAF charges to their rooms so they could get some rest before the evening activities. Larry Ray was hoping that they actually did get some rest, since he had a special night out in Paris planned for them.

They all met again in the early evening. Larry Ray was getting concerned, actually jealous, that the Air Marshal and Air Commodore were looking extremely rested, or was it just pleased.

Larry Ray, with Ted's help, had arranged for an evening at the Lido de Paris, the most famous cabaret in Paris, if not the world.

Ted had arranged for VIP seating and the most expensive dinner and show combination, Soiree Triomphe. Larry Ray knew that Ted would pass the Lido costs on to CAC. He sure hoped the EAF purchased the CC-260, or the Company might deduct some of these Paris expenses from his own pay.

The Lido was only a couple of blocks down the street from the hotel on the north side of the Avenue Champs-Elysees, just across from Fouquet's. It didn't make much sense to take the hotel limo to travel just a few blocks. However, if someone is getting the VIP treatment at the Lido, they need to arrive like a VIP.

Incidentally, Bea and Dee were excused from going to the Lido. As good as they looked, it would be like taking beer to a champagne party, as they say in Alabama. Anyway, Larry Ray knew Bea and Dee should rest up, because once the EAF officers returned from watching the Lido girls do the can-can for a couple of hours, he was sure they would be ready for some special rest.

It was an exceptionally fun and very expensive evening. However, if a company is looking to show-off for a potential customer, then there is nothing like the Lido to make your point.

During the final round of Louis XIII, the Air Marshal commented, "Gentlemen, I propose a toast in honor of the CC-260, and also to Mr. Hardy to thank him for the best, and I do mean best, aircraft demonstration I have ever attended. The EAF looks forward to having your aircraft and to a long professional relationship with you."

They all smiled and clinked their glasses and drank.

Larry Ray replied, "Thank you, Air Marshal Saad and Air Commodore Riad, for your kind words. We at CAC are excited about the EAF having the best military cargo aircraft in the world. Here's to enjoying a long relationship with the EAF. In addition, we would like to extend our special thanks to both of our other special guests, Colonel Barnes and Ali, for being a part of our team!"

Larry Ray expected that Colonel Barnes wouldn't be upset being called a member of their team. Actually, after all they had had to drink, he was sure the Colonel would just go with the flow. Speaking of flow, he continued, "Let's have another round to toast our USAF and MAPS colleagues! OK, maybe that will require two more rounds!"

Larry Ray was feeling exceptionally happy. It was a great ending to a very, very good day!

As they returned to the hotel in the limo, Larry Ray was now thankful for the ride, as he was not sure any of them could walk all that well. As they passed through the lobby, the EAF officers were each handed a note from Bea and Dee, which Larry Ray believed said something to the effect about their beds being made ready for their return, whatever that meant. They all slurred their good nights and agreed to be ready to depart for the airport by mid-morning.

The next morning, they all met once more for breakfast in the Le Cinq restaurant. Again, Larry Ray was pleased with the extremely positive comments on the visit by the EAF officers. When the group had finished and arranged for their luggage to be brought down, they headed for the coach limo at the front entrance.

Talk about difficult good-byes! It was obvious that both the Air Marshal and Air Commodore were very sad to be leaving Bea and Dee. Larry Ray would encourage Ted to provide them a bonus for their hard work. Well, maybe not so difficult, but certainly very well-played.

The drive out to Le Bourget was relatively quick and the CAC jet was standing by at the Jetex executive terminal. As they boarded, they switched seat partners, as agreed upon between Larry Ray and Ali. Ali sat in the forward two-seat arrangement opposite Air Marshal Saad, and Larry Ray sat in the aft four seat arrangement with Air Commodore Riad and Colonel Barnes. Since that arrangement appeared acceptable to the Air Marshal, no one made any comment.

It was the time and the opportunity for Ali to make his "Special Play" to draft the Air Marshal for his team. Once airborne, Larry Ray played flight attendant and served some French wine. It was a surprise that there was any left after the visit. As they were cruising east, capturing a speculator view of the Swiss Alps, Ali made his play.

"Air Marshal Saad, I trust you will agree that not only does the Cargo Aircraft Company make a great aircraft, they also know how to take care of their customers."

The Air Marshal smiled and nodded in agreement.

Ali continued, "As you know, my company has been selected as their local Support Contractor if the EAF acquires the CC-260." Ali wasn't going to mention at this time that he already had the contract.

Air Marshal Saad replied, "Ali, this trip has only confirmed that the CC-260 is a great aircraft and would be a valuable addition to our EAF fleet. Also, considering that the American government is essentially providing the first six at no cost, I believe you can count on getting that contract." And that's exactly what Ali was hoping to hear.

Now Ali had his opening. "That is so good to know, as we are looking to expand my company, MAPS. The CC-260 support contract will allow us to grow. However, I have one concern."

As he said this, Ali saw that he now had the Air Marshal's complete attention, as Saad leaned forward toward him. "As you know, MAPS currently supports mainly military helicopters and business aircraft. We do not have very good experience or knowledge regarding military cargo aircraft. Accordingly, I was wondering, since you will be very involved with the CC-260 introduction and operation, if you would be interested in being a consultant to MAPS to help us be successful in supporting the CC-260? Please be assured, I am not suggesting anything illegal. We will only need you to advise us on commercial technical aspects of the aircraft, but nothing related to military operations. Of course, this would be a private consulting agreement between you and myself, which we would not make public or file in any reports with the government."

When the Air Marshal hesitated, Ali quickly added, "Your advice and council would be extremely valuable to us. Therefore, I am considering a consulting fee of eighty thousand gineih per month." Ali knew that eighty thousand Egyptian pounds equaled about five thousand dollars per month, and could immediately see that he had the Air Marshal's interest, since this would amount to about fifty percent of his annual pay. It wasn't for nothing that the art of negotiation was born in the Middle East.

The Air Marshal thought for a minute or two, then replied, "Ali, I agree that my advice can only help you be successful with the

CC-260 contract. Also, there is no problem in my being an advisor to MAPS, as long as we stick only to commercial technical issues. However, I may require the Air Commodore's assistance on some technical issues. To cover his added expense, I would actually need one hundred ten thousand gineih."

Ali tried not to smile at this counter offer of seven thousand dollars a month. Maintaining a serious look, he answered, "Air Marshal Saad, we only have an introductory contract at this time, which we hope, as you continue to add aircraft, we can increase. The best I can do at this time is ninety-five thousand gineih!" This last offer on Ali's part amounted to six thousand dollars.

As the Air Marshal mulled over this final offer, he thought to himself that although he would need some assistance from the Air Commodore, since the Commodore worked for him, he could get by giving the Commodore small token rewards whenever he needed his help. Satisfied with this arrangement, the Air Marshal smiled and extended his hand to Ali, saying "We have a deal!" As they shook hands, he added, "Let's seal it with another glass of wine, or better yet champagne"

Ali went aft to get the champagne. When he passed by Larry Ray, he commented, "The Air Marshal would like us all to join him in a glass or two of champagne to celebrate the good work of this team." By Ali's use of the word team, Larry Ray knew that the Air Marshal was on-board Ali's team. *Well, another good reason to have another drink*!

While Ali was making his play, Larry Ray, Colonel Barnes, and the Air Commodore passed the time comparing notes on what countries to visit or not to visit, based on their personal experiences. As they drank their way across the Mediterranean Sea, they all agreed that Egypt was one of the best countries for work or play!

After another hour or so, and another bottle of champagne or so, they landed at Cairo International and taxied up to the Sky Flight executive terminal. An EAF military car was there to pick up the EAF Officers. As the FBO ground staff unloaded their luggage and placed it in their car, they all said their farewells. Larry Ray took another opportunity to remind the Air Marshal that time was of the essence, since the aircraft were on the open market.

Larry Ray had arranged for one of his private taxis to take Colonel Barnes over to the US Embassy. He then suggested that he and Ali take a minute to compare notes in the Sky Flight executive lounge. Ali had limited his drinking in order to avoid saying say too much, as he kept in mind that Larry Ray was not on the Home Team.

They took a table in a corner of the lounge. When the hostess came over to take their order, of course, Larry Ray ordered a drink. Ali begged off saying he had to go to a business meeting. He thought, *Those US southern boys must have some special training to be able to drink so much and remain standing.*

Ali wanted to keep this meeting short. "Larry Ray, I wish to complement you and your Paris team on arranging a most successful visit and aircraft demonstration. The Air Marshal assured me that he will be supportive of the EAF acquiring the CC-260 aircraft. I will remain in direct contact with him to keep reminding him that time is of the essence, as you have already informed him, as well as to monitor their progress and let you know of any problems"

Larry Ray really wanted to ask what it had taken to sign-up the Air Marshal for Ali's team. However, he really didn't have a need-to-know status. Plus, Ali wouldn't tell him anyway, so he replied,

"Ali, good work. I will be here for a few days and hopefully will be asked by the Air Marshal to have our contracts people come over to negotiate the contract. Also, I will work with our Washington office and Colonel Barnes to see if we can add some pressure from the US Embassy to get the contract signed by hinting that another country is after this FMF free money. Let's keep in touch and win this game!"

With that, Larry Ray gulped down his drink, said goodbye to Ali, and had another of his private taxis take him downtown to his normal base of operations at the Marriott Hotel. On the trip to the hotel, he wondered how he was going to obtain a debriefing from Ted on the day-to-day, or more so, the night-to-night "Special Plays" of Bea and Dee. Oh well, as they said at home in Alabama, "Let sleeping dogs lie." Time to get ready for the for the next play!

12

ELEVENTH GAME - SAN FRANCISCO 49ERS HOSTS LOS ANGELES RAIDERS

49ers lose 3 to 9

Montana started, despite continuing concern over his health. He was held to 160 passing yards as the Raiders eked out a 9–3 win. The 49ers had many chances to win this game. A final drive was stalled by a penalty on a pass interference on Rice inside the ten-yard line. It was the second game of the season where the 49ers didn't score a touchdown.

Cairo- CC-260 Contract Game Plan

As Ali walked into his home, he was not surprised to see Tasha and her brother, Helmy, sitting in the living room having a glass of wine. Although he was certainly happy to see them, he thought, *I have already surpassed my yearly quota of wine.* Aloud he said, "Aha! The people welcome back the conquering hero! Let me get a real drink and I'll give you the play-by-play of the Mobile, Washington, and Paris games."

Once he had his drink, they clinked glasses and all took a sip. Then Ali launched into the rundown of his trips. "Let me assure you, the CAC team surely know how to play this game. Along with a very professional CC-260 briefing and a very thorough demo flight, they rolled out the red carpet in Paris. It is clear they have made this sort of "Special Play" before. Per their arrangements, we stayed at the best hotel, dined at the most exclusive restaurant, and received the VIP treatment at the Lido show. Tasha, I assure you that I behaved myself during the Lido can-can ladies' performance."

Tasha giggled and gave him an affectionate punch in the arm. Helmy looked amused.

Ali continued with his summary. "The play that was discussed when we first stopped in Paris on our way back to Cairo, prior to this trip, consisted of assigning two very attractive female security guards to accompany the EAF Officers at all times, and I do mean at all times. That went extremely well. Not that I doubt their intentions to protect and provide full services to their clients, but I expect they have some very compromising pictures to ensure that the two officers follow their game plan."

Tasha raised her eyebrows at this, and Helmy gave a discreet cough.

"Fortunately, I did have the opportunity on the return flight to have a private discussion with Air Marshal Saad to see if he wished to consult with me to provide advice on cargo aircraft technical and operational matters. Of course, he was interested, and after a short negotiation, we agreed on a monthly retainer of ninety-five thousand gineih. I will simply deposit the six thousand dollars in a bank account that he will set up under an alias at a local bank. He also committed that he would reward the Air Commodore to support this purchase with a little cash, less workload, and regional inspection trips. We will start this retainer immediately, as I want to have the Air Marshal locked-in before he can ask for more reward."

Helmy responded, "And did you discuss a time frame?"

Ali nodded. "We all emphasized that time is of the essence, since politically free money in Washington DC is always subject to being highjacked. So it looks like all of our ducks, or I should say, sphinxes are in a row!"

Helmy and Tasha laughed at Ali's play on words, as he threw his final pass.

"Helmy, I believe the ball and the play is now in your and Tasha's hands to score for our team!"

Helmy answered, "Ali, good work! I'm not sure I can say hard work, but you have certainly done well for our team. I will get the ball moving at the EAF and, Tasha, you keep the pharaohs on your Procurement Committee from taking the ball away from our team."

With that, Helmy finished his wine and got up to leave. As he headed toward the door, he said over his shoulder, "I'll leave you two to work on your wedding plans, now that we have the gifts all in order!"

After Helmy departed, Ali commented to Tasha, "Our being unofficially engaged has worked to our benefit so far, whereas a very public wedding would bring extra attention to the business relationship between MAPS, the Depart of Defense, and your Committee, especially with all three of us involved in this CC-260 purchase. It could result in someone in our government looking into the MAPS contract and payments from CAC. Also, from what I saw at the Cargo Aircraft headquarters in Alabama, there are a couple of executives there who would immediately blow the whistle and point the finger at us at the first sign of any US Government investigation into this sale."

When Tasha looked questioningly at Ali, he took her into his arms, and kissed her tenderly, while she nestled contentedly against his solid frame. Finally, Ali murmured in her ear, "Why don't we consider having a very quiet private wedding ceremony. That would allow us to keep our combined rewards within the family. We can always renew our vows with a formal celebration sometime later."

Tasha beamed at him and returned his kiss. Then she laid her head on his shoulder. "It's a great idea. I'll talk with Helmy. I expect he won't mind at all, especially since he is paying for the wedding!"

Meanwhile, Larry Ray had checked into the Marriott and was settling into his executive suite. Fortunately, the in-room bar was stocked with bourbon. It did make sense to always stay at the same hotel so they could learn how to accommodate you. As he started on his first drink, he composed a message to Ahmed in order to bring him up to date. Larry expected Ahmed would be able to deduce the real message he was sending.

"Mr. Sharif, Greetings, Larry Ray here in Cairo. I wanted to let you know that your tour director in Paris arranged for an excellent visit for my guests and myself. Our guests were very pleased with all of the sights and events, and were especially impressed with the their two dedicated tour guides. They have mentioned that they really enjoy traveling with us and look forward to many more trips. We have all agreed to expedite the contract for the next trip."

Larry Ray expected that Ahmed and Ali had a special arrangement whereby Ahmed and perhaps a few other Cargo Executives would receive a reward from Ali. He knew he could not make an end run on Ali without Ali complaining to Ahmed and getting him in trouble at the Company. However, it was looking like his play with

Tasha was going to get him a reward. Maybe in more ways than one.

He needed to get some rest as he was due to meet with the EAF the next morning, hopefully to agree to start negotiating the contract. He had his CAC Contracts and Product Support team on standby to come to Cairo. *Well, there was always time for a nightcap or two!*

The next morning, prior to Larry Ray's meeting at the EAF, the local team was already pushing the go buttons. The MOD, Helmy, called Air Marshal Saad, to ask him about the CC-260 inspection and demo flight. The Air Marshal commented on how great the CC-260 was and that it would be an excellent addition to the EAF. Helmy then recommended, which was actually an underlying order, that the EAF immediately begin and expedite the contract negotiations, as he, Helmy, had it on good authority that other countries and politicians were interested in both the aircraft and free FMS funding.

The Air Marshal replied, "Minister, I understand and certainly agree that time is of the essence, to borrow our supplier's words. I know that the Cargo Aircraft salesman, Mr. Hardy, is here in Cairo, and I am scheduled to meet with him this morning. I will make his day by advising him we are ready to start contract discussions immediately."

Helmy grinned into the phone and thought, *We are actually moving the ball!*

After he finished the call, the Air Marshal wondered if the MOD was somehow also on Ali's team. If he was, then his plan to leverage the contract negotiations to increase his consultant retainer might be a more difficult play than he was expecting. *Only time would tell*!

EAF Contract Play Book

Since CAC now had an official "Support Contractor" in Cairo, a MAPS car was waiting for Larry Ray in front of the hotel. As with the previous visit to EAF headquarters, MAPS had all the base entry passes for him and their vehicle. After he had cleared security at the main gate of Almaza Air Base, the car pulled up to the entrance of the headquarters building. Larry Ray was escorted up to Air Marshal Saad's office on the top floor. As he entered, the Air Marshal greeted him like a special friend. Air Commodore Riad was there as well. The three men moved to the sitting area where an assistant served them tea. Larry Ray again knew it would take several cups of tea and lots of small talk before they would be able to get down to business.

Once the pleasantries were over, the Air Marshal got right to the point. "Mr. Hardy, we both wish to thank you and your excellent staff in Paris for the very informative and enjoyable, and I do mean enjoyable, visit to France. I can formally advise you that the EAF is very interested in taking the next step to initiate the contract discussions for the six CC-260 aircraft and a spares package. We appreciate that for this special deal that time is of the essence, as you have so eloquently put it, so we are available to start these discussions whenever you can have your team here!"

Larry Ray smiled, trying not to look too pleased. It was clear that the Air Marshal had been influenced to play the game, so Larry Ray fielded the pass that had just been thrown to him. "Air Marshal and Air Commodore, that is very good to hear! I have had my Contracts and Product Support team on standby, so they can be in Cairo tomorrow evening and we can start the contract negotiations the day after."

Before he could say anymore, the Air Commodore interrupted, "Mr. Hardy, usually before starting the contract negotiations, we have our aircraft technical and configuration staff discuss all of the technical aspects so that we can agree upon the aircraft configuration. As you know this can take some time, so I suggest we not rush into the contact negotiations."

Not only Larry Ray, but also the Air Marshal himself, thought that the Air Commodore was making an end run to set himself up for an incentive. Larry Ray had expected him to already be read into the game plan. However, Larry Ray had seen other end runs along similar lines in doing business in the third world.

Before the Air Marshal could remind the Air Commodore who he worked for, Larry Ray jumped back in to save them all from an embarrassing situation. "Air Commodore, you are correct. Usually, we do spend some amount of time to configure the aircraft to the customer's specification. However, as we pointed out in my Proposal, we are offering the EAF six CC-260 aircraft that have already been built to our and the USAF standard configuration. The price in my proposal is based on the existing configuration. Additionally, I understand from our Washington DC office that the amount of the FMS grant, otherwise considered free money, has been based on that configuration and the price in my Proposal."

The Air Marshal breathed a sigh of relief, thinking, *This salesman really knows how to handle a difficult situation.*

Before the Air Commodore could reply, Larry Ray quickly continued by throwing him a face-saving pass. "I assure you both that the existing aircraft configuration is the gold-plated USAF standard. Actually, after delivery, I expect you may wish to remove some of their so-called bells and whistles. Also, with our technical support, MAPS can easily and inexpensively accommodate any small configuration changes you may require."

The Air Commodore, knowing he had been blocked, conceded the point. "Mr. Hardy, thank you for that clarification. I am only concerned that the EAF receives what is best for us."

Meanwhile, the Air Marshal thought, *We are going to have a serious father-to-son talk after this meeting.*

They then agreed to start the contract discussions the morning after the CAC team arrived. Larry Ray proceeded to provide the names of the Contacts and Product Support team so they could be cleared for access to the base. He was using a two-man minimal team because, since everyone was playing by the "Special Plays" game plan, there was not a lot to discuss.

With the contracts play in place, it was time for Larry Ray to take his leave. He said his farewells and was escorted to his car waiting in front of the headquarters building.

Once Larry Ray had left his office, the Air Marshal delivered a strong rebuke to the Air Commodore. "Commodore Riad! Before I take disciplinary action on your failure to adhere to our chain of command, please explain your actions."

The Commodore replied respectfully, "Air Marshal, I apologize if I was out of line. I was only following the tactic we have used in the past to position the EAF to obtain the best position when negotiating with these companies."

Saad ignored the Commodore's excuse and continued his

reprimand. "You know this is not a normal transaction and that there is higher level military and political oversight on this purchase, or should I say gift, from the United States. You need to expedite this process, not impede it. Do I make myself clear?"

The Commodore thought, *What is clear is that my boss has been influenced to support this deal.* He didn't know whether it was being ordered by the Minister or incentivized by his new friend Ali Omar. The Commodore still wanted to improve on his reward, and it appeared he would need to make another play. But for the present, since there was no way to ask the Air Marshal to improve his offer, he took the formal approach and complied.

"Air Marshal, I will follow your lead and support getting this business completed as quickly as possible," while thinking to himself, *This is not over.*

As the Air Commodore left his office, Saad thought, *Riad might prove difficult. He suspects there is more incentive in play than the small reward I offered him. Just ordering him to play ball may not be the best move. I'll mention this potential problem to Ali as I expect he has the resources to take care of it.*

Meanwhile, once Larry Ray returned to his hotel, he sent the message for the CAC Contracts and Product Support team to make tracks to Cairo. He had already been advised by VP Marketing Mark, who had agreed with President Frank, to send a couple of lower level types who would just follow Larry Ray's lead to get the contract and spares package signed with minimum negotiation. Larry Ray also needed to close the loop with the US Embassy. Therefore, he arranged for an after-work meeting with Colonel Barnes at their favorite, or at best, inconspicuous restaurant, The Umami Sushi & Teppanyaki.

Before taking his well-deserved lunch break with a well-deserved drink or two, he composed a short message to Ahmed to alert him of the Air Commodore's potential end run:

"Sphinx (*Ahmed*), as I mentioned, the demo trip worked very well. I have met with Karnak (*AM Saad*) and Darius (*AC Riad*) and we have agreed to start the contract discussion the day after tomorrow. It appears that Karnak is following the game plan. However, Darius seems to be making an end run. Appears he may be looking for some "Extra Point$." Suggest you alert Ramses (*Ali*) to this play."

With that out of the way, Larry Ray decided it was time to take a break. Later he would get ready for his evening play.

Air Attaché Play

Of course, Larry Ray was sitting at a corner booth enjoying his second drink as Colonel Barnes walked into the restaurant. They said a quick "Hello," and the waiter, who Larry Ray had on "incentivized" stand-by, quickly took the Colonel's drink order as he sat down, and just as quickly served it.

Colonel Barnes smiled and began the conversation. "Larry Ray, I must compliment you and your Paris team on one of the best "influence the customer" plays I have ever seen. In fact, that "security service" play was a work of art." As he raised his beer, the Colonel added, "Well-completed!"

Larry Ray took a moment to savor the praise before responding, "Colonel, thank you. I want you to know that my company really appreciates your assistance and support for our project."

Larry Ray stopped to drain his drink and signal for another, then picked up where he left off. "I assure you we look forward to adding you to our team. As you know the next plays are to get the contract signed by the EAF and then have the DSCA authorize the payment through the Direct Commercial Sales process. We expect they will look for your stamp of approval on the contract. Colonel, I can assure you that we are offering these whitetail aircraft at a very fair price. Like all of our CC-260 aircraft, they are fully configured to meet each one of the EAF operational requirements. Again, as we mentioned in Paris, time is of the essence."

The Colonel looked pleased by Larry Ray's including him in the game, and assured him, "I'll keep you informed on the daily status of the contract discussions, as well as let you know about the flow of the funding from Washington."

It was now time to take a break from business discussions and look at the menu and order their dinner. Larry Ray kept up the small talk throughout the meal. When the after-dinner drinks arrived, Larry Ray decided it was time to request a "Special Play" from the Colonel. This issue was related to the spares package, which wasn't his responsibility. However, Mark had requested, well no, had actually ordered him to smooth the field for this play. Although the reasoning made sense, he suspected there was another "Special Play" in process.

Larry Ray smiled and once more began with a positive approach. "Again, Colonel, it is a pleasure to be working with you and I looked forward to doing more in the future. By the way, there is one more item which will involve the US Embassy's support."

Colonel Barnes raised his eyebrows, and Larry Ray knew he had the Colonel's attention.

"We have already agreed with the EAF to add a standard spares package to the contract. It's only around ten percent. However, it contains all the critical parts they will need for day-to-day operation and minor repairs. As you know, we have already selected MAPS as our local Support Contractor and have some of his people in training in Mobile on supporting the CC-260 aircraft. We just recently contracted for a very large shipment of CC-260 spares by ship to support the Royal Saudi Air Force fleet of fifty CC-260's. Since the ship was transiting the Suez Canal enroute to Jeddah, just down the Red Sea, we arranged for it to stop off and deliver a large spares consignment to MAPS, since they will be the North African regional spares depot for the CC-260. This consignment also included the spares for the EAF. It will be beneficial to have them available on-site as we will start delivery of the aircraft immediately after contract signing."

Larry Ray paused to wet his whistle, allowing the Colonel to process all that he had just said. Satisfied that the colonel might see where this was leading, Larry Ray was ready to deliver his punch line.

"Accordingly, we will be advising the DSCA to make the spares payment directly to MAPS. I expect they will request you to manage this payment, which may involve confirming the EAF spares are available at MAPS. You know, Ali would be pleased to show you his operation. Plus, it will be good for you to understand his business as we will be working with him in the future."

The Colonel was thinking, *This advance placement of a spare's consignment is a little unusual.* However, all that Larry Ray mentioned made sense, so who was he to disagree. Therefore, he answered, "Larry Ray, if the DSCA requests the Embassy's assistance on confirming the spares are available and on-site, we will be happy to help!"

Larry Ray did a mental "spike the ball," and after another round, sent the Colonel back to the Embassy in his taxi, while he had yet another drink, then got the waiter's name for his expense report and paid the bill.

Once back at the hotel, he sent a short note to Mark to confirm he had made the spares play with the Colonel and it looked like a good run.

As he settled in for the evening, he reflected on how well things had gone this day. It looked like all the ducks, sphinxes, pharaohs, or whatever were all in a row in order to do this deal. His only concern, as he called it a night, was whether he had his reward in place. Hamm, he would need to revisit that play.

13

TWELFTH GAME - SAN FRANCISCO 49ERS HOST WASHINGTON REDSKINS

49ers win 37 to 21

The renewed 49ers overwhelmed the defending champion Redskins, with a 23–7 halftime lead and winning 37–21. Montana threw two touchdown passes, one over 80 yards to Rice, and he ran in a third touchdown. Super Bowl MVP Williams of the Redskins passed for three touchdowns.

Cairo - Sign-Up

Larry Ray slept in late and felt a little groggy. He thought, *This hotel needs to have a better quality of bourbon.* Since the CAC Contract and Product Support guys were arriving in the early evening, he actually had a day without a busy schedule. He had made reservations for himself and the two others at the Le Méridien Cairo Airport hotel, which was on the airport grounds just across the street from the terminal. He would keep his suite at the Marriott, yet appear to be one of the boys by staying out at the airport low cost hotel. He would identify his room out there as a conference room so the CAC bean counters wouldn't have an issue with him having two hotel rooms.

Larry Ray was still concerned that the Air Commodore could

delay the game by not following the game plan, and decided he had better discuss this with Ali. Larry Ray planned to set up a meeting with him in the afternoon, as he would be out by Ali's office to meet the CAC team at the airport. He also was concerned with his reward from Tasha. He needed to make sure it was more than just her friendship. And it was clear that Ali was going to be the banker.

Looked like he needed to run two separate plays to ensure he received his reward for wining this game. In fact, he could actually double down if he could make a separate deal with each of them. *Why not!* However, it was also clear to him that Ahmed and Ali had some kind of arrangement, so he needed to tread carefully when he asked.

After a very late breakfast, which doubled for an early lunch, Larry Ray packed enough clothes to survive a few days at the Le Méridien. He had his taxi take him out to the hotel, where he checked in and made sure the other rooms were ready for the two CAC guests. He then went over to the MAPS office for the meeting with Ali that he had arranged.

As he walked into Ali's office, his jaw almost hit the floor when he saw Tasha sitting there. After Ali had received Larry Ray's request for a meeting to discuss issues, aka rewards, for the EAF players, he suspected Larry Ray might be thinking of making an end run on Ahmed's deal. So, he called Tasha and they decided it was time to assure Larry Ray that he would be rewarded financially. He would have to continue to lust after his other desired reward!

Ali shook his hand. "Larry Ray, I believe you have met Tasha Mostafa? As you know, she is the sister of the Minister of Defense, as well as a member of our Government."

Larry Ray, almost never at a loss for words, responded, "Ms. Mostafa, it is a pleasure to see you again after our short meeting at the US Embassy reception last month."

Tasha replied, "Larry Ray, a pleasure to see you as well. I have just finished a meeting with Mr. Omar to discuss his company's support of many of the Egyptian military programs that my Subcommittee funds. I was glad to be informed that your company has selected his company to provide support for the EAF's new CC-260 aircraft. I can assure you that, from my standpoint, it appears that the EAF is going to move forward with the purchase. Therefore, I expect we will get to see a lot more of you here in Cairo." With that she got up to leave, adding, "I'll leave you gentlemen to your business discussions."

As they said their goodbyes, Larry Ray wondered what play was actually going on. Tasha's presence was some sort of message. Hopefully, Ali would provide the answer. As they both sat down, Larry Ray tried to mentally sort it all out, as her being here could be no coincidence.

He led off with, "Ali, I'm impressed that you apparently have a good relationship with the Chairwoman of the Committee that manages the funding of Egyptian military projects. Can I assume that she is supporting our Game plan?" What Larry Ray really meant was, *Is she on your team?*

Before he could go any further, Ali spoke up. "Larry Ray, I have a very good working relationship with Ms. Mostafa. We often discuss the funding and status of various military projects that my company supports. She certainly can provide her opinion on the status of a project like your CC-260 aircraft purchase. Please appreciate that Ms. Mostafa, just like members of your congress, cannot sign up to be on a company's team. That being the official position, I will confide that I do take very good care of her."

Larry Ray figured that he was probably speaking in financial terms. However, if asked in a court of law, Ali would say he was referring to their personal relationship. Larry Ray smiled and thought, *OK, since he is taking care of Tasha, she must be on his team.* Therefore, Larry Ray knew that she would have the resources to reward him. He had heard what he wanted to hear, so he moved on to the official reason for the meeting.

"Ali, again it looks like you have everything under control. My Contacts and Product Support team arrive here shortly. We are all set to start the contract negotiation with the EAF tomorrow. I did meet with the Air Marshal and Air Commodore yesterday and both appear supportive of going forward with the purchase. However, the Air Commodore brought up a couple of issues which could slow down the process. I believe that the Air Marshal and I addressed his concerns. Also, I expect the Air Marshal can influence his actions. You may need to keep an eye on those two."

Ali nodded as if he was already aware of the situation.

Prompted by that positive response, Larry Ray continued, "Additionally, while myself and the contracts man are reviewing and finalizing the aircraft purchase contract with the EAF, my management has directed me to send the Product Support guy over to your facility to inventory the spares consignment to identify and confirm that all the items listed in the EAF CC-260 Spares Proposal are on site. Then, as you and Frank Moore have apparently agreed, we will include the MAPS Spares Package in the aircraft contract."

Larry Ray wasn't sure why the spares had already been delivered to MAPS. However, spares were not his responsibility.

Since it was time to go over to the airport and meet the CAC contracts team, Larry Ray did his best to make his case. "Ali, this is not my first rodeo, as we from CAC probably say too often."

Ali thought to himself, *That's an understatement*, and prepared himself mentally for what was coming next. Then he turned his attention back to Larry Ray, who continued, "I know it takes a team of CAC and local players to win this Game. The key to winning, as with our US football teams, are the quarterbacks like myself. I know that having you on our team is essential to winning and I hope you know I am the key to this win. So, let's stay in close contact and take care of each other." That said, Larry Ray exited to meet his new arrivals.

After Larry Ray left, Ali thought, *I still don't know what a rodeo has to do with selling aircraft. However, it is clear that Larry Ray needs taken care of.* Ali would pass that ball to Tasha.

Larry Ray showed up at the arrivals area of the main terminal just in time to see his two co-workers coming out of the building. He greeted them and pointed out that the hotel was directly across the street from the terminal, an easy walk for them all. After they checked in, he suggested that since they had been traveling for most of the day, they should probably get some rest and meet early in the morning to discuss the play for the contract negotiations.

Although Larry Ray also took a break, he did not, however, get any rest, because his team was about to win this sales game and he wasn't sure that his reward was in place. He called the private phone number he had for Tasha, and when she didn't answer, he left a message that he would like to have a quick meeting at their special place at eight that night.

Harry's Pub

Of course, Larry Ray was at the Pub well before eight o'clock. He hadn't heard back from Tasha, so he could only be hopeful she would show up. Sure enough, just as he was finishing his first beer, she walked in the door and immediately went over to his corner booth and sat adjacent to him, while placing her small electronic jamming device on the table.

She said, "Larry Ray, I was so glad to get your message. I did try to call you at the Marriott, and left you a message."

Larry Ray remembered that he never mentioned to her that he was also staying at the Le Méridien. He also didn't mention it now, as he didn't wish for any more confusion. He only said, "Tasha, thank you for coming. I wanted to bring you up to date on our project. As Ali may have told you, I have a Contract and Product Support team in town and we begin contract negotiations tomorrow. It should go quickly if our local team follows the game plan. It really shouldn't be too difficult to have the EAF accept free aircraft."

Before he could say more, she offered, "I can assure you that I understand from Ali and my brother that all is in order to expedite the contract discussion and have it signed within a few days. I also expect the spares package purchase will be approved as well. You can relax and enjoy this success."

"Tasha, thanks for the confirmation. Although this will be a big success for my company, as I mentioned to you before, there is not much reward in it for me, the one who has put this all together. When we last met, you commented that the local coach would reward his key players. Do you have an update from your coach?"

Tasha decided it was time to put this matter to bed, and not in the way Larry Ray was thinking. She replied, "Yes, I do. First, tell me what is the size of the bonus your company will give you on this six-airplane sale."

Larry Ray quickly answered, "It's peanuts for a three-hundred-sixty-million-dollar sale. The bonus to the salesman is three thousand dollars per aircraft, so eighteen thousand dollars in all."

Tasha thought, *Goodness! How miserly can they be*? Well, she was about to make his day. She and Ali had already agreed to not connect Larry Ray's reward to Ali's local team, as they still didn't trust that this Alabama boy knew how to handle big rewards

Tasha began carefully, "Well, while our coach appreciates his local key players, it can be difficult to pass rewards to a player on other teams." Before he could interrupt, she quickly added, "However, since that discussion, we have found a solution to this matter.

She leaned in and said in a quiet voice, as if not to be overheard. "My Government Committee has some discretionary funds and the authority to disburse them to individuals or companies that engage in good works for our country. I believe in Washington you call them lobbyists. Larry Ray, you are now an unofficial lobbyist for Egypt. I also recommend we do not publicize this role for you. Once this deal is finalized and all FMS payments have been made, you will receive three hundred sixty thousand dollars from us for your lobbying on our behalf. We can work out the transfer details when we get together later to discuss our future business strategy, after this contract is finished."

Larry Ray's jaw just about hit the top of the table. Although, he wanted to play like he was used to big money, his expression gave him away. He took a long slow drink of his beer so as to look calm and cool. Then he sat back, smiled, and said, "Tasha, thank you, you have just made my day. No! My year! I knew we would make a good team. I will push to have this contact signed ASAP, and then we can meet to discuss our strategy. Let's toast to a win-win all around!"

They clinked their glasses together in celebration, then both agreed that they had busy days ahead, so they called it a night. As she left, Tasha gave Larry Ray a light kiss on the cheek, while murmuring, "Strategy sessions can be fun." *Might as well keep leading him on to ensure he remained motivated.* It didn't occur to her that she might be playing fast and loose with Larry Ray's heart.

Tasha also realized she would need to tell Ali that he needed to make an additional one percent on the thirty-six million dollar spares package.

On his way back to the hotel, Larry Ray was smiling as he thought about all the ways he was going to enjoy spending his reward. The sooner he got the contact signed, the sooner he would be enjoying the fruits of his labors!

EAF Headquarters

After meeting for breakfast at the hotel, Larry Ray, the contracts man, Fred Knight, and the Product Support man, Jim Evans, arrived at the EAF headquarters mid-morning, and followed the usual routine. Since they were all pre-cleared, they went directly to the headquarters building and were escorted to a large conference room on the top floor. There they met Air Marshal Saad and Air

Commodore Riad.

Following the introductions, and the usual hour or so of drinking tea and talking about everything except the contract, Larry Ray decided he had to get the negotiations going, or, at this pace, it would take weeks.

So, he initiated the action. "Air Marshal Saad and Air Commodore Riad, I know you both have busy schedules and we do not wish to take up all of your time, so perhaps we should get started on the contract discussions."

Air Marshal Saad nodded. "Yes, let's proceed. I'll leave you with the Air Commodore, who has the responsibility and authority to negotiate all areas of the contract. Of course, I'll be approving it whenever the Air Commodore tells me it's ready." And with that, he left the conference room.

The Air Commodore had already been given his marching, or negotiating, orders on the aircraft contract, so he began, "Gentlemen, I am aware that the configuration of the aircraft is already established and time is of the essence. Therefore, let us, as you Americans say, cut to the chase. Let's go through all of the Terms and Conditions, and quickly identify any areas requiring discussion."

They gathered around the conference table with their copies of the document, and Fred Knight proceeded to lead them through the multi-page terms and conditions contract, page-by-page and paragraph-by-paragraph. The Air Commodore paid close attention, while Larry Ray and Jim Evans almost fell asleep, since most of the details were something only a lawyer would be interested in seeing or would understand.

To the Ticket-Holders: We could print in detail the total negotiation of the one-hundred-fifty page contract for six sixty-million-dollar aircraft. However fortunately for you, there is a page limit! You really only need to understand the basic major contract elements that were addressed:

1. Aircraft Description. This is the Detailed Specification, which in most cases could take weeks, if not months, to agree upon concerning the configuration of an aircraft. Since the aircraft being offered were already built, known as whitetails, and the aircraft were essentially a gift from the US Government, the specification became a "take it as is, or you don't get it" negotiation.

2. Price & Payments. Since the US was gifting them to the EAF, there was very little to negotiate on this point.

3. Pre-Delivery Inspection. The CAC did not wish to take the time to host an EAF technical team to visit Mobile and try to find things wrong with the aircraft. Therefore, they proposed to have a pre-delivery inspection after arrival of the aircraft in Cairo.

4. Warranties. With delivery of commercial equipment, there were usually warranties for a period of time on any breakdowns or other equipment failures. However, once a military product was delivered, there would be no way to monitor the operation. Therefore, except for the delivery inspection, the aircraft would be sold "as is" with no warranties.

The EAF had arranged for lunch to be provided in the conference room, one way to signal support for the understanding that time was of the essence.

As they finished reviewing the main body of the contract, the Air Commodore brought up a couple of areas which required more clarification. Fred assured him he would be able to obtain answers from the home office overnight.

The spares package listing was an appendix at the end of the contract. Jim Evans took over when they reached that point. There was nothing to negotiate on the spares other than to confirm that what they were buying was on-site at MAPS.

The Air Commodore suggested that he and Mr. Evans meet at the MAPS office the next morning to conduct an inventory of the consignment of EAF spares. He was also interested in meeting with Ali Omar again, as he suspected Ali was the one who would be rewarding the local Team.

They finished the contract review by midafternoon, and Larry Ray was pleased with the cooperative attitude of the EAF throughout the proceedings. It was clear to him that someone at a higher level was supporting this play. Most likely Ali had worked his magic with Minister Mostafa. They all agreed that the Air Commodore and Jim Evans would spend the morning at MAPS and then reconvene in the afternoon to go over the inputs from CAC.

Additionally, Air Marshal Saad wished to have a meeting on the process involving the US Government payment for the aircraft and spares. Larry Ray would need to obtain confirmation from the DC office on that payment process.

Larry, Fred, and Jim finally said their good-byes, glad that the tedious discussions were over, and successfully, at that, and returned to their hotel. Larry Ray needed time to send a message to Ken Doyle to obtain information on the funding for the aircraft and spares. He also needed to update Ahmed on the status of the negotiations.

As they entered the lobby of the hotel, Fred commented, "Larry Ray, this is my and Jim's first visit to Cairo. Since the negotiations are going so well and so fast, we may only be here a short time. Is it possible to make a quick trip out to see the Pyramids and Sphinx?"

Larry Ray thought, with a concealed groan, *Just what I need! To be a tour guide.* However, he didn't want Fred and Jim going off touring on their own, because if something happened to them, it could delay the whole play. So, instead, he replied, "Sure, I would be pleased to arrange to take you out there after dinner. It will still be light and a lot cooler then. I have a few things to take care of first. I suggest you both have an early dinner here at the hotel and I'll call you in about two hours to go out to Giza."

Fred and Jim smiled and thanked him enthusiastically.

Once in his room, Larry Ray composed two messages, one to Ken Doyle at the Washington office with copies to Frank, Mark and Ahmed. Larry Ray thought, *As all salesman know, when you have good news you copy the world!*

Subject: EAF CC-260 Contract Status:

The CAC Team here in Cairo is pleased to report that the contract negotiations for the six CC-260 aircraft are moving very well. We have already obtained EAF agreement to not request any changes to the aircraft configuration. We expect to have the entire contract and the spares package agreed by close of business tomorrow. Accordingly, the EAF and Ministry of Defense will be requesting confirmation and timing of the FMS payments. Ken, please provide this information to us ASAP. Thanks, the CAC Cairo Team.

Next, he sent a separate coded message to Ahmed:

"Tour update from Egypt. All is going extremely well with our tour. It is clear the Paris tour achieved its purpose in having all the tourists agree with the Egyptian tour plan. So far Tut *(Helmy Mostafa, MOD)*, Karnak *(AM Saad)*, and Ramses *(Ali Omar)* have been the favorite stops. Darius *(AC Riad)* was not as good as we had expected. Suggest you have our local guide revisit that stop. We expect to finish the Egyptian tour very soon. Hope your Washington tour is going as well as ours."

With his messages sent, Larry Ray visited his mini-bar to get ready for yet another tour.

Giza Tour

Larry Ray met Jim and Fred in the lobby and his private taxi was waiting for them in front of the hotel. He thought, *Here we go again out to the Pyramids! I should work part time as a Pyramid tour guide as I have been out there so many times.*

Fortunately, the traffic in the evening for the twenty-mile drive west across the Nile wasn't too bad. The first stop was to pull up in front of the Great Sphinx of Giza for a round of picture taking. Then the short drive over to the parking lot by the Great Pyramid of Giza, for more picture taking.

Then the fun began. Larry Ray's taxi driver had arranged for two camels with guides to take the two visitors on the standard tour of the Giza Pyramids. The largest was the Pyramid of Khufu, the middle one was the Pyramid of Khafre, and the smallest, but not the least by any means, was the Pyramid of Menkaure. The three smaller pyramids were known as the queens' pyramids. The Sphinx was close by, watching over everything.

Once Fred and Jim went swaying off on their camels, Larry Ray had his driver take him over to the nearby Marriott Mena House Hotel, which had a bar that served drinks to westerners. He knew the Pyramid camel tour would take about three drinks, if he drank at his normal pace. His driver would pick up Jim and Fred at the end of the tour and bring them over to the Marriott for drinks and more pictures of the Pyramids, which made a dramatic vista from the Mena House.

As he finished his second drink, Larry Ray thought contentedly, *This is all going very well. I not only will get my small standard bonus from CAC, but also a big bonus from my Egyptian friends. I'll think I'll have another drink to those bonuses!*

Larry Ray was actually on his fourth drink when Jim and Fred returned from their Pyramid tour. They explained that they couldn't resist paying the extra fee to look inside the large Pyramid of Khufu, but were disappointed that there weren't any mummies in there.

"Yeah, about that," said Larry Ray. "The mummies live in the Cairo Museum. Let's save that for next time." Fred and Jim beamed at the thought they might be returning to Cairo in the future.

Larry Ray ordered another round of drinks for all of them. They agreed that Fred would spend the morning at the hotel to review the information they had requested from the CAC home office. Larry Ray would take Jim over to the MAPS office for his meeting with the Air Commodore. Although Larry Ray was not involved in the Product Support contract, he would tag along to be aware of the Air Commodore making any trouble.

The sun had set and, with the stars backlighting the pyramids, it was time to return to the airport hotel to rest up for the next day's activities.

MAPS Office

It was a short trip the next morning from their hotel to the MAPS office adjacent to the Air Base. Jim Evans knew that it was not normal spares business practice to place a large consignment of spares in a country before a contract had been signed. However, it was also not Jim's first rodeo, so he knew there were "Special Plays" in process. He decided he would just go along with the play call.

Larry Ray and Jim were escorted to Ali Omar's executive conference room and were greeted by Ali and a couple of his inventory specialists, as well as the Air Commodore. They proceeded to go through the list of each of the spare components that were included in the EAF thirty-six-million-dollar package.

The Air Commodore made a few comments that it was difficult for him to match the spares to an aircraft he was not that familiar with. Jim continued to assure him that this package was exactly tailored to the EAF configuration. After completing the review of the listing, the MAPS inventory specialist suggested they walk through the dedicated CAC CC-260 spares storage area to do spot checks to confirm that the items were actually on-site.

Larry Ray and Ali let the four of them go off on their spot check. Once they had left, Larry Ray expressed his concern regarding the Air Commodore. "Ali, everything is going very well and it appears to me that the local team is playing together very well, except I am concerned that the Air Commodore may try to throw a block in our play."

Ali replied, "I agree, and after you and Mr. Evans finish, I'll have a "father to son" talk with the Air Commodore to encourage him to follow the game plan."

Larry Ray felt better, as he was sure that Ali had more clout with the local players than himself. So, he said, "Good, I'll leave that with you."

They had several cups of tea and as usual talked about the weather, and the Mobile, Washington, and Paris trips, still trying to figure out the real role of the two Paris Security Specialists.

Once Jim and the others returned from their tour, they all sat around the conference table. It was the time for the Air Commodore to make his play. "Gentlemen, I wish to thank you for a very good overview of the proposed spares package. Although I respect your experience and position that the consignment contains all the correct items and matches the contract listing, I am not familiar enough with the CC-260 configuration to provide my one- hundred-percent stamp of approval on this package. I will review my concerns with Air Marshal Saad. We can review this with him when we meet this afternoon for another round of contract discussions."

There was nothing more anyone could say. Ali dismissed his inventory specialist and bid the CAC team farewell. He then turned to the Air Commodore and asked him to stay, so that they could discuss some other EAF business.

Once Larry Ray and Jim had left, Ali said, "Air Commodore, you and I know how this game is played. Also, you and I are not the star players. However, please appreciate that my company really needs this CAC business."

Just then Ali's secretary interrupted with an apology and informed them that the Air Commodore had an urgent phone call, which he could take in a private office next door. The Air Commodore excused himself and went into the adjacent office.

He picked up the phone and heard, "Air Commodore Riad, this is Mr. Kahn, the manager of your bank. I am sorry for the interruption. We have just received a wire transfer from a Swiss bank to your account in the amount of four hundred eighty-two thousand Egyptian pounds. That's the equivalent of about thirty thousand dollars, at today's exchange rate. We were instructed to notify you immediately of this transfer. Also, there was a short message, "Welcome to the team!"

The Air Commodore cordially thanked Mr. Kahn for the call, and thought, *What an amazing coincidence that I have been made a member of the team just as I was about to make my end run*!

He was all smiles as he returned to Ali's office in high spirits. "Ali, that was good news, not only for me, but for all of us. I do need to get back to the headquarters so I can submit my approval for the spares package as proposed."

This time Ali smiled. They quickly said their good-byes. Ali thought, *Forget about rodeos. I have played this local game before*!

The Sign-Up

After lunch at their hotel, this time with no drinks, Larry Ray and the CAC team prepared to return to the EAF headquarters for what they perceived was going to be a long afternoon. They were not aware that Ahmed had arranged for Ken Doyle to send a message that morning from Washington to the Ambassador and Colonel Barnes with a blind copy to Ali which Ali immediately forwarded to Helmy and Tasha. It read:

"Secure Communication to US Embassy- Cairo

185

Sender: Washington DC office – Cargo Aircraft Corporation

The US Department of Defense and the Senate Armed Services Committee both strongly endorse the US FMF grant to provide the Egyptian Air Force with six CC-260 military cargo aircraft and spare parts. Please be advised, we have been informed by our contacts in the Senate that there is a move in the Senate Committee to redirect this FMF Grant to Jordan. As you know King Hussain recently visited Washington and was promised significant US Government support. We suggest you contact the key players in country to expedite the CC-260 purchase so that the FMF funds can be fully committed to Egypt."

Larry Ray and the team arrived at the EAF headquarters and were again escorted to the conference room on the top floor adjacent to Air Marshal Saad's office. The Air Marshal and the Air Commodore were already there.

After the usual greetings and tea, the Air Marshal stood up and said, "Mr. Hardy, Mr. Knight, and Mr. Evans, I am pleased that these contract and spares discussions have progressed so well. The Air Commodore advises me that the open contract issues are simply clarifications which can be addressed later. Also, he is in agreement that the spares consigned at MAPS will meet our ability to fully support the aircraft." He paused to smile, then finished with, "I know you gentlemen would all like to spend more time in our great country. Nevertheless, I propose we have the formal contract signing by our Minister of Defense tomorrow morning here in this room."

Larry Ray, Fred, and Jim were astounded, not to say totally pleased. But Larry Lay was never at a loss for words, especially in this type of situation. True to form, he responded smoothly, "Air

Marshal Saad and Air Commodore Riad, we of course would like to spend more time in your beautiful country and take whatever amount of time you would require to assure you that you are receiving one of the finest military aircraft in the world. We already appreciate the time you have provided out of your busy schedules to meet with myself and my team. I'm sure Fred and Jim agree with me that we are at your service and certainly do not wish to delay this purchase. We will have all the contract documents finalized, printed in duplicate, and delivered for the Air Commodore's review by midafternoon. We will be standing by at our hotel to convene here tomorrow for the signing of the contract. We welcome the EAF as a member of the CC-260 worldwide team!"

With nods all around, Larry Ray, along with Fred and Jim, said their good-byes and took their leave.

Now, Larry Ray had seen some fast plays in other countries. However, he was really impressed with whoever was coaching the local team. Once back at the hotel, he knew that Fred and Jim would need most of the afternoon to finalize and print the execution copies of the contract. This would give him time to send messages to CAC Mobile and Washington to announce the imminent contract signing and take most of the credit for the sale. *OK, all of the credit for the sale.*

Although, Fred and Jim would be returning home soon after the contract signing, he would need to stay in Cairo to monitor the spares funding flow through the Embassy to MAPS. Plus, he needed to work on receiving his local reward, or, hopefully, rewards.

Once the guys had finished and sent the execution copies of the contract over to the Air Commodore, Larry Ray felt that they deserved a night out on the town. Although he disliked tourist attractions, he knew they would enjoy going out to Sahara City, a night club out by the Pyramids which had belly dancers and western drinks.

Of course, what happens in Sahara City, stays in Sahara City, so suffice it to say that both Fred and Jim awoke the next morning with major hangovers, and hoping that no one had taken any pictures!

They had a message at the hotel that the contract signing would take place at 11:00AM the next morning. Although Larry Ray was the CAC team leader, he was not authorized to sign contracts, so Fred Knight would get the honors. Fred would return to Mobile with the signed contract. He would also probably try to take all the credit for the favorable negotiation.

They all returned to the top floor conference room. This time along with the Air Marshal and the Air Commodore, they were joined by the Minister of Defense Helmy Mustafa, US Ambassador Knox, Air Attaché Colonel Barnes, and Ali Omar. As always, it took time to get through all the introductions, be served tea, and discuss many trivial issues.

Finally, the MOD said, "Gentlemen, I do not wish to rush through this significant event. However, let me start by thanking our American friends for bringing this project to the EAF. I do agree with both the Air Marshal and Air Commodore that the Cargo Aircraft Company CC-260 aircraft will be an excellent addition to the Egyptian Air Force. We especially appreciate the dedication of the CAC team in bringing this project to the EAF, and the US Embassy in supporting their efforts. I suggest we go ahead and sign the contract. I look forward to having a flight in the aircraft after it arrives. I hear the Air Marshal checked out as a good pilot."

That made them all laugh, and in this jovial atmosphere, Fred Knight and the MOD proceeded to sign the contracts. With that done, after a little more small talk, they all departed.

Both Fred and Jim had already booked a late evening flight to London with a connection to the US and Mobile. Larry Ray guessed they didn't want to stay over for another night at Sahara City.

He would have a drink with them before they left for the airport. He was already thinking about getting all the funding flowing. Especially that coming his way.

Later on, Larry Ray sent a message, again to the world, that the contract for all six aircraft and the spares package had been signed at full price. That would certainly make the Executives and bean counters happy. He informed them that the MOD and the EAF had requested an update on the FMF funding, although they actually hadn't. However, he wished to pass the ball to Ken Doyle to put pressure on him to run his play. Well, it was time for the Washington players to show what they could do.

Larry Ray called it a very good day, week, month, or whatever, as he sat in his suite having a bourbon and thinking about how to handle his rewards!

14

THIRTEENTH GAME - SAN FRANCISCO 49ERS AT SAN DIEGO CHARGERS

49ers win 48 to 10

San Francisco scored big as Montana threw three touchdown passes and Craig had two rushing scores and a touchdown reception. DuBose added a rushing score. Four San Francisco backs as well as both quarterbacks, Montana and Young, rushed for 203 yards, beating the Chargers.

Washing DC- CAC Corporate Office

Ken Doyle was certainly pleased to hear that the contract for the sale of the six CC-260 aircraft to Egypt had been signed. However, he was aware that the ball had been passed to him and he was responsible for scoring the transfer of FMF funds. He needed to review the game plan with the local team, and also start making his plays on the US Government bureaucracy field. First he reviewed his notes regarding the FMF-FMS process:

Congress appropriates funds for FMF (Foreign Military Financing).

The FMF program provides grants to help countries purchase defense equipment produced in the United States.

FMF funds the purchases made through the FMS (Foreign

Military Sales) program.

FMF also funds the purchases made through the Direct Commercial Sales program, which oversees sales directly between foreign governments and private US companies.

The State Department's Office of Security Assistance sets policy for the FMF program, while the Defense Security Cooperation Agency, part of the Defense Department, manages it on a day-to-day basis.

Military personnel in U.S. embassies overseas (Attachés) play a key role in managing FMF within recipient countries.

OK, with these facts firmly in mind, Ken was ready to proceed with the Washington play.

Ken already had made the Congressional appropriation play which he called "Resume Speed," alluding to the hometown of the Chairman of the Senate Armed Services Committee. He now had to run a play on the Defense Security Cooperation Agency. Since the recently retired Director of the DSCA, General Al Hancock, had joined the Cargo Aircraft Corporation as the new VP of Defense Business, and now had an office down the hall from Ken, it was time for the new VP to earn his pay.

Ken walked down the hall to Al's office. Since Al had only been there a short time, Ken might need to do a little hand holding on this play. After a short conversation about how the General was adjusting to corporate life, Ken made his pitch. "Al, we are so glad you have joined our company. In the past we have had many potentially highly profitable international FMS sales opportunities. However, we lost them to our competitors due to our inability to convince your old organization that what we had was best for the country and the international customer. We really need your guidance on how to obtain DSCA support for our international business."

Al smiled. "Ken, I am here to take charge and win those campaigns for you."

Ken thought, *He sure talks like a General.*

Al asked, "I am aware of the CC-260 sales campaign for Egypt, but how far have you made it to the goal line?"

Ken then gave him the short version of the Washington game. "Al, the Senate Armed Services Committee has already approved a grant for Egypt to purchase six CC-260 aircraft for three hundred sixty million dollars, plus a spares package of another thirty-six million. So almost four hundred million dollars. The documentation for this grant has already been sent over to your friends at DSCA. Now, since this is a grant using US funds, it has been requested that DSCA make this a Direct Commercial Sale. Our CAC sales team has been successful in getting the contract for the aircraft and spares signed by the Egyptian Minister of Defense yesterday." There was no need to tell Al that there was a local team in play as well.

When Al nodded his approval, Ken went on with his briefing. "As you may know, the six aircraft are whitetails sitting on the ramp at Mobile ready for delivery. So, the sooner they get delivered, the better. You may also be aware that the international sales of CC-260 aircraft is the most profitable business for CAC and the Corporation."

Al stood at attention, like the General he was, and stated, "I am sure I can encourage my friends or previous staff at DCSA to expedite the FMF payments through the DCS process. I will talk today to the general who took over my position."

Ken thought, *So far so good,* and said aloud, "Thanks, Al. There is one area that may need some special attention. As is standard procedure, when the CC-260 is introduced to an overseas customer, CAC usually arranges for a local company which already provides support to the customer for their military aviation aircraft to take on local support for the CC-260. This provides a base of operations for training and storage for spares. CAC has already selected a very well-respected local contractor, Military Aircraft Parts and Services, or MAPS, for short. This company has already been approved by both the CAC and Corporate Review Committees." Ken intentionally omitted the word consultant, as that term might make the General a little nervous.

Now for the part where Al would be given an opportunity to earn his pay, although Ken knew what he had to say next might seem a little unconventional to the General. "After MAPS had been selected and approved, it was just a coincidence," and here Ken's thoughts interrupted, *oh yes, just another amazing coincidence,* "that CAC was delivering a large CC-260 spares package by sea on a commercial freighter to the Royal Saudi Air Force in Jeddah. As usual the RSAF had ordered three times what they needed, so it was easy to downsize the RSAF order and drop off the EAF spares as a consignment at MAPS while the ship transited the Suez Canal, prior to going into the Red Sea down to Jeddah. This actually saves the US money and provides the EAF with more spare parts, since CAC does not need to add the shipping charges to the EAF Spares package. Now that the EAF CC-260 spares are already sitting in Egypt, we need to have DSCA do a DCS to MAPS for the spares." Ken knew this was a highly unusual request, as all DCS payment had to be made to a US Company.

OK. Al knew that the direct payment of already allocated FMF finds to CAC was a standard process, so he would, of course, ask his ex-staff to make the payment sooner versus taking their good ol' usual time. That way he could take a lot of credit for cutting through the DSCA red tape and getting the payment expedited. All that jibed.

On the other hand, the direct payment to a foreign company was very unusual and would require someone at DSCA to take a risk and actually make a controversial decision. Guess it was time for him to, as they said in this office, lobby the general who had just filled his former position.

Al decided he might as well make this sound as difficult as possible, so he replied, "Ken, the direct payment to a US company can take a lot of time. I certainly know the process and will suggest to my ex-staff how they can shortcut the process and get approval for the payment to CAC at the earliest possible date. However, the direct payment to MAPS is not currently permitted, so I will have to help DSCA create an "exception" to allow it to happen. I'll provide you with an update on both processes as soon as I discuss them with my friends at DSCA."

Ken was satisfied with Al's response. He just hoped now that he had handed Al the ball, hopefully he could make the play. Ken nodded, then left and returned to his office to document that the success or failure of both DSCA DCS payments to CAC and MAPS was now in the hands of the new VP.

After Ken left, Al knew he needed to meet with his successor and determine the actual status of this FMF deal, as well as to teach him how to manage an "exception." It was very difficult to have a private meeting anywhere in or near Washington, so they might as well hide in plain sight. The perfect place would be the Army Navy Country Club in Arlington. It was actually less than a mile from both Al's and the DSCA offices.

Thanks to US tax dollars, there were actually two country clubs, the one in Arlington near the Pentagon, and the other out in Fairfax just past Tysons corners. Both looked like southern mansions. There were over 500 acres of rolling, wooded landscape at both sites. They included fifty-four championship golf holes, thirty-two tennis courts, six of which were indoors, six swimming pools, a fitness center, and golf and tennis pro shops. Their dining facilities offered various venue options, whether serving a private dinner for two, or catering an event for several hundred people. Since Army Navy Country Club membership was restricted to active or military officers and family as well as senior officials from select government agencies, Al knew this would be an ideal location, and the ambiance would be exceptional.

Al planned to meet his DSCA colleague at the Arlington Club rooftop terrace, which was a private dining room overlooking the Washington Monument with views of the golf course and tennis courts. It wouldn't be crowded, and if anyone did happen to see them, it would just be two members having a drink together.

Al made the call to the current head of the DSCA, General Mike Howell, to invite him for drinks at the Club. There was no question that General Howell would meet with him, for they had met several times before when the General needed Al's advice on how to manage the DSCA bureaucracy. They agreed to meet at five o'clock.

Like most Washington senior military staff, politicians, lobbyists, and US and International company executives, they both had small apartments close to work. Their homes or mansions were well out past Dulles Airport, as even with their high salaries, they couldn't afford the living accommodations they were accustomed to anywhere close to their offices. The typical routine was to come into town on Monday morning and go out to their estates early Friday afternoon. That left four evenings of free time to be wined and dined by lobbyists or any friends with an expense account.

Al was already sitting in the far corner of the glass enclosed dining room with a bottle of the General's favorite wine, Laithwaite's Barons de Rothschild Lafite Réserve Spéciale Pauillac. At two hundred dollars per bottle, Al was pleased that he had an unlimited expense account. Plus, at the Army Navy Country Club, he only had to sign the check and the bill was sent directly to the CAC Corporate office where a bean counter would charge it off to miscellaneous business expenses, since by law a military person was supposed to pay for their share of any business meetings with contractors or suppliers. Also, the company preferred not to have a military guest's name and rank on a company expense report.

General Howell and Al discussed the normal stuff—weather, the latest political rumors, and the usual complaint that DSCA never had enough money to get the job done, as they enjoyed their first of many glasses of Bordeaux.

After the first bottle and some expensive *hors d'oeuvres*, Al decided he had better get down to business. "Mike, thanks for taking the time to help me with this bottle of wine," which made them both laugh. "I hear that things are running smoothly at DSCA. I'm glad this posting is working out so well for you. I find that being in a senior position in Washington DC really positions one for a variety of post-retirement executive positions. I hope, when you elect to pull the plug, that you are as fortunate as I was at attaining a senior position with a major defense contractor. I found the key is to develop a strong working relationship with several of the major defense companies so they will come knocking on your door when you retire." Al's subtle message was, *It'll pay to work with me.*

"I have found that these private companies do not seem to have well laid-out schedules like we have in the military. Just today, our Cargo Aircraft Company advised me that they have signed a contract with Egypt for six CC-260 which are aircraft just sitting on their ramp ready for delivery. They understand that a grant for an FMF Direct Commercial Sale is in progress. I expect some of the folks from Mobile are sitting outside your office looking for this money?"

General Howell now knew why he had been invited to this meeting. He held the cards to the timely completion of their sale. He knew the funding was all approved and in work, so a little push from him would certainly pay off with more meetings with his close friends.

The General replied, "Al, you know these grant FMF-DCS transfers can take a long time. But I do know the money has been appropriated. Therefore, I will give the system a little kick in the pants to make the payment to CAC."

"Mike, thank You. Let's have another bottle of wine so you are ready to hear what those fellows at CAC told me next."

Mike smiled and thought, *I may not enjoy this next bottle as much as the first one.*

After signaling the waiter for more wine, Al plunged in. "As you know, a small portion of the Egyptian FMF grant was for the spares package. Well, some bean counter at CAC decided he could save their company and the EAF a lot of money by diverting to Egypt a portion of a big spares' shipment headed to Saudi Arabia. Therefore, thirty-six million dollars' worth of EAF CC-260 aircraft spares are already on-site at a CAC support contract facility in Cairo. They suggest that DSCA just go ahead and make the DCS spares payment to their contractor in Egypt." Before Mike could object to such a non-standard procedure, Al added. " When I was at DSCA, we did make "exceptions" like this on a case-by-case basis." *He hoped Mike didn't want names and dates* "The key is to have the US Embassy in Egypt certify that the spares are on-site at an authorized and EAF-approved facility."

Mike didn't like the word "exception," so he asked, "Al, why don't we, the DSCA, just pay CAC? Then CAC can pay their local contractor for the storage and administration."

Al had expected the General might come up with this simple resolution to this problem, so he was ready. "Although that appears to be straightforward, you do know that throughout the military procurement systems the prices for spares are marked-up a very large amount? Also, since the EAF spares are on-site, the CAC and EAF contracts people have inventoried the spares at MAPS and confirmed at the contract prices that all of the thirty-six million dollars' worth of spares are there. If DSCA pays CAC the full amount of thirty-six million dollars, then CAC will only pay MAPS for handling the spares at their actual value which I believe is around twenty-five million. Otherwise, it could appear in a financial audit that CAC is paying MAPS a large commission over the actual price of the spares."

"If DSCA pays MAPS the full thirty-six million, then the Egyptian government and our Senate Appropriations Committee will see that the EAF received the full thirty-six million that was funded. Then MAPS can pay CAC for the spares, less their small handling and storage fee. That way there is no visibility of CAC spare parts mark-up. Mike, I assure you that all US military suppliers play this same game, so there is no need to bring attention to this issue."

General Howell blinked, thinking that Al was playing the old shell game of "guess which shell has the money under it?" They both took a long sip of wine. The General was not sure if it was the wine or not, but Al's logic did make some sense.

"Al, although it appears to be somewhat unconventional, I will see if and what it will take to make the spares payment direct to the CAC subcontractor, with oversight by the US Embassy in Cairo."

Al was careful not to appear too appreciative, and tried to keep his tone "business as usual," which he knew it wasn't. They finished their wine, and Mike agreed to give him an update in a day or so.

As they left together out the main entrance, the General said, "Al, next time we get together for a bottle of wine, I'm buying, as long as you promise not to give me any more work assignments."

Al chuckled, and answered, "Sounds like a deal," thinking, *Which I hope this turns out to be.* Then they each requested a taxi, as it appears, they had both planned to do some serious drinking.

Al would meet with Ken in the morning with the encouraging news that the FMF-DCS funding to both CAC and MAPS was in the works. Ken would also need to alert his team to arrange for the US Embassy in Cairo to support the direct pay to their local subcontractor play. Al thought, *This commercial business gig isn't bad. I sure can pay for a lot better wine than was allowed on my military expense reports.*

DSCA Funds the Game

The next morning General Howell arrived early at his office in the Pentagon. He had only been in charge of DSCA for a little over a year. He wasn't familiar with all of the regulations related to FMF/DCS fund transfers, since, at his level, he didn't deal with these details. Therefore, he was hesitant to issue an order on the Egyptian program without having any background.

He could ask several of his staff to outline the various procedures, which he most likely would still not understand. Or, he could do as many newly-appointed executives did, just ask his secretary how to do it. Ms. "know it all" Wright had been there forever and probably could run the Agency better than he.

Ms. Wright, like the General, was always at work early. *Might as well get the ball rolling*, thought General Howell, and asked Ms. Wright to come into his office. He remained behind his very large government-issued desk and motioned for her to take a seat. Since it was not required to waste time discussing weather, family, or non-work issues with low-level staff, she had her notebook and pen in hand, ready to take orders.

He started in his military command voice. "Ms. Wright, it has come to my attention that several senior Government officials are monitoring our handling and progress on making the already approved FMF Direct Commercial Sale payment to the Cargo

Aircraft Company for the sale of their aircraft and spares to Egypt. Please find out who in our Agency is in charge of making this payment and advise them immediately to. . . "

He broke off as he looked down at his notes from the meeting with Al Hancock, which he proceeded to read verbatim, ". . . make the payment to the Cargo Aircraft Company for the CC-260 aircraft. Then transfer the funds for the spares package to the US Embassy in Egypt. Upon the Embassy's confirmation that the spares are there, finally have the Embassy make the payment to the CAC subcontractor Military Aircraft Parts and Service Company."

When he was sure that Ms. Wright had taken down all that information, he finished with, "Have whoever is in charge advise me of the expected dates of these two transfers. Let me know if you have any difficulty handling what I believe is a simple task."

He stood up from his desk, which signaled that the discussion was over. As she left, he thought, *Either things will go as in previous cases like Al said, or someone will alert me to a problem which I can then assign to someone to solve. Actually, funding a sale to a third world county is way below my level.*

Well, this was also not Ms. Wright's first rodeo. Once she returned to her desk, she reviewed the weekly activity report which apparently the General hadn't bothered reading. It stated that the FMF grant funding for the six CC-260 aircraft and spares package for Egypt was in process for payment to CAC in Mobile Alabama within a couple of days. However, there were no instructions for a direct payment through the Embassy in Cairo for the spares package.

Ms. Wright had survived many years working in the Pentagon by not challenging orders from a general. Although she was not aware of there ever being a direct FMF payment to an overseas company, who was she to argue with General Howell? Consequently, she did as the General had requested and prepared a formal order document directing that the payment for the Egyptian CC-260 aircraft spares be sent to the US Embassy in Cairo. After they confirmed that all the spares were on-site at the CAC local subcontractor Military Aircraft Parts and Service Company, they were to make the payment directly to MAPS.

She placed the FMF spares payment order in a folder with several other documents for the General to sign and placed them in his IN basket. Since generals didn't need to waste their valuable time reading administrative documents, General Howell later picked up the folder in his IN basket, quickly signed the documents, and threw the folder in his OUT basket.

Shortly thereafter, Ms. Wright picked up the folder, and sent the order for the Egyptian spares payment to the department handling this FMF case. She didn't expect any problems, as the activity report indicated that a Major White was in charge of this department. She didn't expect a major to challenge a general's order.

Amazing how direction from a general can make things happen! Ms. Wright handed General Howell a document the next afternoon which confirmed that the FMF payment had been made to CAC in Mobile for the aircraft. Also, another FMF payment for the spares had been sent to the US Embassy in Cairo with instructions that, once they confirmed all the CC-260 Spares were on-site, they would transfer the funds to the local company, Military Aircraft Parts and Services.

The General thought, *That was sure easy and fast. I'll let General Hancock know. I'm sure this will result in another bottle or two of wine.*

15

FOURTEENTH GAME – SAN FRANCISCO 49ERS AT ATLANTA FALCONS

49ers win 13 to 3

San Francisco limited the Atlanta Falcons to 177 yards of offense for this win.

Cairo

While the DC team was moving the money, Larry Ray remained in Cairo to monitor the situation, but more importantly, to figure out how to move his money-reward back to the US. He needed to have another meeting, or session, with Tasha to lay out a plan for his reward, or maybe rewards. With the fund transfer imminent, he left her a message that Harry's Pub was having a special event that night at 8:00 PM. He was pleased to receive a reply a short time later that "his friend" would be there.

He had already received the notice from the Washington office that the FMF funding would be made to both CAC and MAPS within the next few days. The only caveat was that the US Embassy had to confirm that the entire package of spares were on-site at MAPS. He knew that was a no-brainer as his spares guy and MAPS already had accomplished that audit. He would get in touch with Colonel Barnes to encourage him to accept the CAC and MAPS audit in order to expedite the FMF payment to MAPS.

While the DC team was moving the FMF money and Larry Ray was dreaming about his reward, the local Cairo Team was also having some special activities. There was no question that Tasha and Ali, being in love, were anxious to get married and start a family. Of course, Tasha's' brother Helmy, the Minister of Defense, as the leading male member of the family, strongly supported sooner versus later. Now there was another factor that supported the sooner versus later wedding.

The Local Team Merger

Ali had received a message from Ahmed that the DC team had scored and the FMF Funds for the spares were being transferred to the US Embassy for payment directly to MAPS. Ali was once more impressed with the CAC expertise at making all the plays to ensure the sale and reward the teams. So, as one of them had said earlier, it was time to get their sphinxes in order. The next play was called "Keep it in the Family."

There was an Arabic-Egyptian tradition called *mahr*, which was a mandatory payment, in the form of money or possessions, paid by the groom to the bride at the time of marriage. It was the reverse of the western tradition of a dowry. As Ali, Tasha, and Helmy already knew the value of their reward, Ali could commit an amount of his *mahr* to Tasha. It was an amazing coincidence that Tasha and her brother Helmy just happened to have a shared family bank arrangement where each had full access to the account. Again, it was a family matter.

While Larry Ray was in his hotel suite contemplating how to spend his reward, a *Katb el-Kitab*, the official Islamic marriage ceremony, was being held at a very small mosque in Al-Shorafa about twenty-five miles south of Cairo. It was remote enough that there was low probability of anyone recognizing Ali, Tasha, and Helmy. Only a couple of close friends were in attendance. Most of the other attendees were security personnel to ensure no outsiders came into the mosque during the short ceremony.

They had previously agreed that they would hold off announcing the marriage and taking the honeymoon until after they had finished the CAC game.

Tasha had agreed to another meeting with Larry Ray, since they didn't want to give him any reason to raise concern about his reward. She and Ali had already discussed several ways to give Larry Ray only his monetary reward. They would have to ask him to be patient as no one was getting anything until the team funding arrived.

Harry's Pub

As in the past. Larry Ray was sitting in a corner booth finishing his first, *or was it third*, beer when Tasha arrived. Once she was seated and had been served, Larry Ray announced, "Tasha, thanks for coming, as I have great news on our game. Our Washington team have finished their game and the grant payments for the six aircraft and the spares are being made in the next couple of days. The aircraft are being prepped for the delivery flight to Cairo as soon as the payment for the aircraft arrives at CAC. The DSCA is transferring the payment for the spares to the US Embassy for transfer to MAPS once they confirm all the spares are on-site." He took a long drink of his beer so all that info could sink in and be appreciated.

He continued, "I expect that in another week my work here will be finished. I sure do not wish to leave without having our business positioning meeting, and receiving my rewards."

Tasha noticed that he used the plural of rewards and didn't want to disillusion him just yet on a part of what she knew he was thinking. She offered, "Larry Ray, that's great news. I'm impressed with how your company knows how to work the territory."

Tasha then leisurely sipped her beer and thought she would have a little fun. "I have learned that for you Alabama cowboys, this was not your first rodeo." They both laughed. "Please, do not worry. My committee has also played this game before. However, we must wait until the aircraft have arrived and the payment for the spares has been made. As you mentioned, that should only take a few more days. Over the next few days, I will work on getting your reward ready, then we can celebrate when we have our business positioning meeting before you leave town."

That was all Larry Ray needed to hear tonight. His job now was to encourage the quick delivery of the aircraft and have the Embassy make the spares payment.

Tasha finished her beer and said, "I am sorry to leave you so quickly. However, I must run as I have other commitments this evening. I'll make it up to you next time."

They shared a quick hug and kiss on the cheek as she left. Larry Ray thought he would start celebrating early, and ordered another beer.

US Embassy

The next morning Larry Ray was moving a little slow. He had received confirmation overnight that the aircraft payment had been received at CAC. The six CC-260 aircraft would all be arriving over the next few days. He called the Embassy to see if Colonel Barnes needed any assistance in auditing the spares at MAPS. He was a little surprised to be told by Colonel Barnes that the Colonel and Ali had already agreed for the Embassy to accept the CAC and MAPS spares audit document as on-site verification. Also, that the spares payment was going to be transferred to MAPS later that day.

MAPS

Ali was pleased to be informed that the first CC-260 aircraft would be arriving the next few days. He was even more pleased to be advised by his bank that MAPS had received a thirty-six-million-dollar transfer from the US Embassy. Now was the time to play 'Who do You Trust.' He sent a message to Ahmed confirming that the payment for the CC-260 spares had been received. He confirmed that MAPS would make the agreed payment to CAC for the spares as soon as CAC guaranteed the Support Agreement for the ten-year contractual period. In terms which only would be understood by the CAC team, MAPS would transfer the agreed payment for the spares as soon as CAC made the remaining eight-million-dollar payment to MAPS. Ali knew he had good leverage by withholding the almost twenty-nine million until he received the eight million.

Although it appeared to be a complicated process of moving a few million dollars back and forth, he knew that CAC was managing several accounts to hide who was paying who for what, or as the Americans say, cooking the books.

CAC

Frank Moore already knew that the spares payment had been

made to MAPS long before he received the message from Ahmed. Both Larry Ray and Ken Doyle at the Washington office had sent messages earlier that day. Since the first two aircraft had already departed for Cairo, it was time to finish this game.

Frank knew that his Finance VP, Jim Smith, would strongly object to making a final payment of eight million dollars on the MAPS support contract long before it was due, especially since the only money available was the recent FMF payment from DSCA. If they were ever to become aware of it, they would be suspicious with the timing of transferring large amounts of their money to an overseas contractor especially when it coincided with the recent signing of the contract. It just might be considered as an illegal undisclosed commission using FMF funds.

Fortunately, Jim was attending an Aerospace Finance Conference in Las Vegas. He suspected the main topic was which game provided the best odds for winning at the casinos. He needed to get the payment made to MAPS without creating a paper trail leading back to him. He knew that Jim's second in command was fairly new to CAC and the aircraft business. He apparently was hired to assist Jim in understanding the world of computer control finances. He asked his secretary to have Jim's assistant come to his office.

Once 'Charlie-what's-his-name' arrived and they were seated across from each other at Frank's impressive conference table, Frank started with, "I hear from Jim that you are doing a great job of bringing the Company in line with the latest financial processes. As you know, Jim is away at a conference. We need to make a small payment to one of our many overseas Support Contractors and I do not know who in Jim's department takes care of these things. Since you are filling in for him, can you take care of this for us?"

Of course, Charlie said "Yes," even though he had never processed an actual payment to anyone.

Frank proceeded to explain Charlie's assignment. "The Company is our Support Contractor in Cairo, Military Aircraft Parts and Services. My secretary will give you the payment portion of our agreement with them. It states we will pay the full amount over a period of time. They just started supporting our recent highly profitable sale of six CC-260 aircraft to Egypt and now they need money to build a large hanger to service our aircraft. So, let's just go ahead and make that payment now."

Charlie was in no position to debate a direct order from the president, so he simply replied, "Yes Sir, I'll take care of it immediately."

Frank was a little concerned what account Charlie would charge for the payment. However, that was a Finance department decision.

The new finance guy was impressive—or trying to impress the boss—as later that day Frank received a note from the Finance Department that the eight-million-dollar payment had been made to MAPS.

Frank then sent a message to Ahmed to advise him that MAPS had been paid in full. He added a post-script which read, "I expect that MAPS will now honor their part of *our* deal." Only a couple people would know what that referred to. It was time for MAPS to make their play and end this game.

Cairo

It was late afternoon in Cairo. Ali had asked Tasha and brother Helmy to meet at Helmy's villa in Mirage City on the golf course.

Once they were all seated on the patio overlooking the golf greens and enjoying an expensive glass of wine, he said, "The Cargo Aircraft executive team has finished running all their plays. We have received the full payment to MAPS that they promised. At present, we have two of our own plays to run to finish this game."

Helmy and Tasha couldn't help but lean in a little closer for Ali's next words. "The first play is to send the payment for the spares, less our handling fee, to CAC. Of the thirty-six million dollars we received for the spares, Ahmed's team is expecting MAPS to be paid fifteen percent, or almost five and one-half million dollars, equal to our fee. I will sign the consulting agreement with his Jordanian company, JET, and transfer these funds to his bank in Amman. Now, Ahmed believes we are only being paid the fifteen percent. It appears he missed the fact that I had negotiated a twenty percent handling fee with their VP of Finance. So, we have another almost two million coming to us."

"We also have to cover those small incentives to the two EAF players. We have already agreed for Air Marshal Saad to consult to MAPS at six thousand dollars per month, which equals seventy-two thousand for the first year. We will not renew that consulting contract with him unless another similar deal comes our way. Furthermore, I already incentivized Air Commodore Riad with thirty thousand dollars. Now, I understand from my new bride that she has "betrothed" three hundred sixty thousand to her best new friend Larry Ray."

Helmy and Tasha nodded. No surprise there, since Tasha had already mentioned the amount of the reward she had promised to Larry Ray.

Ali continued, "Looks like after we deduct around five hundred thousand from our almost two-million-dollar bonus, we can add the other amount of just over one million to our account. That will total exactly 11.3 million dollars. I know we had originally agreed to a three-way split of the ten million. I recommend we keep to that and hold the 1.3 million as working capital at MAPS only to be used by us to attend business meetings in various South Pacific beach resorts to investigate business opportunities."

They all smiled at that suggestion, as they contemplated future visits to various exotic tropical paradises.

Ali took a deep breath, as though a little worn-out from his lengthy briefing. "Now for the wrap-up. If we are in agreement, then MAPS will transfer the ten million over to one my private accounts I now share with Tasha. I will then transfer three and one-third million to the account Tasha shares with Helmy with her promise not to touch that account. I don't think anyone will be able to follow that transfer trail. On the same note, in taking care of Larry Ray, and I only mean financially, I am not comfortable at just handing him a large amount of money that could be traced back to us, even though he may be a nice guy and a great salesman. I'm sure that between us, we can come up with a workable plan, for, as the Americans say, that's why we get the big bucks. You know, I really love all those American slang sayings."

Tasha looked affectionately at Ali and said, "Are you about finished, my love?"

Ali grinned back at her and answered, "Yes, my dear. And I hope there are no questions, because, quite frankly I don't think I could go through it all again." But he just had to add, "As you know, this was not my first rodeo." The comment prompted Tasha and Helmy to roll their eyes.

They all clinked glasses and settled back to enjoy their wine, while reflecting on the fact that they had made millions of dollars by being in the right place at the right time.

16

FIFTEENTH GAME - SAN FRANCISCO 49ERS HOSTS NEW ORLEANS SAINTS

49ers win 30 to 17

San Francisco and the Saints both where at 9 wins and 5 loses. Craig alone rushed for 115 yards of the 49ers' 152 yards for two scores. Montana threw for 233 yards and a touchdown.

Zurich

Ahmed was pleased to receive the messages from CAC in Mobile, Larry Ray in Cairo, and Ken Doyle in Washington that the Egyptian contract had been signed, the FMF funds transferred, and the first aircraft had been delivered. He was even more pleased to be advised by his bank in Amman that his company JET had received a wire transfer for almost five and one-half million dollars

Now he had to reward his team for such a well-played game. Most people believed that Swiss banks were the best for handling private transactions or moving money. Although they were certainly good at keeping private transfers between Swiss banks, Ahmed knew that the American NSA had hacked into the system which wire transferred funds to overseas banks. It was not as easy to monitor banks in the Middle East. With all the overwhelming amount of oil, imports, tourists, and arms business transactions which were handled in a somewhat sloppy method, the NSA could not figure out what all went where. Kind of like hiding in plain sight.

Ahmed knew he could easily hide his share between his several accounts in Amman, Zurich, and the Cayman Islands, but it was going to be more difficult to get the rewards to his other team members. He had the account number for Mark in the Cayman Islands. That would simply require moving the reward in reasonable amounts between a couple of friendly banks in the Caymans.

Ahmed smiled as he recalled that the CAC players had never discussed or agreed to the amount of their rewards. Mark expected they would be receiving a big payday, or kickback, from MAPS of somewhere between four to five million dollars. Frank had not run this type of spares play before, so he probably wasn't sure what to expect. Also, he would be concerned about taking a big reward from FMF funding. Ken would also be nervous regarding playing with FMF funds.

Since Ali had assured him that MAPS would reward Larry Ray, all Ahmed had to do was identify who were the key players on his own team, besides himself, and split the pot. He certainly wasn't an accountant, so he took out a blank sheet of paper, and not a cocktail napkin this time, and listed the rewards for each, with a brief reason for their reward:

Ahmed (*who picked the local team to made it happen*)
= $ 2.5 million

Mark (*key coach who had previously run this game with him*)
= $ 1.5 million

Frank (*rubber stamped the plays Ahmed had called*)   = $ 750k

Ken (*already receives a large Corporate bonus*) = $ 250k

JET/Amman (*future business expenses*) = $ 400K

He would soon shred this personal memo, and would not document any of these transactions, as paper-trails have a habit of coming back to haunt you. The transfer from Amman to the Caymans was straightforward. He was sure Mark would be pleased when he checked the status of his account there. However, getting the rewards to Frank and Ken would be more difficult. But if those Alabama guys could say, 'This is not our first rodeo," then Ahmed could come back with, "Now it's time to do the laundry," as Al Capone used to say.

Ahmed had done his due diligence in understanding the ins and outs of money laundering. He knew that Capone, with his Mafia buddies, had perfected the art of commingling their profits from illegal activity with those from legitimate business activity. There were many types of money laundering, one of which was the "foreign investment method," which occurred when funds were delivered to a foreign partner. The money would then appear to be the property of the foreign partner. This step was known as placement. The next step, known as layering, took place when the foreign business would invest in a legitimate business with the money placed with them.

First, Ahmed would receive funds from the foreign business interest MAPS. Then Ahmed, in the guise of his company JET, would buy shares of CAC stock equal to each reward. The final step, known as integration, would occur when the money could be obtained by selling the stock or reaping profits that the stock would generate. Ahmed would instruct his US stock broker to transfer the appropriate CAC shares to each of Frank's and Ken's US brokers.

Since they both received shares of CAC stock as part of their salary and the bonus programs, it would be difficult to identify these additional stocks from all the others in their accounts. It would take a day or two to make all of these transactions.

Ahmed knew his team would all be satisfied with their rewards. He was curious how Larry Ray was doing with receiving his reward, or rewards.

To the Ticket-Holders: The preceding information was not meant to condone this practice or encourage the use of this system by any reader. It was merely used as an illustration.

Cairo

Larry Ray had seen all the messages reporting that the CC-260 EAF sale was complete and the new aircraft were arriving in Cairo soon. His job here was finished. However, he had advised the home office that he was staying a couple of days to solidify some relationships for the long term. He didn't know whether he should contact Tasha and ask for his rewards, or just wait a little while longer.

He then was pleased to receive a message which said, "A thank you gift will be delivered to your hotel suite at 7:00 PM this evening." Even though it was not signed, he knew who it was from. *Interesting that she was coming to his hotel room to deliver his reward.* He had thought she would be concerned about being recognized in a public place like the Marriott Hotel and that she would want to keep their business meetings private.

Nevertheless, he called down to housekeeping and requested that his suite be cleaned, flowers provided, the minibar fully stocked, and new sheets put on the bed. *As the Boy Scouts say, "Be prepared."*

By the time 7:00 PM rolled around, he had already had a few drinks to relax and calm his nerves. He jumped up when his doorbell chimed at exactly seven. As he looked out the door peephole, he saw a black hood and immediately thought he was about to be kidnapped. On a second look, he saw it was someone in a black *niqab*, the garment Arab women wore to cover all of their body and face, with only a slit for the eyes. This was quite a cover up from a *hijab*, the normal compulsory garment Muslim women wore to cover their upper body and head, but not their face.

He now understood how she had planned to get to his room without being recognized. He quickly opened the door, as Tasha joked, "Larry Ray, don't tell me you didn't recognize me by the look in my eyes?" They both laughed. He wanted to hug her, but didn't quite know how to embrace her through the loose fitting *niqab*.

As Tasha proceeded across the suite to the sitting area, she shed the *niqab*. Larry Ray was impressed to see she was wearing a very short, low-cut cocktail dress. He quickly poured her a glass of wine and refreshed his drink, while Tasha complimented him on leading his team to victory. She thought, *No need at this time to discuss how all the other players also helped to make it happen*

They took a seat on the sofa, where Tasha snuggled up close to him while they reviewed how well the sales game had gone. Tasha commented, "I understand from Ali that you have kept all the promises you made to him. Therefore, I want to do the same and keep the promises I made to you." He noticed that she had said promises, so it sure looked like it was going to be a rewarding night.

"First of all, my government wishes to express their gratitude to you for arranging for Egypt to receive the six CC-260 aircraft and spares at no cost. That "thank you" is the three hundred sixty thousand dollars that we mentioned as your monetary reward. However, since we all know that carrying or transferring large sums of money can be difficult and risky, we have developed a system that we hope will work well for you."

Tasha pulled a picture from her purse. "This is the Bronze Wadjet. I'm sure you know who that is." Tasha smiled, as she knew he wouldn't know the Wadjet from a wombat, whatever that was. Larry took a look at the picture she showed him, a bronze statue of a very strange-looking creature.

Tasha continued, "But just to refresh your memory, the Wadjet was the goddess of the city of Dep, located east of Alexandria on the Nile Delta. This statue dates back to the 21st or 22nd dynasty in the Third Intermediate Period, which was about 1070 to 712 BC. Egyptians often used bronze statuettes of this type as votive offerings, that is, objects offered in gratitude for the fulfillment of a previous vow. Once inside the temple sanctuary, the worshipper would ceremonially present the figure to the deity as a repayment for a favor. So, this should be very appropriate for you."

Larry Ray grinned at her remark.

Tasha stated, "This statue is an original artifact. It stands only thirteen inches tall. My associates are packaging it to look like an Egyptian souvenir, and it will be delivered to you tomorrow."

Larry Ray was about to comment that he had no interest in old Egyptian artifacts, when Tasha added, "However, in case you do not wish to have this beautiful statue sitting on your fireplace mantel as a souvenir, our Cultural Attaché at the Egyptian Embassy in Washington will be happy to come to your home in Alabama and purchase this artifact from you for $360,000 in cash."

Larry Ray thought, *What a great idea! This solves all my concerns about having to transfer a large sum of money from here to there*. He replied, "Tasha, as much as I would like to keep that statue as a memento of our friendship, I think the money is a better remembrance. Also, packaging it as a souvenir will make it easier for me to get it through customs when I return to the US. You folks sure to know how to handle rewards," he finished in his "Aw, shucks, ma'am" voice.

With that business out of the way, Larry Ray had a couple more drinks and Tasha another glass of wine, while discussing the potential for future business together. As Larry Ray was about to blurt out, "When do I get my other reward?", Tasha murmured, "Larry Ray, it is getting late. It's time for your other reward. Why don't you go and get dressed for bed and get ready for it."

He gulped down his drink, smiled, and headed for the bedroom. While he was in the other room, Tasha poured him another bourbon and slipped a little green powder into it. She had a play for the evening, however it wasn't the one Larry Ray was thinking.

When he came back to the bedroom door dressed in his pajama bottoms, she exclaimed, "Well, that was quick! Come over her and finish your drink, while I finish my wine."

Larry Ray sat down beside her and started chugging his drink as fast as he could in order to get to the next play. Tasha took her last sip of wine, and added, "Larry Ray, I am going to go to the bathroom to get ready to present you with your special reward. Please finish your drink and go warm up the bed, as I don't like cold sheets, especially when I do not have any clothes on. I also expect those pajamas may get in our way."

As Tasha went into the bathroom and closed the door, Larry Ray drained his drink, threw off his pajama pants, and jumped into the bed. Tasha took her good ol' time doing nothing in the bathroom other than turning the water on and off. When she finally exited fully dressed, Larry Ray was passed out on the bed under the covers.

Tasha thought, *Well, that sure worked.*

She pulled out a small bottle of her perfume and sprayed it around the bed. Next, she pulled a pair of black lace panties from her purse and dropped them on the floor. Lastly, she placed a note next to his pillow, which said, "Larry Ray, you sure know how to handle a reward. I look forward to doing more business with you, T."

Tasha then put her *niqab* back on and left the suite, placing the 'Do Not Disturb' sign on the outside door handle.

Larry Ray awoke very late the next morning with the worst hangover he had had in a long time. He immediately noticed that he was alone and was pleased to smell the scent of her perfume. As he sat on the edge of the bed to read her note, he saw the panties on the floor. Although, he didn't remember a thing, it appeared he had received his reward with honors. He smiled, fell back on the bed, and went to sleep again.

His phone ringing woke him the second time. The front desk had a package for him and would send it up to his suite right away, He threw on a robe and answered the door when the bell rang. After the service boy handed him a package, he closed the door and as he opened the package, he saw it was the Egyptian statue in Tasha's picture. Also, it was wrapped as if it was just an "off the street" souvenir. He thought, *How can something so funny-looking be worth so much?* He set it beside his suitcase and started to get ready to leave Cairo and return to Mobile. He smiled as he placed the black panties in the trash, thinking, *What would US customs say if they found them in my suitcase?*

His return to Mobile thru Europe went on schedule and he made it in one long day, chasing the sun westward. As expected, he had no trouble getting his souvenir through customs when he arrived in the US.

He went into the office the next day and was pleased to receive congratulations from all the executives on a job well done. *OK, lots of nice words.* However, no one was giving him the monetary reward he thought was due to him. Fortunately, he had outsmarted them by running his own reward play.

The next day, before he could figure out how to cash in the statue, he received a call from a Mr. Mohamed, who said he was the Egyptian Cultural Attaché at the Embassy in Washington. He mentioned that he understood that Mr. Hardy had a very valuable Egyptian artifact in his possession which he might be interested in selling. Once Larry Ray confirmed he was the Mr. Hardy with the artifact and certainly was interested in selling it, they agreed to meet at the Mobile airport the next afternoon.

Larry Ray was waiting just outside the arrivals area of the airport when the Egyptian Attaché, in a business suit and pulling a medium size roller bag, exited. It was clear that he knew who was meeting him. The two men shook hands and walked to the airport private business club where Larry Ray had reserved a small conference room. This was all business, and neither man wished to waste time with a lot of small talk.

Once seated, Larry Ray handed Mr. Mohamed the statue still wrapped as a souvenir. The Attaché opened it, carefully inspected it, then said, "Mr. Hardy, thank you for taking good care in transporting this very valuable artifact to its new home here in the USA. We plan to display it prominently at our Embassy in Washington." Then he motioned toward the roller bag. "This contains the $360,000 that was agreed upon between you and our Government."

As Mr. Mohamed opened the case, Larry Ray thought, *Even though I kind of trust this guy, I'm going to make sure no one tries to take a share of my reward.* It wasn't hard to count the money that was packaged in ten-thousand-dollar bricks with a bank seal on each one. Larry Ray counted thirty-six separate packages and closed the suitcase.

Mr. Mohamed smiled and said, "You also get to keep the suitcase." Larry Ray thought, *Did he just make a joke?*

As Mr. Mohamed placed the statue in his small carry-on bag, he apologized, "I'm sorry to have to leave so soon. However, I booked an immediate return flight to Washington. Thanks again for your service to Egypt."

He stood, they shook hands again, and both left the conference room.

Once back at his home, Larry Ray already had a plan to secure his reward. He had recently reserved safe deposit boxes at three local banks close to the airport. That would allow him to spread the wealth and not have all of his nest eggs in one basket, so to speak. Plus, it would be convenient in case he needed to quickly leave town. He thought contentedly, *All is good.* What he didn't appreciate was that even though the game was over, it still wasn't the end of the season.

Don't leave the stadium yet!

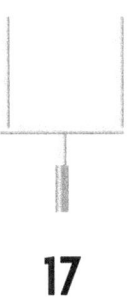

17

SIXTEENTH GAME – SAN FRANCISCO 49ERS HOST LOS ANGELES RAMS

49ers lose 16 to 38

The 49ers clinched the NFC West despite a three-way tie with the Rams and New Orleans (all finishing 10–6) and despite a 38–16 slaughter by the Rams that put them into the playoffs. Jim Everett threw four touchdowns while Montana and Young combined for 291 yards but no scores. San Francisco won the division on tiebreakers and the Rams were the wild card, while the 10–6 Saints were eliminated from playoff contention.

Washington DC- The Pentagon- DSCA

Within the Department of Defense, the DSCA oversees global security cooperation programs and funding for the Office of the Secretary of Defense, Joint Staff, Department of State, Geographic Combatant Commands, the military departments, and US industry. It is responsible for policy, processes, training, and financial management involving approximately 161 partner nations, 775 Security Cooperation Officers in 135 US embassies, 391 Humanitarian Assistance projects in 75 countries, 13,000 active Foreign Military Sales cases worth $403 billion, and training for

7,344 international students from 141 countries.

With over 10,000 government employees and all of the above-mentioned activities, it would hardly be expected that anyone would notice a small FMF transfer to a small company in Egypt. However, a DSCA lower level SG 8 bean counter just happened to see a report that the US Embassy in Egypt had reported a transfer of thirty-six million dollars of FMF grant funding to an Egyptian company in Cairo.

Over the next few days, he was able to determine that this transfer was directed by General Howell, who was in charge of DSCA. Being the new guy, he was not one to challenge a direct order from a general. He mentioned this matter to a few of his colleagues and they all advised him not to rock the boat. Being good soldiers, airmen, or sailors, who were they to ask a general to explain his order?

However, some people just won't let a sleeping dog lie, so he unofficially passed an unsigned memo about the FMF transfer to MAPS onto the DOD Office of the Inspector General. This office had the responsibility and authority to initiate audits, evaluations, and investigations relating to programs and operations of the Department of Defense.

A lower level Office of Inspector General staffer, Johnny B. Good, received the unsigned message. At first, he considered just throwing it away. However, as he thought about it, if there were any inappropriate transaction and he was credited with making the discovery, it would certainly enhance his career. So, he noted all the key information and shredded the original message. No use taking the chance of someone else receiving credit, if this turned out to be a big deal.

Although he knew by the message that the head of DSCA, General Howell, had issued the order for the direct payment to the Egyptian company, he wanted to have more details of the transaction before he suggested to his management to challenge the order. He started by sending a message to the Air Attaché at the Embassy in Cairo requesting the background on the direct FMF funding of the spares for the CC-260, as well as information on the local company, Military Aircraft Parts and Services.

Cairo – US Embassy

Colonel Barnes was concerned at receiving a message from the Office of Inspector General requesting information on the FMF payment to MAPS. He knew it was unusual, if not illegal, to make FMF payments to non-US companies. However, since the direction had come from General Howell, the head of DSCA, he never questioned it. He knew this could be a career-disrupting event, so he needed to be careful to be sure he did not take a direct hit.

Colonel. Barnes did a thorough search and review of FMF procedures and restrictions. It was verified in the DSCA administrative manual that direct FMF payments to non-US companies were not permitted. There was no mention of any procedure to override this restriction. It looked like his best position would be, "I was just following orders, Sir." He also alerted the Ambassador not to touch this "tar baby," but if he was contacted by anyone on this matter, to just refer them back to Colonel Barnes

The Colonel had been around long enough to know he just couldn't make a quick reply pointing the finger at DSCA. He needed to show the OIG that the Embassy was following standard procedures and only following the direction from one of the many

US Agencies they support, as they always did.

Also, he needed to meet with Ali Omar to alert him that there might be an investigation by a US agency on the direct payment to MAPS. Fortunately, he had copies of the CAC/MAPS audit that confirmed the itemized spares matched the listing in the contract and the amount to be paid. He had actually wondered, when the Embassy transferred the thirty-six million dollars to MAPS, how much actually flowed back to CAC. This could really get interesting.

He placed a call to Ali and asked him to come meet him at the Embassy. He didn't want to make a special visit to the MAPS office or indicate how well he knew Ali. They would meet the next day. In the meantime, he prepared a detailed account of the Embassy's support of the CAC sale to the EAF. Of course, there was no mention of private meetings with Larry Ray, and he certainly made the trip to Paris for the aircraft demo sound like a trip to central Africa—all work and no play!

Next, he sent a message to his new good friend, Larry Ray Hardy, as the Colonel might need to consider, or even be forced into, early retirement if he couldn't pass this 'tar baby' back to the OIG office. He also thought it would be good to alert him and CAC that one of the alligators from the DC swamp was sniffing around their business.

Ali arrived early the next morning. After they had coffee and got up to date on local events, Colonel Barnes mentioned that one of the Washington agencies - he didn't want to frighten him by mentioning the Office of Inspector General – was conducting a review of the CAC spares transaction. As far as Ali was concerned, he had cooperated with CAC, the EAF, and the Embassy, so he didn't believe he had done anything wrong. Colonel Barnes, not being aware of the actual mark-up on the spares package and how much MAPS had received, also believed all was OK, since both he and Ali had only complied with DSCA and CAC direction.

They reviewed the spares audit documentation to be sure they were both playing by the same game book. The Colonel told Ali that he was essentially going to reply that the Embassy was only following orders from DSCA.

Likewise, if asked by anyone, Ali would respond that MAPS was only following direction from their customer, CAC. The Colonel said he would keep Ali informed of any further communications that might affect MAPS.

As they said their farewells, Ali handed the Colonel a flowery envelope. Before the Colonel opened it, he said, "Colonel Barnes, that is an invitation to my wedding reception. As you may be aware, Arab weddings are usually small private affairs. However, we do pull out all of the stops for the reception. We had our wedding a few days ago, and now are having the reception next weekend at the Almaz rooftop ballroom at the Marriot Hotel on the Nile."

The Colonel smiled and answered, "Ali, thank you. I'll be very pleased to attend. Who is the lucky bride?"

This time Ali gave a sly smile as he said, "I believe you know her, or certainly know of her. She is Tasha Mostafa, who is now Tasha Omar."

After he left, Colonel Barnes thought, *This Egyptian situation is now really getting more interesting.* Was it more than an amazing coincidence that the government official responsible for funding the military happened to be the sister of the Minister of Defense, both of whom had recently authorized the purchase of the CAC CC-

260 aircraft? And that now she was married to the CAC Egyptian Support Contractor? *What a small world!* Colonel Barnes decided he had no choice but to add a note on this "merger" to the audit report, or he might later be accused of collusion.

Once Ali returned to his office, he decided he should advise Ahmed as to what Colonel Barnes had told him. He also decided to mention his new bride to Ahmed at this time so that Ahmed would not hear about the "merger" of his players from someone else. After he sent this message, he called Tasha and suggested that she invite her brother over for a drink that evening to discuss their play for a potential investigation of the CC-260 spares purchase from MAPS. He was not overly concerned, since all the payments had been to CAC approved contracts. Plus, he had his money and wasn't about to give any back.

Washington DC – Office of Inspector General

While he was awaiting a reply from the Embassy in Cairo, Mr. Good sent a request to DSCA asking them to verify that the price paid for the EAF CC-260 aircraft was commensurate with the configuration of the aircraft.

Mr. Good was learning more about international military aircraft FMF-FMS projects every day, and felt he was beginning to understand the process and procedures. It appeared that the payment to CAC was by the book. However, there was still one unsettled issue with using FMF funds, the question being whether the EAF had received an aircraft of value equal to the FMF payment or had CAC overcharged for the aircraft?

The next day he received from DSCA the detailed EAF CC-260 aircraft specification with a comparison on the price of thirty-six million dollars per plane with recent USAF purchases of aircraft in a similar configuration. It was clear to him, even as a novice on military aircraft configuration, that it was almost impossible to have an exact comparison of any two aircraft. Apparently, the DSCA had determined the configurations were close enough for government purposes. However, being an auditor, it appeared to him the EAF had paid for a Cadillac version where the USAF purchased Chevy's. There was a possibility that CAC may had exceeded US Government guidelines on profitability on military items, which also applied to FMF purchases.

Looked like he needed to make a visit to CAC in Mobile to further his education.

Washington DC – DSCA Office

The request from the Office of Inspector General for the configuration comparison and the DSCA reply were handled way below General Howell's level. However, nothing ever got by his secretary, Ms. Wright. When she saw the request from the OIG in the weekly staff report, and also that a reply had been made, she went into the General's office and told him they needed to have an off-the-record discussion.

Once the door was closed, she opened with, "General Howell, as you well know, I have been with DSCA for many years, most of which have been spent working with the senior level management. I have seen a considerable amount of political infighting, so I am always keeping my eyes open for anything unusual. I'm sure you recall the recent FMF grant program to supply CC-260 aircraft and spares to Egypt?"

The General replied, "Sure do, that was one of my first major projects." Meanwhile he was thinking, *I hope my good friend Al Hancock didn't talk me into a bad play.*

Ms. Wright continued with, "As I said, I've seen a lot here, so when I see in the weekly staff report from our Air Force Department that the Office of Inspector General has requested background information on the FMF direct payments to CAC and their Support Contractor, I suspect they are beginning an investigation." That made the General sit up a little straighter. "So, accordingly, I recommend you have a meeting with everyone involved in that project and arrange for any replies to any OIG requests be reviewed by you."

He replied, "Ms. Wright, thank you for bringing this to my attention. Please go ahead and set up that meeting as soon as you can."

After she left his office, he called his friend General Hancock. *Or was that maybe friend?* Once Hancock came on the line, General Howell said, "Al, I hear that your CC-260 sale to Egypt was completed a couple of weeks ago."

Al replied, "Mike, it sure did and I'm delinquent in sharing a few bottles of wine with you to thank you for your support and expediting those payments"

Before Al could say anymore, General Howell interrupted, " Al, before we celebrate too much, I need to alert you that the OIG is asking a lot of questions regarding the FMF payments on that Egyptian program, especially our direct payment to your Support Contractor. I suggest we both monitor this OIG activity and keep each other informed on what we see or hear from them."

The unspoken message by both Generals was, *Somebody is in*

trouble and I hope it's not me.

After the call, General Hancock asked Ken Doyle to come over to his office. Once Ken arrived and sat down, the General didn't waste any time on small talk. "Ken, what the hell have you gotten me into? I just had a call from the head of the DSCA and he advised me that the Office of Inspector General has started an investigation into your CC-260 sale to Egypt."

Ken was taken back at the General's strong tone, and responded, "Al, slow down, the CC-260 sale to the Egyptians was by the book." *At least, I hope so*, thought Ken. "This happens every once in a while, when some politician gets outmaneuvered and his pet project didn't get FMF-funded. Just relax, and be careful the OIG or DSCA doesn't make us the scapegoat for something we didn't do."

Al replied, "OK. General Howell and I have agreed to keep each other informed, so let me know if you hear from Cargo Aircraft of any issues with the sale."

Ken left Al's office, and wondered if the OIG had the ability to audit private citizen stock transactions. He now needed to send a message to Frank Moore to alert him and his team to this developing situation. He hoped that all of their plays were either by the book or a well-kept secret.

Zurich - CAC Corporate Office

At first, Ahmed was not overly concerned with the message from Larry Ray, as it sounded like it could just be a normal DSCA-OIG audit. However, his concern increased with the message from Ali, which added more details supplied by Ali's discussion with Colonel Barnes.

What really caught his attention was the announcement of Ali's marriage to Tasha. He thought, *What a great end run!* The local Egyptian team had a much bigger play than he could have imagined. Such a marriage would not cause too many raised eyebrows in Cairo. However, the amazing coincidence that the head of the local company that supports the Cargo Aircraft Company marries the government official who approved the use of US FMF funds for CAC aircraft, which were purchased by her brother, might generate some attention from one of those US Government investigative agencies. He needed to alert his players in Mobile and DC.

Ahmed composed a message that only a few players would understand.

"Closer (*Mark Maddox-VP Marketing),* I have just been informed by Roadrunner *(Larry Ray),* Eagle *(Ken Doyle)* and Ramses *(Ali)* that the alligators in the swamp may be looking for prey in Mobile. Suggest you alert your hunters to be on the watch for them. Also, a couple of the local businesses, Ramses and Cleopatra, have been merged."

He knew that would cause a lot of concern at Mobile. Furthermore, since this again was not his first rodeo, Ahmed was aware that the direct payment of FMF funds to MAPS was against the law. He also suspected the large advance payment to MAPs would not go over well. And although he certainly trusted Ali and his players not to be whistle blowers on the rewards given back to his team, he wasn't so sure that one of his own players might not give up his reward to avoid going to jail. He knew it was time for him to implement his exit strategy

18

SEVENTEENTH GAME -NFC DIVISIONAL PLAYOFFS-SAN FRISCO 49ERS HOST MINNESOTA VIKINGS

49ers win 39 to 9

For the third time in a year San Francisco hosted the Vikings. For the second time it was in the playoffs. Minnesota had just defeated the Los Angeles Rams 28-17. Montana threw three touchdown passes in the first half and Rice caught all three. Vikings quarterback Wilson was picked off two times as the 49ers won 34-9. This was San Francisco's first playoff win since Super Bowl.

Mobile, Alabama – Cargo Aircraft Company

Before Mark had received the message from Ahmed, he had been informed by Larry Ray about the message Larry Ray had received from Colonel Barnes regarding the audit of the EAF spares at MAPS, requested by the Office of Inspector General. Mark hadn't been overly concerned until he received Ahmed's message, which sounded far more serious. He called the President's office and told Frank's secretary the he and Larry Ray needed to schedule a meeting with Frank on the Egyptian sale as soon as possible. He wasn't aware that Frank had just received a detailed message from Ken Doyle on the same subject. Frank's secretary called back almost immediately, saying they were to come up to his office right away.

Once they were all settled at his conference table, and the secretary had served them coffee, Frank decided he wanted to hear their side of the story first.

Mark started with, "Frank, both Larry Ray and I have received messages regarding our recent sale to Egypt. Colonel Barnes, the Air Attaché at the Embassy in Cairo, advised Larry Ray that the US Office of Inspector General requested an audit of the spares positioned at MAPS. Colonel Barnes met with Ali Omar and they both confirmed that the consignment of spares matched the EAF contract. So apparently there are no issues there."

Ken thought, *Well, at least that's a good start.*

Mark continued his rundown. "Then I received a brief message from Ahmed in Zurich that he was also aware that the OIG was looking into the Egyptian sale. He didn't have any details other than there could be cause for concern in the fact that our Egyptian Support Contractor, Ali Omar, has married the government official who supported using the US FMF grant funds to Egypt to purchase our aircraft. She is also the sister of the Minister of Defense."

Mark looked over at Larry Ray. "Larry Ray, I believe you have met Tasha Mostafa, who is now Mrs. Tasha Omar?"

Larry Ray choked and spit his coffee out onto the conference table, spraying some on Frank. *Probably a negative impact to his career in more ways than one.*

With a grimace, Frank wiped the coffee off his tie and the table, then growled, "Larry Ray, I'll take that as a "Yes, you know this Tasha whatever her last name is!"

Larry Ray struggled to give a weak reply that he had met her at the Embassy reception some time ago.

Frank and Mark were not professional interrogators. However, they could tell when someone was being less than truthful. They were both thinking that they might have bigger problems than just a salesman having an affair on the road.

Frank took over the discussion. "Gentlemen, I also have heard of the OIG interest from our Washington office and it could be a lot more involved than a simple audit of spare parts. The head of the DSCA, General Howell, has mentioned a concern with the FMF-DCS payments, especially the direct payment to MAPS. I have also been advised that an auditor from the OIG will be here tomorrow to review our documentation on this sale. I expect he'll spend most of his time with the Finance department. However, let's alert all our staff to be on their best behavior. That's all for now."

As Mark and Larry Ray were leaving, Frank called out, "Mark, please stay a minute, as I have an administrative matter to discuss with you."

Once the door was closed, Frank asked, "Mark, do you know if Larry Ray was playing around with this Tasha person?"

Mark had his suspicions, but had no proof until he could talk to Ahmed. "Frank, he has a reputation as a playboy, and he has been married several times, so it's not out of the question. Let me make a couple of calls and I'll get back to you."

"OK, this could get very serious, so we need to consider another "Special Play.""

To the Ticket-Holders: One special play often used in football is the "reverse play." A form of it has been adapted to international business.

Reverse: In football terms, this is a trick play which often begins as an end-around. In a reverse, a ball carrier running parallel to the line of scrimmage in one direction hands off to a teammate coming in the opposite direction. This abruptly reverses the lateral flow of the play. If the defense is slow to react, the second ball-carrier might make it around the end of the line to a nearly open field.

Executive Reverse: In the international sales game, this play is a little easier to understand and make. This play begins by trying to do an end-run around the problem. The executive hands off the problem to a teammate coming in the opposite direction. This abruptly reverses the flow of the play. In this play the teammate gets to carry the problem. This new ball carrier might make it around the end of the line to a nearly open field, or he may get tackled, which is another word for indicted.

CAC Executive make a "Reverse" Play

Frank knew he needed to pass off this problem. Also, that Mark and Ahmed were not good candidates for this play, as they also knew this play. He decided to mix it up a little and pass the problem, that is, point the finger at Larry Ray, VP Finance Jim Smith, and General Counsel Vince Holliday,

He then called in his secretary and said he wished to document the direction he had verbally given to Larry Ray, Jim, and Vince at the start of the Egyptian sales campaign. He dictated an internal document, which essentially stated that they had the responsibility to ensure that all discussions, memos, and agreements related to the sale to Egypt comply with all US and Egyptian laws. He told his secretary to date the memo with the same date that he recalled giving this direction.

His secretary knew this was a CYA memo. Since she was approaching retirement, she was not about to question the boss, so she did as she was told.

Frank had now handed off the problem ball!

OIG visits CAC Mobile.

John B. Good arrived at the CAC office early the next morning. He had asked to first meet with the President and then spend a day or so with the Finance department reviewing their files pertaining to the sale of aircraft and spares to Egypt.

He was immediately escorted to the President's office. Frank met him at his door and gave him a warm greeting and they both sat down at his conference table. Frank's secretary provided coffee and, according to her, some home-made biscuits. While they enjoyed their mini-breakfast, Frank provided Mr. Good with an overview of the Cargo Aircraft Company and their history of being a first class supplier to the US Government. He also mentioned his time overseas endorsing US Government policy on supporting favored foreign countries with military equipment. Good's impression was that Frank sounded like he was running for office.

Frank ended his speech, saying, "Mr. Good, I assure you that my staff has been directed to give you their full cooperation. I wish I could be of more help to you. However, my position requires that I focus my attention on aircraft production and future development projects. As you will see, international sales are a small portion of our business. Therefore, I delegate that responsibility to my very experienced international sales management team."

Frank then slid a document over to John B. Good. "This is a copy of the direction I gave my staff regarding the potential sale of aircraft to Egypt. I trust they will have all the answers to your questions." Frank added to himself, *And I hope the ink is dry on the memo I created yesterday.* Talk about passing the buck!

John didn't want to raise any alarm or provide any indication of the target of his visit. So, he simply replied, "Mr. Moore, it is a pleasure to meet you and to visit your Company. As you know we do these types of audits all the time. I expect with your Company's history, all will be in order. I'll stop by when I finish and provide you with an overview of my findings."

Understanding that this discussion was over, Frank called in his secretary to escort Mr. Good over to the Finance department.

CAC Finance Department

Frank had alerted his VP Finance, Jim Smith, of the visit of the OIG auditor. He deliberately had not mentioned it was specifically related to the FMF funding of the Egyptian aircraft and spares.

Although Frank remained hopeful that this investigative audit would not result in any further action, he was aware that they had paid MAPS a lot of money to be the CAC Egyptian Support Contractor and MAPS had done very well on the spares consignment. His strategy was to blame his lower level department heads and accuse them of withholding key information from him. Actually, that was how he had survived so long and been so successful.

Mr. Good was escorted to Jim's office. This was also not Jim's first rodeo. If there were to be any problem with the Egyptian payments, his play was to pass the ball, or problem, to some of his staff and those guys in the Sales department. He welcomed Mr. Good, but offered no coffee, acting like he was too busy to deal with these types of details. Jim had arranged for one of his newer staff to take care of Mr. Good. He had also told his department to bury this auditor with paper. That way it would take forever for Mr. Good to plow through it all to try to find the information he wanted. Possibly he would just get frustrated and go home.

John was escorted into the CAC finance department field of cubicles. He was provided with a small work station and told to simply ask the department secretary to provide him with any files he wanted to see. Following his simple request to see the files on payments related to the Egyptian sale, he was shortly overwhelmed with stacks of financial files. A less dedicated auditor might have made a cursory review and called it a day. He suspected there was a needle buried in the document haystack, and he was going to find it!

Actually, he was glad to be left alone, since he didn't want to alert anyone at CAC if he discovered a problem. While he was conducting his audit, he was treated like he had a communicable disease. He was escorted to lunch in the company cafeteria where the conversation stuck to the weather and sports.

Persistence paid off, and John B. Good did find the documentation that confirmed his suspicions. The first irregularity was regarding the payment from CAC to MAPS. Yes, CAC had clearly hired MAPS to support the sale, but there was no accompanying statement of work to justify the initial payment of two million dollars. There was also no sound reasoning to advance the multiple-year payment for another eight million. Now, it appeared that this additional eight-million-dollar payment had been authorized by a lower level finance manager, who had used a portion of the FMF money for this payment. This could be considered paying a commission with FMF funds, which was clearly illegal. So, clearly two whistles on this play.

Now for the yellow flag. The spares transaction was a far more serious matter. Buried in the finance department documentation was the repayment that CAC had actually received from MAPS for the thirty-six million dollars of FMF-funded spares. That repayment only amounted to 28.8 million dollars. That means MAPS netted 7.2 million dollars, or twenty percent of the original payment. Good knew that the industry mark-up for subcontractors' handling of spare parts on a US Government program was around five percent.

As another matter of interest, he had become aware of the connection of MAPS to senior level Egyptian politicians and military officers.

He had discovered a lot more than he expected. He didn't want to alert the CAC executives to his findings until he could review them with OIG management to see if they agreed with him. He decided not to meet with the CAC President or any other Company employee, so as to keep what he had discovered on the down-low.

At the end of the second day, he returned to Washington without telling anyone at CAC. Instead, he sent a note to both Mr. Moore and Mr. Smith, advising them that he had been unexpectedly recalled to Washington and thanking them for their hospitality.

The quick departure concerned Frank. He felt it could either be a good sign or a bad sign!

On the other hand, Mark Maddox had been monitoring the ongoing audit. He was surprised at the way Finance was handling this. They should have had tight limitations on what the auditor could see. As this was not his first rodeo, *Hey! Was there any other way to put it?*, he decided it was time to start working on his exit strategy.

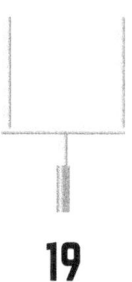

19

EIGHTEENTH GAME NFC CHAMPIONSHIP GAME- SAN FRANCISCO 49ERS AT CHICAGO BEARS

49ers win 28 to 3

San Francisco played at a very cold Soldier Field in Chicago. It was less than three months after San Francisco's loss on the same field. San Francisco cinched the game in the third quarter with Montana's third touchdown of the game. San Francisco limited the Bears to just one field goal.

Washington DC – Office of Inspector General

Soon after he returned to his office, John B. Good noticed he had received a reply from the US Embassy on the CAC-MAPS spares audit. He saw that the on-site consignment of spares did match the CC-260 contract. At first, he wondered why the Air Attaché had mentioned the local wedding, until he quickly made the connection from CAC to MAPS to the Government to the Minister of Defense. As someone once said, 'The Plot Thickens." He organized all of his findings on CAC payments using FMF funds, in addition to the information about the relationship of these key players.

He then requested a meeting with his senior manager. After he had presented all the results of his investigation, his manager commended him. "John, excellent work. I believe you have not only found the smoking gun, but also discovered the shooter. We need to take this up the chain of command to the Deputy Inspector General for Investigations, Jim Keller. He has a good track record as a lawyer and previous prosecutor in the DC Federal Courts."

John and his manager made the trip up to the Deputy Inspector's office and presented their findings. After reviewing their report, Jim smiled, saying, "Fellows, good work. I believe you have just found major violations of the Foreign Corrupt Practices Act and financial fraud by one of our largest defense contractors. I'm going to take this to the IG. Please keep this matter to yourselves for the time being. We do not want to alert either CAC or the DSCA of these violations, as they might go into "destroy the evidence'" mode before we can get what we need."

Jim met with the IG later that day. Of course, he took almost full credit for the discovery of the FCPA violations.

The IG responded, "Jim, I agree that we have a serious violation of the FCPA, as well as financial fraud by CAC. I don't understand why DSCA General Howell ordered the direct FMF payment to this MAPS company in Egypt. There may be a lot more conspiracy going on than we have seen so far. And Jim, you'll be interested to know about another amazing coincidence that may be related to all this. I have recently been alerted by the FBI of a potential money laundering scheme going on between a CAC salesman and the Egyptian Embassy. Even more remarkable, this same CAC salesman was working on that recent CC-260 FMF sale to Egypt."

Jim couldn't believe that the amazing coincidences just kept piling up.

The IG meeting the next day with the FBI went very well, since their small money laundering case had just became a lot more serious with a major FCPA violation. Besides Jim, the IG had included John Good and his manager in the meeting because the IG knew neither he nor Jim had all the answers to the questions the FBI would be asking.

At the end of this meeting both the IG people and the FBI agreed it was a solid case and they needed to bring it to the attention of the US Department of Justice, more specifically, the Criminal Division's Fraud Section. This section had over one hundred federal prosecutors who investigated and then prosecuted multi-district and international white-collar crime. These cases usually included corporate investment fraud, marketing fraud, and government procurement fraud, as well as violations of the Foreign Corporate Practice Act.

The IG arranged for John Good, Jim Keller, and a senior FBI agent to meet with the Chief of the Foreign Corrupt Practices Act Unit within the Department of Justice at their offices over on Pennsylvania Avenue, about halfway between the White House and the Capitol. The Chief had also invited a couple of his staff lawyers.

The discussions took most of the day. By the time they finished, they all agreed this was a serious case which required immediate attention before the trail of evidence went cold or disappeared. The Chief recommended that the FBI obtain search warrants and schedule a raid on the CAC headquarters in Mobile, along with the homes of the President, Frank Moore, the VP Finance, Jim Smith, the VP of Marketing, Mark Maddox and the Salesman, Larry Ray Hardy. They passed on the General Counsel, Vince Holliday (out of mutual respect?).

They had no authority to approach the Egyptian Embassy in Washington. Also, there wasn't much they could do about the Corporate VP, Ahmed Sharif, in Zurich until they indicted him and asked Switzerland to extradite him to the US.

They also elected not to raid the CAC Corporate office over in Crystal City, partly out of consideration for a neighbor, and because they believed they could obtain all they needed in Mobile.

The IG's office was also conducting its own investigation of General Howell at DSCA and they wanted to keep that low key for the time being.

Mobile – CAC Office and Executive Homes

The FBI were experts at conducting raids on businesses and homes looking for fugitives, or in this case, documents. They usually conducted these types of raids in the early morning hours, as there were too many nosy people around during the day who might alert the subjects.

All was quiet at the pre-dawn raid at the CAC office, since the subjects were either still asleep or just waking up. Seizing evidence was the first step, so there was no plan to arrest anyone today. They would arrange with the local police to keep an eye on the key subjects to see if any of them made a run for the hills.

The raid on the offices took several hours, as the files they needed to seize were spread over several departments. Fortunately, John Good had given them a list and location of the suspected departments and the offices of the several executives. Otherwise, they would have needed a moving van in order to gather up all of the company's documents related to international business activities.

The raids on the homes were conducted after Frank, Jim, and Larry Ray left for work. The only hiccup was that Mark Maddox was not to be seen, even though he was reported to be in town. Maybe he was having a sleepover with a friend. They left an agent at his house and put out an alert to the local police to pick him up if he was spotted.

Frank Moore arrived at his office just after the FBI had left the premises, and the CAC headquarters was buzzing with rumors for the cause of the FBI raid. Frank immediately called a meeting of all his key staff in the executive conference room. Once they had taken their seats, he asked all those whose office or department had been raided to remain. He excused the others.

Once they had left, he saw that only Larry Ray, Jim Smith, and three of Jim's Finance Department managers remained. Frank addressed them. "Gentlemen, we have a very serious situation. It is clear to me that someone in our company has committed a federal crime. I want you three finance department managers to get with your staffs and provide me a listing of all the documents confiscated by the FBI. Get going on that now."

Once the three managers had departed, he asked, "Larry Ray, do you know where Mark is?"

Larry Ray replied, "Frank, I saw him in his office yesterday morning. He left after lunch and said he had some personal business to take care of. He said he would see me today, but I haven't seen him nor heard anything since."

Frank asked Larry Ray to go to Mark's office and see if he could uncover anything that would tell whether Mark had any travel plans or outside appointments scheduled for today.

After Larry Ray left, Frank said to Jim, the last man sitting, "It looks like that OIG auditor found something very serious to result in this raid. We need to be prepared for the worst, as Mark received a recent message that our Support Contractor in Egypt has some special connection to a lady in their government and the Minister of Defense. You know that neither Mark, Larry Ray, nor Ahmed mentioned any such connection in their recommendation to have MAPS as our Egyptian Support Contractor. It appears to me that, if they didn't know, they should have. Jim, go review all the documents we received on MAPS. Let's see if we can lay the responsibility for whatever this is on the Marketing department and the Zurich office."

A short time later, Larry Ray returned to Frank's office. "Frank, Mark is still not here and there were no outside appointments on his calendar. His secretary has also not seen nor heard from him. He is not answering his phones. The secretary said it appeared he had stopped by last evening after hours, as his desk was clear and some of his files were missing. Also, he had left this envelope addressed to you in his Out box."

Frank took the envelope and opened it. There was a one-page letter from Mark to Frank which said that, effective immediately, Mark was resigning from the Cargo Aircraft Company for personal reasons. Although Frank was quite surprised, he almost immediately thought, *We have a scapegoat!*

Frank didn't share Mark's announcement with Larry Ray, since he knew, if Mark had a reason to run, then he had better keep an eye on Larry Ray. He closed the letter and said, "Larry Ray, it looks like Mark had to take care of some personal business. So please take care of any urgent Marketing business while he is away."

Once Larry Ray was out the door, Frank called the security office and told them to monitor Larry Ray's activities, especially if he made any travel plans.

Unknown to Larry Ray, while the FBI was raiding the CAC offices and, later on, the four homes, another FBI team was visiting all of the local banks with search warrants for information on the accounts and any safe deposit boxes of the four CAC executives. The FBI agents were pleased to discover the three safe deposit boxes of Mr. Hardy each containing fifty thousand dollars in cash.

Of course, the FBI had also been monitoring any large cash withdrawals from the Washington DC accounts of the Egyptian Embassy. They had previously arranged with those banks to provide the serial numbers of the bills of any large cash withdrawals. What an amazing coincidence to find that the serial numbers on some of the bills in Mr. Hardy's safe deposit boxes matched those of some of the cash withdrawals by the Egyptian Embassy in DC.

Washington, DC – Cargo Aircraft Corporate Office

The news of the FBI raids created a lot of discussion and concern, especially for Ken Doyle and General Hancock. Ken knew he had fairly well insulated himself from any direct responsibility in the funding for the aircraft sale to Egypt. Lobbying was still not a crime, especially in Washington DC. Additionally, he had only rubber stamped the CAC strong recommendation to appoint MAPS as their Support Contractor in Egypt.

General Hancock was a lot more concerned. Not so much for himself, as he had only encouraged his friend General Howell at DSCA to authorize the direct payment to MAPS for the aircraft spares. But he was really dreading the next call from General Howell.

Washington, DC – DSCA Office

After General Howell had heard of the FBI raids on the Cargo Aircraft Company, he was smart enough to know he had been led astray by his now ex-friend, General Hancock. He also knew when to admit defeat. He called his secretary, Ms. Wright, into his office. He then dictated to her his resignation from DSCA, indicating that it should coincide with his retirement from the USAF, both due to personal reasons. Ms. Wright had an idea of what was happening and hoped his direction on the MAPS payment would be considered a lack of experience and he would be able to stay out of jail.

Zurich – CAC Corporate Office

The FBI had an agent assigned to Switzerland with an office in Zurich. Apparently, he had friends in high places for such a plum assignment. The FBI had a good working relationship with Interpol and the Swiss government, as long as they didn't ask any questions regarding any private bank accounts. They had agreed for the Zurich police to accompany the agent to Mr. Sharif's office just to conduct an interview. When they arrived, they found the office door unlocked and no one there. As they looked around it was clear that Mr. Sharif had cleared out the files. There was a single envelope laying in the center of the desk addressed "To whom it may concern." Inside was a copy of his resignation letter to his Corporate office in Washington, DC. Of course, they would issue an alert for him at the airport and train stations. However, they suspected he was long gone. The FBI agent went back to his office and sent a report to DC.

Washington DC- Office of Inspector General and FBI Headquarters

After reviewing and organizing the documents and other information from the Cargo Aircraft Company on the aircraft sale to Egypt, the appointment and payments to the local support Contractor, Military Aircraft Parts & Services, the OIG and FBI advised the US Attorney's office of their findings.

Shortly thereafter, the US Attorney's office in Mobile charged Cargo Aircraft Company with violations of the Foreign Corporate Practice Act, wire fraud, money laundering, and defrauding the DSCA, the United States, and Egypt.

Indictments were issued for the Company, as well as President, Frank Moore, VP Finance, Jim Smith, VP Marketing, Mark Maddox, and Marketing Manager, Larry Ray Hardy. Additionally, the extradition was requested of Corporate VP Middle East, Ahmed Sharif, from Switzerland, if he was found there.

This started a long and expensive legal process for the Cargo Aircraft Company, with an infinite amount of legal briefs.

Prepare to catch the final "Special Play!"

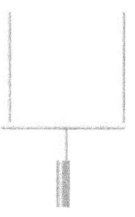

20

NINETEENTH GAME-SUPER BOWL -SAN FRANCISCO - 49ERS AND CINCINNATI BENGALS

49ers win 20 to 16

This Super Bowl was highlighted by the 49ers' fourth-quarter game-winning drive. They were behind 16–13, San Francisco had the ball on their own eight-yard line with only 3:10 remaining on the clock. They moved 92 yards in under three minutes. Then they scored the winning touchdown on a Montana pass to Taylor with just 34 seconds left on the clock.

San Francisco wide receiver Rice was named the Super Bowl MVP. He caught 11 passes for a Super Bowl record 215 yards and one touchdown.

This was the final NFL game coached by Walsh.

Mobile, Alabama - Federal Courthouse

Following a somewhat lengthy legal process of grand jury testimonies, and hours and hours of prosecutor and defense lawyer discussions, the Federal Attorney elected to ask for only two trials.

The first trial involved the CAC Company defendants, President, Frank Moore, VP Finance, Jim Smith, and Marketing Manager, Larry Ray Hardy. There was no action the Federal Attorney could pursue against the VP Marketing, Mark Maddox or the Corporate VP Ahmed Sharif until they could find them in the US or extradite them from a foreign county under an extradition agreement. Courts in the United States held that, according to the United States Constitution, a criminal defendant's right to appear in person at their trial, as a matter of due process, was protected under the Fifth, Sixth, and Fourteenth Amendments.

A joint trial of codefendants was known as a "joinder." A judge could merge the cases of two or more defendants when the issues in the defendants' cases overlapped enough to make a single trial both fair and more efficient. Defendants didn't have to face the exact same alleged crimes for a judge to join their trials. All that was necessary was that the charges be related substantially to the same facts. Joint trials were ordered in complex prosecutions for conspiracy or fraud where multiple defendants were accused of committing a variety of crimes stemming from one set of facts.

The second trial involving the Company was conducted for all of the same alleged crimes.

The pages of testimony for this first trial were copious, but the basic conclusions and subsequent actions concerning the players were as follows:

President, Frank Moore

Although all of the illegal activities took place under his watch, other than signing the Consultant Review meeting report, there was no direct written evidence that he had orchestrated the violations. His verbal direction to the lower level Finance staff could not be substantiated and become the same old "he said, they said" testimony. Moreover, his memo assigning the Egyptians sale responsibility to others saved him from being convicted.

However, the Corporation was not so forgiving. Immediately following the conclusion of the trial, Frank was "promoted" to President of the CAC Parts manufacturing facility out in the "back forty," which had a total of 30 employees. Frank wasn't that upset, as he had avoided going to jail and had enough high-level Corporate contacts that he was sure, after all this was forgotten, he would be able to move up. Of course, considering his new position, there was nowhere to go but UP!

VP Finance, Jim Smith

Jim took the brunt of the Government's wrath as his Finance department had made the eight-million-dollar payment to MAPS using FMF funds. He certainly tried to place all the blame on the Marketing VP and the Zurich VP. However, without any testimony from Maddox or Sharif, it was his word against Larry Ray's, who had agreed to cooperate with the government in exchange for a reduced charge. Jim was sentenced to three years in a federal prison. However, it was an amazing coincidence that Jim was released after six months for good behavior soon after the Governor of Alabama received a significant political campaign donation from the CAC Washington lobbyist.

Marketing Manager, Larry Ray Hardy

Larry Ray, being the ultimate salesman, had sold the Feds on the story that he had been led astray by Sharif and Maddox and was simply following orders. Without Maddox or Sharif there, it was hard to argue against his position. Also, he had pointed the finger at Finance and Legal for not doing their due diligence.

His defense on the money laundering charge was a work of art.

He reported that the statue had been given to him by an unknown party in Egypt. He said he thought it was a souvenir thank you gift from the hotel. He was surprised with the visit from the Egyptian Embassy guy. He had put the money in safe places while he took some time to investigate the transaction and then he was going to turn the information and the money over to the FBI. Although everyone in the courtroom rolled their eyes, it was an award-winning story. Plus, he was a witness for the government, and they usually didn't beat up their own team. Of course, Larry Ray did not believe it was necessary to tell them how much the Egyptians had actually given him, nor that he had set a large chunk aside for a rainy day. There was no way to find out from the Egyptian Embassy how much was actually paid for the Wadjet artifact. After all, this wasn't the Egyptian Embassy's first rodeo!

Larry Ray was sentenced to two years' probation and prohibited from international travel. He was moved from the Marketing Department to the Accounting Department. His new responsibility was auditing expense reports. His sign over his cubicle read BTDT, as in, Been There Done That! Of course, this five days a week job allowed him to spend most weekends at his new condo on the beach in Gulf Shores, Alabama, about an hour south of Mobile. He liked to mention it was an inheritance from a distant relative, Aunt Cleo, short for Cleopatra.

General Counsel – Vince Holliday

Although he was not indicted, the Corporation was not pleased with his oversight of international business at CAC. Shortly after the trial, he was moved to his new position as Legal Assistant at the same "back forty" facility as Frank Moore.

Cargo Aircraft Company

A day prior to the start of their trial, the Company and US Attorney agreed to a plea bargain, whereby CAC pleaded guilty to a violation of the Foreign Corrupt Practices Act. They paid a fine of forty million dollars, which was supposed to be equal to the profit CAC made on the CC-260 sale to Egypt. The Government accounting types said it was their best estimate of the profit, as the CAC books seemed to use an unknown accounting method.

Washington Office

Of course, everyone in the Washington office was shocked to learn of the corruption at the Mobile offices. There was one executive who was very thankful that he had not been caught up in the mess. General Hancock had kept his head down and avoided any accusations other than those from his no longer friend General Howell, who had recently resigned from the USAF and DSCA. Hancock had heard of the shakeup at the senior level at DSCA, which wasn't that surprising to anyone, as it happened quite often in government organizations. Hancock had thought the Pentagon War games were tough. He now was on a quite different battle field.

Cairo

The Egyptian team had monitored the US trial of Cargo Aircraft and the Executives. It appeared that without Ahmed or Maddox there to testify, there was no one to reveal the rewards back to the Cargo Aircraft Team. The trial hardly made any news in Cairo, as rewarding local business teams was standard procedure around the world.

Cayman Islands

At the Ritz-Carlton Golf Club on Seven Mile beach on Grand

Cayman in the exclusive beachside lounge BAR JACK, which boasts the island's best sunset viewpoint, two suntanned patrons sat down to enjoy a few of the finest piña coladas in the Caribbean.

Mark Maddox and Ahmed Sharif clinked their glasses together, as Mark said, "Ahmed, here's to our success, or should I say survival on the Egyptian sale. Also, to the continuation of our business here in paradise. It will much easier to manage the investments of all of our Support Contractors, now that we are living here on Grand Cayman. However, we may wish to consider changing our company name from **C**ayman **I**nvestment **A**ssociates, CIA, as those initials sometimes can have an interesting connotation."

They both laughed, and Ahmed replied, "I hate to say I'm glad someone blew the whistle on the Egyptian deal. Those winters in Zurich were really getting to me. This is truly my style, lots of sand, rum drinks, and no camels."

They both laughed again as they drank in the piña coladas and the sunset.

Marketing Director

Since Robert McTelall had no documented involvement in the Egyptian sale, he was not indicted. However, his reputation was tainted for just being in Marketing at CAC Mobile. After the dust of the accusations settled, he had made a few calls to his friends at the Corporate office. . . .

This Season is Over!

The Next Season Highlight!!

London England

The new Cargo Aircraft Corporate VP Business Development-UK, Robert McTelall, was having his first staff meeting at their London office on Grosvenor Square. He gave the usual speech covering his experience, avoiding any mention of Egypt, and highlighting the great sales potential for Cargo Aircraft Military Products in the UK. He ended by saying, "You all need to know. . .

. . .this is not my first Cricket Match!"

The "Playing" Field for the next Season

www.ingramcontent.com/pod-product-compliance
Lightning Source LLC
Chambersburg PA
CBHW070002120726
47909CB00003B/777